JACOB'S LADDER

ST. NACHO'S BOOK 3

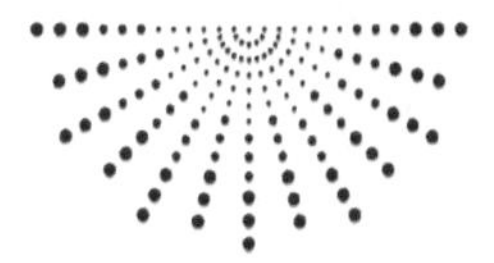

Z.A. MAXFIELD

For those who have the courage to start over.

CHAPTER ONE

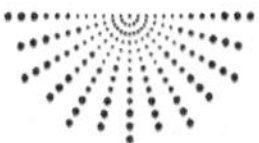

I stood outside the door to the restaurant kitchen, giving myself a much-needed break. Unlike the waiters and busboys, who sneaked outside to smoke, I liked a cloud-gazing break when I could get one. I was more than content to watch the changing sky and often sat outside in one of the cheap resin chairs during the endless morning bakes. While the busboys took long drags on their cigarettes, I scanned the blue horizon, particularly fond of the days when storm clouds rolled in from the sea.

I had a Dr. Brown's—cream soda this time—although I harbored a marked preference for either ginger ale or Cel-Ray. The ice-cold bottle sweat cool droplets onto my hand in the muggy heat. I liked those kinds of days the best, when what felt like tropical moisture got pulled up and inland from the south and the air was sultry and felt thick on my skin. Southern California always seemed too hot and bone-dry, even though I was close enough to the beach that seagulls congregated in the parking lot of Il Ghiotto, where I worked as a pastry chef. Lately I'd needed more and more in the way of these breaks. It was a fact that I was just about out of patience with cannoli and tiramisu.

I took another pull of my soda, closing my eyes when the flood of sweet syrup became crisp bubbles that snapped and popped in my mouth, imparting a creamy vanilla flavor and bringing me an indefinable step closer to the place where I grew up.

Maybe it was time to head up the coast to see my brother, Daniel, whose recent moodiness and epic bouts of self-pity inevitably made me feel as though I had no right to complain about anything.

I got to my feet with some care and pushed my empty bottle into the recycling bin on the way back inside the sweltering kitchen. I'd come into work even though I wasn't feeling well at all. I'd been by turns tired and dizzy all morning, and now a scratchy throat announced the beginnings of a cold. I didn't know how much longer I could hide my condition from the others in the crowded kitchen.

"You don't look so good, man." Arthur, my assistant, gave me a wide berth.

That certainly answered my question.

"Yeah." I headed for the sink to wash my hands. "I think I'm—"

"Jacob, I'm going to need something gluten free for the Ramirez rehearsal dinner to…" The assistant manager, Phil, reached out a hand and felt my forehead. "Shit. Go home. You have a fever, and none of us want to get sick." Phil had some say in these matters.

I backed away from his touch. "But—"

"No arguments." Phil walked to the sink and washed his hands as if I were unclean. That stung for some reason. "I don't need the swine flu or whatever it is you've got. Don't you read the papers?"

"No." I turned and started unbuttoning my chef's coat,

yanking the fabric a little more forcefully than necessary. One of the buttons popped off. "I don't need to be treated like a leper, Phil."

Phil turned around and winced. "I know, Jacob. I apologize. I'm paranoid about getting sick right now with Hannah's due date looming. Head home. Arthur can take it from here. I'll call you to check on you later."

When Maurizio, the owner, got in later, I knew Phil would make my excuses, and it wouldn't be a big deal as long as the work got done. I glanced at Arthur, who nodded.

Sighing with relief, I told Arthur, "Flourless chocolate cake with raspberry coulis."

"What?" Arthur's eyes looked blank.

"It's gluten free. For the Ramirez party."

"Ah, all right." Arthur turned and headed back to work. It was a lot of responsibility they were piling on Arthur this morning. He'd never been in charge of the baking alone.

I started to say something more when Phil stopped me. "He'll be fine. Just go, damn it. The sooner you go home and rest, the sooner you'll be back. Please don't let it be something bad."

I snorted. "God didn't let me survive a suicide bomber in Tel Aviv to die of the swine flu."

Phil rolled his eyes. "Go home."

"I'm on my way." I tossed my coat into the laundry on the way out and stepped into the moist air. I wondered briefly if I should call Sander and see if he wanted me to pick up anything on the way home, but the fever was making my bones ache, and I thought if Sander was lucky enough to be able to sleep in, I didn't care to wake him. Sander's job as a bouncer for a local strip club kept him up late at night even though he was making the rounds of auditions for film and television roles during the day. Since I worked from the early morning until late afternoon, our schedules were ideal when Sander didn't have anything else to do but sleep in.

As far as I knew, Sander didn't have a call that morning, so I rode home as usual on the bus, then let myself in to our small apartment quietly and removed my clogs in the tiled entry.

As I neared the bedroom where Sander slept, I heard the unmistakable sounds of laughter. Thinking that Sander was up watching television, I didn't announce myself but simply walked through the bedroom door. In retrospect, I realized there had been an extra pair of shoes, or three, next to Sander's expensive trainers on the entry-hall floor.

That's what I got for allowing my life since returning to America to make me complacent.

Of the four men in our bed, only one seemed to think my presence there—my horror at finding my lover engaged in an orgy—wasn't laughable. The other men were certainly laughing. They laughed while they put on their clothes and all the way down the hall and out the door.

"I didn't expect you back this early." Sander picked up a tiny can of some energy drink off the nightstand and took a sip.

"I'm sick." I practically fell onto the bed next to him, causing him to get up and stand against the wall. "And apparently, you're an asshole."

"That was nothing."

"How many people do you have to fuck at one time to consider it something?"

"It's not like that."

I was sick *in*side now as well as out. I wished I felt better. I could hardly work up a good case of righteous indignation if I could barely lift my head off the pillow. "How many times?"

"How many times what?"

"How many times have you jumped into bed with whoever took your fancy while I was stuffing fucking cannoli to keep food on the table?"

"I *work*!" Sander fired back, happy now to have some sort of argument of his own, his own reason to be indignant. "I spend my nights shoving drunks around a titty bar so I can help out."

I was tired and let my mouth run. "You work so you can get newer and better headshots by expensive photographers and to pay for gasoline and insurance for your car so you can pursue your dreams, while I slog back and forth to the restaurant on the bus. It's not like I see a dime of your damned money. It's not like I've asked for it."

Sander got quiet. "Shut the fuck up. It's not like that."

I was too tired and sick to care. I reached into the nightstand for a couple of extra-strength pain relievers, then chewed the tablets to get them to work as fast as possible. "Could you get me a glass of water, please?"

"Get your own damned water." Sander had apparently decided that the best defense was a good offense. "And while you're at it, you could have a little consideration. I've seen this new flu on the news, and people die from it. You could at least sleep on the couch until you're not contagious anymore. *Motherfucker.*"

I'd been living with the man for almost a year and realized I had no idea why. Sure, he was pretty. Big and buff and blond with a perfect eight-pack of abs and an out-of-control libido that seemed like a damned good thing at the time. He wasn't the brightest man, but the way he ate the special dinners I prepared for him in the early days of our relationship, so enthusiastically and with such childlike delight, had charmed me.

I'd realized a while back that Sander wasn't exactly faithful and put off the moment when I'd have to do something about it, because, for the most part, he was discreet. Until today.

"You need to find another place to live." I rolled tiredly to my side and lurched to my feet, intending to get myself a bottled water from the kitchen. That seemed a long way away.

Sander followed me, itching for a fight. "And you need to

dream on. This is where I live. You don't like living with me, then you move on."

"If I do, I'll have to give the manager notice," I told him. The sisters who owned the place managed it, and their reputation among the tenants was legendary and not in a particularly good way. It took looking the other way when their eccentricities became uncomfortable in order to live in the building, which was a trade-off because it was priced far below market value. The older sister ran it like it was her own little low-rent kingdom, and we were her serfs. Just seeing her was like an audience with the Wizard of Oz. Fortunately she liked me, and her equally frightening but less quirky sister was very fond of cannoli. "Since the place is in my name, you'd still be out of here on your ass."

"My ass would land right side up at least."

I gazed at Sander for a minute to see whether that was some kind of a lame joke. Nope. Didn't look like it. I turned my back on him—which I knew he hated—and growled, "Just leave me alone, you dumbass."

"Who are you calling a dumbass?" Sander gripped my shoulder and spun me around. He wrapped his massive hand around my neck and shook me hard. The rage that always simmered beneath the surface of his skin started to bubble over, and even I had a moment of true alarm when his grip got tighter and his face darkened with pure fury.

Any other day it wouldn't have—*couldn't have*—happened. As attracted as I was to big, brutal men like Sander, I was combat trained in Krav Maga. I believed I would always be able to take care of myself, and up until that point, I had. But just as all my instincts kicked in, I almost blacked out from the damned flu. My first move, my instinctual move, was to snap the palm of my hand into Sander's nose and break it, but because I was unable to follow through and put him on the ground for good, it only enraged him. Sander let loose a curse and struck me hard across the face.

"You fucking broke my nose!" I could see his panic. "My fucking *face*. You asshole. What are you thinking? Just because I got a little on the side?"

"It was instinct." I tried to pick myself up off the ground but slid a little in the blood that had spattered from Sander's nose. "I'm sorry. I'll—"

"You're *sorry*?" Sander kicked me in the ribs, sending a blast of pain throughout my entire body. I saw flashing lights dancing in my field of vision as I rolled into a ball.

"You just killed my career." Sander delivered another vicious kick.

Daniel always accused me of not knowing when enough was enough, and I had long since come to the conclusion that he might be right. I laughed weakly.

"Like you had one."

In light of the fact that my lover was beating the shit out of me, my laughter seemed reckless, but I'd reached the free-floating part of a physical beating where I felt nothing. I'd been there before: that magical dimension between someone else's rage and utter darkness. I'd decorated the space with memories from childhood and the ruined scraps of family life. It was as familiar to me as the sight of my own face in the mirror. I felt my cheek split under another blow from Sander's fist.

Well. Maybe not anymore.

Sander gripped a handful of my hair and pulled my head up until we were nose to broken nose.

I tried to move my head to spit the blood from my mouth, but Sander held me firm. I spit anyway. The blood I'd been holding sprayed all over Sander's pale blond hair. Sucked for Sander.

"Aren't you afraid you're going to get whatever it is that I have? Swine flu?"

As an escape technique, that worked rather well. Too well, actually. Sander dropped my head, and it hit the cabinet door on the way down. The blow split open the skin under the hair behind my ear.

As he left, I called after him, "You see? This is why we can't have nice things."

Getting the last word in...priceless.

I don't have a clue how long I lay on the kitchen floor, drifting in and out of consciousness. Truth be told, the numbness was better than I'd felt all day. I listened while Sander dressed, and then heard him race around shoving his crap into a suitcase. When the door finally slammed shut behind him, I allowed my tense body to relax. It wasn't the first time we'd brawled, but it was the worst. I had been utterly unable to defend myself. Until today neither Sander nor I had ever realized how far it would go if I couldn't use my strength or my experience to put a stop to it.

Even if we should have.

The phone in the pocket of my baggy pants rang, and I fumbled with the flying pig-printed fabric until I could wrest it out.

"Hello?" I answered, absurdly trying to hide the fact that I was beaten half-dead from whoever was calling. Like hiding my stupidity from a phone solicitor counted for anything when I was physically unable to crawl to the front door of my apartment and ask my neighbors for help.

"Jacob, it's Phil. I'm hitting the road early today because I'm now suffering from an assortment of what are probably psychosomatic flu symptoms. You need anything before I head to the valley?"

I closed my eyes and laughed again. "Yeah, Phil. I do." Already I could hear the neighbors banging on my door and, somewhere off in the distance, sirens. I hoped they weren't for me. There was more than one person in my apartment complex who looked out for me. The most likely person at the door was one of my landladies.

"Mr. Livingston?" I imagined I heard the pitter-patter of aging feet in leather come-fuck-me-pumps so old *they* had bunions within which to house the bunions of their owner. "I can't stand it! I'm coming in with the key, Mr. Livingston. That brute just ran out of here covered in blood and—" When she saw me, she covered her mouth in horror. "*Oh*."

Great. Today was apparently *Seven Year Itch* day, and Madeline, the femme fatale of the daring duo, was rocking a platinum blonde wig and a yellowing white satin halter dress.

I tried to halt her progress toward me just as she slipped in a pool of blood, but fortunately she caught herself on the countertop, so she didn't fall. I held up a hand.

"Don't get near me, Madeline. I don't want you to ruin your nice dress."

CHAPTER TWO

"Are you sure I can't talk you out of this?" Phil asked for the fifth time.

I swallowed past my bruised throat. My lips were split, and my entire body ached. It was hard for me to talk, but I owed at least that much to the man who had been kind enough to help me.

"I'm sure, Phil. Going to see my brother will make me feel bad enough that getting the crap beaten out of me by my boyfriend won't make me feel like such a loser."

Phil said nothing. He didn't have to. We'd argued about Sander's temper more than once.

"I know. You told me so." I leaned over and carefully picked up my duffel. I stopped Phil when he would have taken it from me. "I can get it."

Phil scowled at me. "I would never, ever say I told you so. Jeez."

"I'm sorry."

"I grew up wondering if my mom stayed with my dad because she had an unusually optimistic personality. But that can't be it, because you're a fucking shit storm of bad news. I'll never figure out why either of you put up with that shit, but I won't blame it on you either. It's not my call to make."

The bus was ready to board. "I'm going to get help," I muttered. I started limping toward the big diesel, walking slower than I needed to because I already knew it would hurt like hell to get up those steps.

"What?" Phil took my arm. "Sander's the one who needs—"

"It's not about Sander." I blinked back tears. Fucking medication. I couldn't hide my emotions at all. "I'm attracted to violence. It's…familiar."

"That's…" Phil frowned.

"Go home to Hannah. Take care of her. She needs it a helluva lot more than I do."

"I hope you feel better."

"Thanks." I looked down at Phil from where I stood on the steps of the bus. "Give her my love."

The bus driver gave me a flinty stare as I dropped my things into the seat two rows behind her. I usually like the seat right behind the driver, but there were two youngish girls there already. I had enough experience to know that no matter where I sat on the bus, I'd still smell the bathroom.

I watched the girls out of the corner of my eye, long enough to see that they were already frightened. I didn't blame them. As someone who often took public transportation and always took this particular bus to visit my brother, I knew they had reason to be afraid. They were lovely, maybe just out of high school, with ebony skin and handfuls of thick brown braids. Guys were already scoping them out as they entered the bus. The girls had probably been told to sit directly behind the driver by their mothers or the driver herself, and they were frozen in their places as if on display.

As the rest of the riders filed past me, I recognized the usual suspects. It was like a roll call of the worst life has to offer, like watching the seven deadly sins take their seats until the bus overflowed. The girls in front of me were already shivering.

An old man in a pair of polyester trousers with a plaid shirt and a worn sweater sat in the seat next to me. I glanced at his face and saw that behind his thick glasses he had a cataract in one eye. He wore a jaunty plaid hat at an angle that reminded me of my grandfather and aimed a toothless grin at me. I couldn't help but smile back.

A glance out the window confirmed that there would be rain before long. I closed my eyes and tried to find a comfortable way to sit. My knees were jammed into the seat in front of me. Even though the man next to me was diminutive, maybe five six, and frail, I didn't want to just stick my legs out and suck up all the space. I closed my eyes and succumbed after only a few minutes to the medication I'd taken for pain.

I slept fitfully with my head pressed against the window. It might as well have been the rock in the story about my biblical namesake. I dreamed my own dreams, some of which still bore traces of the violence I'd experienced the day before. When Sander fled, he'd taken only his clothing with him. Phil got his cell number from me and assured me that he'd phone Sander and tell him to get the rest of his things while I was out of town. Whether he did or not, I didn't particularly care. He'd have his chance, and then I would change the locks.

The motion of the bus soothed me, and the grinding, *rumbly-chumbly* of its big diesel engine lulled me back to sleep.

IT SURPRISED me when I awoke and didn't hear the engines. I'd coughed a little, taking care to turn my head and press the cough into my shoulder, the very model of good, ethical hygiene. When I dragged my puffy eyes open, I realized that the older gentleman who had been sitting next to me had left for parts unknown. So had the girls who sat in front of me. The pain meds had long since worn off, leaving me achy and febrile.

I focused my eyes and saw the face of the bus driver, angry and supercilious at the same time, floating above me. She was a thirtysomething Latina with a pretty face, but the kind of makeup I found theatrical: heavily lined eyes and eyebrows that didn't look natural. She had a hard look, and she was glaring at me, which exacerbated it.

"*Sir?*" she demanded. I squinted at her. Apparently I was late for a party I didn't know about. The light of day was gone, and rain sheeted down the closed windows of the bus. The air inside the vehicle was squalid.

"Yes?"

"Are you sick?"

"I have a cold, yes."

Her eyes narrowed.

"I just need to take some Tylenol, and I'll be fine. How much farther to Santa Cruz?"

"You won't be going to Santa Cruz." She crossed her arms. "You need to leave this bus right now."

"Excuse me?"

Her dark eyes flashed. "I have thirty passengers on this bus, mister, and none of them want whatever you got."

"Is this because of that flu thing? I was in the hospital this morning, and they let me go."

"Did you bring a medical release?"

I shook my head. "No."

"Then you need to get off this bus."

I turned to look at the other passengers. None would meet my eyes except for the man who'd sat next to me earlier. He looked at me sadly, then glanced away as though something had caught his eye in the darkness outside.

The driver tapped her foot on the nonskid flooring. "I don't want to have to say it again, but I will. I don't want to have to ask the passengers to help you off, but I will do that too. Please. Get. Off. The. Bus."

I stood and edged into the aisle, enjoying the fear that showed in her eyes when I rose to my full height. Nobody knew better than I did what a mess I was. I took a step toward the driver, and she flinched.

"Where the hell are we?" I asked. I could see lights past the window, but they didn't seem like anything I'd recognize. A sign for a convenience store maybe. An off-brand gas station. It wasn't exactly familiar. The water rippling down the window glass distorted and obscured whatever the other sign said.

"We're on Highway 101 in Santo Ignacio," the driver told me. "This is the SeaView Motel. We wouldn't strand you in the middle of nowhere, but I'm telling you to get off my bus."

"I'm going," I said, walking past her. "Are you going to open the cargo hold of this barge so I can get my duffel bag?"

"I am. I'll be down in a minute." She reached under her seat for a container of bleach wipes and handed them off to the old man who'd been my seat partner. He took them from her but held them in his hands as if he didn't know what to do with them. Or maybe he just didn't want to do it in front of me.

I disembarked slowly. I was going to feel this day's adventure for a long time. When the rain hit my skin, it began to dawn on me that I was being *thrown off* a Greyhound bus. How rich. If I'd thought for a second that finding my lover in bed with three men and then being beaten half to death by his 'roid-sucking, faithless ass had been rock bottom, being thrown off a Greyhound bus had to be below it somewhere. My very lowest ebb's deeper, fouler, and more craptastic cellar.

I got my duffel out of the locker and watched as the driver boarded the bus. Soon the distinctive growl of the engine ripped through the silence. It rumbled for a minute, and then the bus's pneumatic doors closed with a *psssshhhht,* and the bus roared off down the highway. Without me.

Crazy.

Fucking swine flu. If I'd had it, they wouldn't have let me leave the hospital, would they? I counted myself lucky I'd only been on a bus. If I'd been with that same crew midflight aboard a plane, I'd be making a spectacularly wet, unscheduled *thud* on the ground right about then.

I turned to the motel. There was a flickering lighted sign on a pole that read SEAVIEW MOTEL. The *V* and the *I* in SeaView remained unlit. A red VACANCY sign welcomed travelers.

In you go, Jacob.

CHAPTER THREE

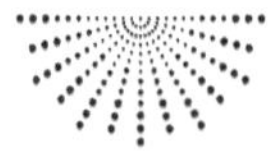

The doorknob on the motel's small office turned easily in my hand, but the door was stuck. I gave it a tug and then pulled harder when I realized it was probably because of the humidity. Rain continued to spatter down intermittently. The old man behind the desk was reading *USA TODAY* and kept me waiting for a minute.

I cleared my throat delicately, afraid to cough in front of someone else that night, lest I have to sleep on the street like I had the plague.

Bring out your dead.

"I see you. Just a sec," the man said, not unkindly, from behind the paper.

I waited until the pages rustled and came down to reveal an average face, about sixty years old, with half-moon glasses.

"Holy cow," the clerk whispered when he saw my face.

Okay, that was going to get old. "That bad?"

"Worse," the manager drawled. "What can I do for you?"

"I need a room for"—I realized I'd have to call Daniel, who might or might not choose to come and get me—"a while maybe."

"Okay." The clerk got out a registration form and handed it over. "Our rooms are all nonsmoking."

"That's fine."

"I'll take it personally if whoever did that to your face blows up my motel."

I got out my wallet. "It was domestic, so that's highly unlikely."

"All right." The man didn't bat an eye. "The little woman box professionally?"

"High-fashion runway model."

"Oh." The old man's lips twitched. "Those are deadly. That's why they hobble them in those spiny high heels."

I laughed and glanced up. "I'd shake your hand, but I have a cold."

"I have hand sanitizer." The man held out his hand. "Carl Lents. I own this place."

"Jacob Livingston. I…" I stopped talking when I felt a tickle in my throat. I coughed into my shoulder and then took his hand and shook it. "I just got thrown off the Greyhound for coughing."

"I hope that's not the high point of your life so far." Carl's lively eyes crinkled at the corners.

"Maybe it is."

The man grinned while he checked my identification and ran my credit card. "Upstairs or down."

I looked out the window into the motel courtyard, empty and slick with rain. At either side of the parking lot the two-story buildings had long galleries and stairs at the far end. *Stairs. Shit.* "First floor."

"There's an acute-care clinic in town, and it'll be open at eight tomorrow morning."

"I saw a doctor this morning at the ER." Was that only this morning? "I have a cold, and I'm spectacularly beat to hell. Nothing a little Vicodin and some rest won't cure."

"If you say so."

I bent to pick up my bag. "I appreciate your concern."

"Yeah. Well. Dead people stink real bad."

I shook my head. "I'll try not to let it get that far."

Carl frowned. "Look. If you need something, it's okay to ask, all right? Call the office if you need..."

I paused at the door. "It's fine. I'll be fine, thank you. Really."

"All right." Carl let me go, and I made my way across the empty lot to the room. The old-fashioned key felt odd in my hand, its tag proudly announcing *The SeaView Motel* in faded gilt lettering on opaque, cream-colored plastic. It looked like it might glow in the dark. When I went on vacations with my family as a kid, we'd play a game where my dad would toss the hotel keys into the pool so Daniel and I could swim down and retrieve them—usually only until Dad had one too many and started throwing them so high they were dangerous when they fell if you got under them. I clearly remembered losing one in the moth-covered security lights at one pool and wearing a key-shaped bruise on my forehead for a week.

Nowadays key cards floated, taking away both the adventure and the danger of the game—and wasn't that just the dilemma of the modern world. Everything had to be *sanitized for your protection*, like the little strips of paper across the toilets in those old motel rooms proclaimed.

I tossed my duffel on the second bed and entered the bathroom, hoping an old curmudgeon like Carl would keep the ancient fires burning. But the toilet was bare of any proclamations.

I peed and washed my hands, then unwrapped one of the hard-plastic mugs and got myself a glass of water. A flash of inspiration made me fill the tiny coffeemaker's carafe as well, and I placed them both on the nightstand next to the bed along with my medications. I could barely peel off my damp clothes and hang them over a chair before the bed beckoned me, welcoming me into the bleachy white envelope of thin linens and old blankets.

There was something I knew I was supposed to do, but I was so tired. My meds and the water I'd brought from the bathroom seemed as if they were miles away. Surely it wouldn't hurt me to sleep for a bit before I took anything. They were only pain relievers, and if I was asleep, it wouldn't matter.

My skin was on fire. There was no other explanation. It burned with pain like a thousand needles, and the agony was shooting straight from my nerve endings to my brain. Every cell in my body hurt. My muscles had tightened, and the swelling on my face and ribs throbbed. Light was dancing behind my closed eyelids, but I couldn't find the will to lift them.

One was lifted for me, and the light blinded me for a minute.

"*Jacob*," a voice spoke above me. "Come back, buddy. Can you hear me?"

The voice wasn't familiar, but it held a kind of paternal sweetness that reminded me of my *zeyde*. Zeyde's voice had been a lightly accented tenor, and it still called my name in dreams sometimes. I didn't hesitate to answer, even though Zeyde was long gone.

"Yasha, Zeyde. How come you don't call me Yasha?"

"Yasha. Okay. Yasha, talk to me. How you doin'? What happened, Yasha?"

"Dunno." *So much pain.* "Musta been Daddy. I didn't let him get Mama, Zeyde. This time he didn't hurt her. Me and Dan stopped him good."

I felt the hands pause on my skin, which was too bad because even though they felt sticky and caught the fine hairs on my arm, they were cool, and it felt nice.

Somewhere above me my zeyde, my grandpa, sighed. "Aw shit."

When I tried to push myself to a sitting position, the man with the cool plastic hands pushed me back down, crooning to me to be still. I felt a pinch and a prick in the back of my hand.

"No." I fought to get up again, to push the pain away and find my feet. My head was so fuzzy, and I hurt everywhere. Someone sticking a pin into my arm was unnecessary and cruel. "Leave me alone."

A second pair of hands grasped my shoulders as Zeyde's voice hummed in my ear. Even though I fought, my strength was entirely gone. Still, I didn't stop twisting in the hands of the beings who held me. All of a sudden I had the most awful feeling that I knew who it was. It made such perfect, horrible sense that I drew in a shuddering breath.

"*Zeyde*," I whispered. "I'm wrestling with the angel, just like Yaakov in the story." I lashed out with a foot, and hands clamped down on it. "Well, *this* sucks. God seems to have sent more than one for me."

An amused voice said, "Shh, Yasha. That's because you're special." Hands lifted me onto another bed, one that moved beneath me. I tried to get off it, and Zeyde grabbed me around the rib cage from behind and held me while others fussed with me and grabbed at my feet.

I turned my head and found a pair of green eyes that held such compassion. Or was that the angel, using Zeyde's voice to trick me into giving up the fight? If I told Zeyde I'd let my lover beat the crap out of me, not just this once, but for a whole year…

Wait. My zeyde's dead.

"Tell me who hurt you, Yasha."

"Fight club," I lied. No way I would let the angel trick me into telling my secret.

The light in the pretty eyes dimmed as if their owner was

disappointed in me. *Shit.* I knew it wasn't my zeyde. My zeyde would never look at me like that.

"Stay still now while we move you."

I struggled. "*Leave me alone.* I just want to go to sleep."

"It's all right if you do," came the reply.

The offer was tempting. It felt like Zeyde was *right there* and so warm. If I dropped my head back, I could imagine it resting on Zeyde's shoulder. Everything would be okay.

Hands moved over my body, taking me away from my zeyde, holding me still while they pulled a strap tight around my chest. Then I remembered again. My zeyde was dead, and I had to wrestle with all these angels until morning to win.

"*Zeyde.*" I wanted to cry. "I'm not strong enough."

"Strong enough for what, Yasha?"

"I can't hold on until morning." I looked at him through unshed tears. "The angels will beat me."

"No, Yasha," Zeyde's voice spoke firmly in my ear. Someone took my hand. "I'll be right here. I won't let you lose."

Maybe my zeyde's a ghost?

"Thank you, Zeyde. I've missed you so much since you've been gone." I squeezed my zeyde's hand. "You're the only one."

A rough hand that smelled like seawater, makrud lime leaves, and something subtler, like a smoky driftwood fire caressed my cheek. I knew my zeyde would stand guard until I was strong enough to wrestle with the angel some more. I turned my head toward his palm and pressed a kiss there because—at last—I knew it was safe for me to rest.

When I opened my eyes, the light was bright enough outside the window next to my bed to convince me it was morning.

"Welcome back, Yasha." Soft hands wrapped a blood-pressure cuff around my biceps.

I was too startled by the use of my nickname to brace myself for the pain of the cuff contracting over my battered arm. "Ow."

"I know this hurts a little because of the bruising. Sorry. I'm Alice."

I looked up into the face of a fortysomething woman in scrubs. She was taking my blood pressure, so I thought it was safe to assume she was a nurse. She had brown hair and kind eyes and wore no makeup.

"What happened?" The last thing I remembered was…What?

"The paramedics brought you here after the motel manager where you were staying found you unconscious in your room. You were so severely dehydrated, I think he might have saved your life. He's here if you want to see him. He stopped by to see how you're doing."

I remained silent. *Wow. I'd almost…*

"He's just outside. Should I tell him to come back some other time?"

"No. It's all right. I should thank him."

"That'd be good," she agreed.

After noting my vitals, Alice drifted out, and in came Carl, the motel owner, with a younger man, maybe my age.

"I hear I have you to thank for some timely medical intervention."

Carl's eyes lit up. "That's the second time I've had to call paramedics for a guest this year. They just don't make tourists like they used to."

Because of my sore face, I fought back a grin. "I'm usually made of sterner stuff."

"When you didn't come or go for a couple of days, I started to worry. And like I said, dead people—"

I rolled my eyes. "Stink real bad, I know."

"Here's someone else you should thank. This is Jason, my son. He's the paramedic I called."

Jason held out his hand. I took it and found his handshake

firm and dry. "Call me JT. Glad to see your color's coming back. You scared us all for a while, Yasha."

I frowned. "What did you call me?"

"Yasha. Isn't that your name?"

"It's Jacob."

"You told me to call you Yasha. You called me zeyde. That's 'grandfather,' right?" He looked at his dad.

Suddenly, what happened came flooding back, including the look in his eyes that had caused me to kiss the palm of his hand. *Shit.*

Carl spoke. "That's right. Zeyde is Yiddish for 'grandpa,' and Yasha is a nickname for Jacob, like Sasha is for Alexander. I had an uncle we called Yasha."

I felt my face catch fire. "I must have been really out of it if I called you zeyde."

JT grinned. "It did seem odd," he murmured. "I don't usually get mistaken for someone who has grandkids.

JT rested his forearms on the railing of the bed and folded his hands together. My heart did a little squeeze thing. JT had green, green eyes—an opaque color like jade—and brown hair. He must have been coming off shift, because his cheeks and chin were heavily stubbled with beard hair that glinted coppery red even in the half-light of the hospital room. He looked tired but sweet as if he was going to go home with his dad and curl up in a chair across from him to play chess. Feed some stray cats. Kind eyes. Soft voice. *Jason Lents.* Not exactly my normal kind of guy but attractive.

"My name is Jacob."

"The problem is, I like calling you Yasha." JT's voice was a caress. He stretched a finger out to trace the tape that held the IV in place on my hand. "I saved your life, so I own it, right?"

"Sure," I said lightly. "As soon as I get out of here, I'll move in with all the other people you've rescued over the years."

"No need to go that far. Maybe you could see to it that you

don't need my services for a while." Green eyes peered at me, serious and probing. "Let me buy you coffee sometime so I can tell you that you shouldn't be content to be someone's punching bag."

I felt slapped. "You don't have to tell me that."

"Looks like I do." JT's eyes narrowed. "Looks like you don't give a rat's ass what happens to you."

"You don't know that." I sounded hoarse, and I hoped Carl and JT thought it was just about cotton mouth. The way JT was looking at me made something compress my heart painfully—like shame. Because I knew I had only myself to blame. I knew what Sander was, and I should have walked away. But what did this virtual stranger know about it?

"Then stay out of trouble."

I looked at his father, who kind of rolled his eyes and shrugged. I looked back down at my hands. "Sure. Sometimes trouble just…finds me though."

Although he exhibited no outward sign of disappointment, JT's intense focus dissipated. "Dad, I have to go get some shut-eye. *You*"—he pointed at me—"do whatever Alice and the docs tell you to do. Don't make me come back here and kick your ass. Figuratively speaking, of course."

Carl winced. "Son—"

JT turned to his father. "See you later, Dad." He gave his dad's arm a squeeze. "I'm outta here."

When the door closed behind Jason, Carl leaned over my bed. "Don't mind my son. He's like that. A whirlwind."

"It's all right. He's probably had a long night."

"Yeah."

A deep silence filled the room. I had never been one to wade in and fill them, and neither it seemed was Carl. Eventually he said, "You're Jewish?"

"Yeah."

"Me too." Carl gazed down at me. "I'm not very observant."

I tried out a smile, but it hurt. "You noticed I didn't leave my room."

"That's not…Oh. I see. Yes." Carl grinned. Another silence followed. "I guess I meant to say I'm not a good Jew."

"I know. Me neither."

"My son is more religious. He thinks it's a crime against God to fight like you do for pleasure or money. He worries about things like that. He's fairly opinionated about it."

I tried to think what that could mean. "Fight for pleasure?"

"Don't get me wrong, I understand that it's a popular thing, and people call it a sport, just not Jason. He has this idea that those fight clubs are barbaric, a return to the kind of blood sport that was popular in ancient Rome."

"Fight club?" I tried to focus on Carl, but even that brief encounter tired me. I tried to think back on what I'd said while I'd been so sick.

"Yeah. No big deal. You just need to know you're going to hear about it from Jason. He'll try to talk you out of ever doing it again."

Something clicked in my memory. "*Fight club.*" I sighed. "I told him I was in a fight club."

"Yeah." Carl's eyes were brown. I wondered where Jason's green eyes came from.

"I lied. I don't…I'm not a boxer. He can rest assured I'll be avoiding anything like this in the future."

"That's good. He was building up quite a head of steam, and he can lecture like you wouldn't believe."

"I see."

"Why would you lie?" Carl asked. "If you're in some kind of trouble with the law—"

"It's nothing like that." I fought the desire to look away. Instead, I stared Carl right in the eyes. "I told you the truth. It was domestic—my boyfriend. I was ashamed."

"*Ah…Yasha.*" Carl sighed sadly.

"It's over anyway. Even I'm not that stupid. Just don't tell… anyone, okay? It's embarrassing enough wearing it on my skin." Despite my determination to hold Carl's gaze, my eyes began to drift closed. "So tired."

"Heal up." Carl started for the door but then turned back. "How long do you plan to stay here in St. Nacho's?"

I dragged my eyes open. "Hell if I know. I never planned to be here in the first place."

Carl started moving again. "You might want to rethink that. St. Nacho's has a way of wrapping itself around you. I only stopped here to fix my truck, and that was forty years ago."

"You've done well though. You must have liked it here."

Carl frowned in concentration as if he was thinking hard or remembering. "I don't think so. Not exactly, no. But it didn't let me go." He left me alone in the room to wonder what the hell he'd meant by that. There were lots of things in my past that wouldn't let me go. But that didn't mean I wanted another one.

Rain began to patter against the window, and the sound was soothing enough that it drove away all my more pressing problems. I'd have to call Dan. Maybe Dan knew where this place was, and he could pick me up. I had been asleep on the bus in the dark when they'd let me off, and I had no clue.

Maybe I'd take a break right here, though, and look around after I got out of the hospital. I'd never heard of St. Nacho's. What kind of a town was called St. Nacho's anyway?

Maybe I'd stick around long enough to find out.

CHAPTER FOUR

"I could have called a taxi," I argued as JT helped me up into the cab of his truck. The thing was an early sixties Ford, a lacquer red F-100 Flareside, solid and beautiful, fully restored. It was a treasure. Not one of the early curvy trucks but big, square, and wide, its grille a toothy horizontal smile of chrome. A moment of intense covetousness caught me squarely in the chest.

"You'd have to wait hours for it to get here from Santa Barbara. St. Nacho's isn't a cab kind of town. On the other hand, if you stuck your thumb out, you could get a lift, probably even from someone who wouldn't kill you for your wallet. So it all evens out." JT had an engaging grin, and he was displaying it a lot.

The ignition was to the left of the steering column. The shift was "on the tree." I sighed and ran my hands over the dash.

"This is a very fine truck."

"I call it Mithril."

I laughed. "I can see that. Tolkien. Gandalf said, 'Mithril! All folk desired it. It could be beaten like copper and polished like glass.'"

JT gave an inelegant snort. "And everyone knows that the 'beauty of mithril did not tarnish or grow dim.' Could I be a bigger geek?"

"Probably not."

JT glanced at me. "Some things feel true and uncomplicated."

I guess I knew what he meant. There weren't any bells and whistles, just a big wide bench seat, a glove box, and a tiny radio in the no-frills cockpit. But it was like looking through a window in time, and it still carried an earthy farm smell and the reminder of a bigger, more optimistic America.

When I looked up, I was caught in his gaze, and I had the absurd thought that he was both surprised and delighted by my reaction. As if we were kindred spirits and the truck was like a bond between us: a secret handshake or a code word that broke the silence and bridged the distance between us.

The individual springs under the car's upholstery were stiff and sproingy, and they creaked as I looked around for a seat belt.

"There's only lap belts." JT seemed to read my mind. "This truck didn't originally even have those. They added them later."

"Cool." I dug between the seat cushion and back by the door and found the one side, then groped around on my other side to find its mate. "So has it always belonged to your family?'

"Yeah. Dad's family used to have a farm up in Castroville."

"Castroville?"

"The artichoke capital of the world." JT keyed the ignition and adjusted the choke when the truck sputtered to life, smoothing it out. "In the sixties, when Julia Child started doing her *The French Chef* show, people started to get into gourmet cooking and fine dining. My grandmother thought it would be a good time to start going into high-end produce—white asparagus, Belgian endive, artichokes, different kinds of lettuce, and baby vegetables."

"You're kidding."

"Nope. And she sent first my grandfather and then my dad around in this truck to the restaurants and farmers' markets in the San Francisco area. Dad was on a trip down to Los Angeles to see if he could open a market there and got stuck here in St. Nacho's by a cracked radiator. While he waited for it to be fixed, he fell in love with the daughter of the man who owned the SeaView Motel."

"That's a great story. He mentioned that this town wrapped around him and wouldn't let go."

"Yeah, well. That was probably my mom who did that. Anyway, his brother took over the farm, but when it came time to get a new truck, my dad couldn't bear to let them sell it. We've had it ever since. It's mine now."

We hit a bump, and it jostled me enough to make me wince. I grabbed the seat next to my leg.

"I'm sorry. It doesn't have the smoothest ride."

"That's all right. She can knock me around a little. I'm not that delicate." It definitely rode like a farm truck. Nothing wrong with that unless you were beaten all to hell.

JT's hands tightened on the steering wheel. "I wanted to talk to you about that. Were you sick with the flu before or after you took that awful beating?"

"Look, I don't know what your dad told you about me, but—"

"He told me that you don't belong to any fight club," JT almost growled. "He told me who beat you."

"Great." My hand tightened on the seat. "Just...great."

"Was that the first time?"

"No," I muttered.

JT stayed silent for a long enough time that I thought he was going to stay that way for the rest of the ride. After a while, when we were stopped at a red light, he turned to me. "I don't understand that. I'm just called in to pick up the pieces. Sometimes more than once at the same place, you know?"

"It's not that simple."

"I know that. Nothing's simple." When the light was green again, JT pulled out into the intersection. "I was shocked to find out is all."

"What?"

"That a guy like you..." He never finished his sentence.

What did he mean by that? I looked out the window and didn't answer.

"I don't mean to pry," he said eventually. "Only that as an outsider, you wonder."

"What do you wonder?"

"When I was an absolute rookie, we responded to a call. When we got there, a woman had been stabbed several times and left for dead on the living-room floor. Her husband was just sitting there, in a recliner, watching the game and drinking a beer. Before the police dragged him away, he said she'd asked for it and he'd given it to her. That's the kind of shit I can't wrap my mind around."

Poor JT. His earnest green eyes were shadowed, like the answer was something he expected to figure out, and the fact that he couldn't made him feel like a failure. Like he lost sleep over it. Those eyes said JT took things harder than most. Maybe being an EMT was an especially tough job for him.

"Nobody asks for that."

"I know that. Of course I know that."

"So what do you wonder?"

"Why, I guess. Why, after the first time, the first blow, the first bruise, does anyone allow it to go on?"

"That's a great question."

"Well?"

"Don't look at me. As you can see, I flunked that test."

JT grunted at me but said nothing further.

When the silence looked like it was going to continue, I ran my hand over the frame of the door, admiring what my dad used to call a wind wing. It opened smoothly, and I let the air wash over me. It was a pity they didn't make those anymore—the little quarter windows that opened to focus a blast of air into the truck. It felt like the human equivalent of being a dog, shoving my head out the window, and letting my tongue loll. I'd always liked playing with a wind wing, aiming it until I felt like I was drowning in air, and since JT lived so close to the ocean this far north of LA, he probably wouldn't need an air conditioner much, even if the truck had one. Which of course it didn't.

What it did have was style: solid cherry-lipstick-colored cool.

We pulled into the parking lot at the SeaView, and the dip as the truck ascended the driveway caused me to clench my teeth until I saw the setting sun reflected on the glassy, waxed hood. My heart burst with longing.

"I'm so in love with your truck," I gushed.

JT's green gaze landed on me and took my breath away.

My face heated. I yanked the plastic bag with my personal crap off the bench seat between us. I wished I'd never told JT my nickname. He seemed like a nice guy, but I wasn't the sort of man to appreciate a nice guy. And even if he had been my type, if I knew anything at all, it was that when one guy beat you half to death, it wasn't a good policy to pin your hopes on the guy who picked you up and dusted you off.

For me it wasn't a good policy to pin my hopes on anything. I wasn't good at picking men. Or rather I was clearly the quintessence of picking the wrong men.

Whatever.

"Thanks for the ride."

"If you're going to stick around for a few days, why don't you let me show you the town?"

"I don't think I'll be here that long." I pulled my key out of my pocket.

"What's long? I could show you everything here in about fifteen minutes." JT leaned one hip against the truck. "I could buy you a beer."

"No." I stopped at the door to the motel room and turned to see he'd followed me and was standing just inches away. Something indefinable teased my senses: that same smell that felt vaguely familiar when he'd put me on that gurney. The laundry soap he'd used on his uniform shirt maybe, the disinfectant, or the latex. A light aftershave that bore the smell of the sea. I'd smelled it when I was so sick I didn't know who I was, and I now realized why it triggered memories of my zeyde. "You smell like the ocean in Jersey."

His eyebrows rose. "You might be the first person who ever said that to me."

"I don't mean that in a bad way."

"That's good, I guess."

"I'm not saying this right." I closed my eyes and concentrated. "It's like popcorn and suntan oil. Driftwood fires. Citrus. You smell like a particularly good day at the beach."

"Everything smells like the beach in St. Nacho's."

"This is different. You make me anticipate…adventure. Salt-water taffy. Strong men and sword swallowers." His face said he was lost. "I guess I've had one too many pain pills."

"Yasha"—he squared his shoulders—"I'm going to ask. Even though you don't want me to. Even though you say you don't know. *Why* did you let someone beat you?"

Sighing, I turned but refused to meet JT's eyes. "Look, I'm a big guy. I've been in the military. I thought I could handle…It turned out, when the chips were down, I couldn't protect myself, and it started me thinking." I was prepared to think, at least.

JT waited, and when I didn't say anything further, he spoke. "About what?"

"About why I made it okay for the possibility of violence to exist in the first place."

"*Yasha.*" JT's infinitely gentle touch found my cheek where it was split and bruised. It was tender, but because I couldn't meet his eyes, I had no idea if it was romantic or merely the professional examination of a wound by an EMT.

"Yasha." I turned when I heard my name a second time. Carl stepped out the door of his office and waved hello. JT and I watched him walk over.

Carl shook my hand. "It's good to see you back."

"Hi, Carl. It's good to be out of the hospital."

Carl shaded his eyes against the setting sun. "Have you given any thought to how long you'll be staying?"

"I'll have to make some calls." I clutched my bag tighter. "I'm not real anxious to do that either."

"Well. Take your time, son. Better to move slowly if you're not sure." From the way he gazed at his son, Carl seemed to be including JT in that.

JT frowned at his father. "Yasha, I'll pick you up at six forty-five."

"*Jason.*" Carl's voice held a warning.

I didn't understand the subtext, but I wasn't planning on going anywhere. "I don't want to—"

"Trust me, Yasha, please." Those jade eyes never wavered. "It's not what you think."

MY HAND WAS sore from gripping my cell phone tightly, but Phil didn't cut to the chase. While it was a simple question, whether I still had a job waiting for me, Phil didn't seem to want to give me a brief answer. Maurizio had apparently panicked at the thought that his pastry chef was, in his words, "circling the drain," and he couldn't be appeased. He'd begun looking for another to hire from the moment I got sick.

"Fucking swine flu," I practically shouted into the phone. "I don't *have* the fucking swine flu. I was in the hospital, and they let me go. Did you tell him that?"

"You know Maurizio. If you're asking if he's started to listen to me at this late stage in the game, the answer is no." Phil paused. "It seems Giorgio is available."

"Oh shit. Well, that's that, then." Giorgio was Maurizio's on-and-off sexual and professional obsession, and if he needed a job, no pastry chef's job was safe at Il Ghiotto.

"Maybe we'll get lucky and he'll hold out for an outlandish salary. Maybe *he'll* get the swine flu."

"Or I'll get it for real."

"Jacob, don't even talk like that."

"Nah. No can do. Swine's against my religion." I pinched the skin on the bridge of my nose, but even that hurt. "Look, remember when I gave you a key in case I lost it?"

"Yeah."

"Can you call Sander's cell and tell him to pick up his crap?"

"You sure you want me to do that?"

"Yes and no. I mean, it's over. I'm not...That was it. I wish I could do it myself, I just can't go into that apartment with him again."

"Glad to hear it. I'll go by your place and talk to your landladies—the freak sisters. See if they'll let me change the locks. I want to make sure Sander leaves your shit alone.

I closed my eyes, remembering. "It's pretty shocking. There's still a mess in the kitchen where I—"

"You want me to have a service in?"

"No. I'll clean it when I get back. I probably need the lesson in humility." Humble, humility, *humiliation.*

Phil murmured his goodbye, even as I reminded him to give Hannah a kiss for the baby.

That just left Dan.

"Hello?"

"Hi, Dan, it's Jacob."

"Jakey! What happened to you? I was expecting you to call days ago. I tried your cell—"

"I had a cold, and it wasn't possible for me to travel."

"You could at least have given me a call."

"I'm sorry. I was really under the weather and had to stop in a town called Santo Ignacio. I've been pretty out of it."

"You never answered. Eventually it just went straight to voice mail."

"My phone ran out of charge. I'm better now. I'm still here."

"Where's here?"

"St. Nacho's. Santo Ignacio. Have you heard of it?"

"No, let me ask BreeAnna." Muffled words floated over me as I waited for Dan to come back on the line.

"BreeAnna says she knows where it is. They have a good brunch there on Sundays."

"St. Nacho's does?"

"A restaurant there. It's famous for the all-you-can-eat Mexican brunch. They have champagne and a guy who plays mariachi music on the violin. That's what BreeAnna says."

"Is it any good?"

Dan paused. "Are you kidding me? How would I know?"

"Yeah." All-you-can-eat wasn't exactly the kind of restaurant that drew the brittle, anorexic BreeAnna, and Dan didn't dare make a move without her. "Dan, can you come and get me?"

Dan said nothing for a long while, and I worried that he'd finally had it with my dropping in for visits whenever things got tough. "Something completely unexpected came up this week, and I can't get away right this minute. It will have to wait for the weekend."

Jeez. The weekend. It was only Monday. I tried to look on the bright side. Dan wasn't cutting me off, even though it was no secret that BreeAnna would have liked him to do just that. She was an ultraconservative born-again fundie Christian who had married Dan in spite of his Jewish heritage when he'd made it big in real estate before the bubble burst. From what Dan hinted at privately—just lately—I thought it was possible she regretted it.

I felt bad for my brother, even if I was exasperated with him. He was a good man, and he deserved a wife who loved him. But while BreeAnna didn't approve of Jews, she at least allowed that we had a place in the natural order of things—if only so she and her church cronies could look down on someone. She had no use for gays that didn't involve pitchforks and tar and feathers.

"This weekend, then?" I asked. "I could always rent a car."

"No, Jacob." My brother sighed. "It's not a good time to be here, but you shouldn't have to do that. If you need me to come and get you, I'll—"

There was some sort of disturbance on the phone, and I knew Dan was arguing with BreeAnna. Maybe he had his hand over the phone, or maybe he held it to his chest. I was fairly certain of the outcome. We weren't the closest of brothers anymore. I didn't understand how that had happened. At one time we'd only had each other. Dan and Zeyde had been my entire world.

Now, half the time we couldn't understand each other, and half the time we were spoiling for a fight. But we both understood that blood was important, and the pain of our shared past made us cling to what was left of our family regardless of our differences. I felt bad for how tough that made things with BreeAnna.

"I have a bit of time off right now from the restaurant, and this—St. Nacho's—seems like a good place to hang out for a while. I've made a couple of friends here. The motel owner is a nice guy. Why don't you call me back later on in the week, all right?"

"Sure." Dan's voice held a false and fragile brightness. "A little vacation. That's probably a good idea."

"I'll wait until I hear from you, then." I let him off the hook like a tired fish and threw him back. "Say hi to BreeAnna for me."

"I will. Have a restful time. You work awfully hard. Take advantage."

"You bet." I hung up.

"Enjoy your stay in lovely St. Nacho's," I said to no one in particular.

A KNOCK on the door roused me from sleep. I couldn't remember falling asleep, actually, so I wasn't at all ready to be wakened.

I opened the door to find JT on the other side, dressed in his blue work uniform.

"Somebody call 911?"

I looked around him stupidly, still shrugging off the effects of my nap. "I didn't."

JT grinned. "I'm kidding. Are you ready to go?"

I backed up so JT could enter the small motel room. Once he was inside, it felt even smaller. I was still marginally disoriented. "I fell asleep. Where are we going again?"

JT looked down at me. "I asked you to trust me. Do you?"

I was silent for so long that JT raked a hand through his hair and let out what sounded like an exasperated sigh. He stood there in his uniform, looking like an overgrown Boy Scout. He'd saved my life. Of course I trusted him. Was that what he was asking? Or did he mean something different? Did he mean for me to notice the way his eyes met mine boldly, or the fact that up close I could see those coppery spots scattered throughout his five-o'clock shadow? Did he mean would I trust him if he made a move on me? Did he mean did I trust him not to? Did I want him?

The way his scent teased me, always noticeable, like a gust of wind off the ocean on a late-fall day, made it hard for me to think. If he made a move, *if he wanted me,* I certainly wouldn't have minded. My heart stuttered, lodging nearer to my throat than usual. "What do you mean do I trust you?"

"Look. In my line of work I see a lot of things. I've done some research on how to help victims of domestic violence. There's a support group here in St. Nacho's, and—"

"Oh *hell no.*" I took a step back toward the bed. No fucking way. This was far worse than any of the scenarios I'd imagined.

"Hear me out. You could just—"

I was so stunned I practically screeched, "How *lame*!"

"You could just go and see what they have to say."

"Are you kidding? I know what they have to say."

JT's green gaze passed over me sadly. "I know you do."

"So is this part of the rescue? Standard follow-up care?"

JT shook his head. "No. I just figured anyone who lives in a relationship where he gets the shit beaten out of him—"

"I'm not like that. I don't want to go."

"I understand that. That doesn't mean you shouldn't. On the contrary, you have nothing to lose and everything to gain by going if only to find out that you were right and you don't belong there."

"Let me guess. You majored in psych in college."

"Minored. I can't stay, Yasha." JT's eyes were warm and sincere. "I'm on a break. I have to get back to the station. I only came to take you—"

I went toward the door and opened it. "I can't go. I'll be a joke. I'll be the only guy there, and I'll…"

JT's eyes were beautiful and sad. "And I'm asking you to *trust me.*"

Heaven help me. I did trust him. But more than that, at that moment, I was charmed by him, and I thought *maybe...*

We left the motel room without speaking. After I opened the passenger door to his truck, he put his hand on the small of my back and took my elbow to brace me, ready to help me up if I needed a boost. I thought, yeah, I can trust him. I just can't trust myself.

CHAPTER FIVE

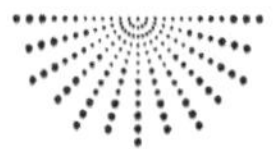

I held my coffee and gazed around at the women, all silent, all clenched within the small circle of chairs. I didn't even know how I'd gotten here, really. One minute I was with JT, and the next I was walking into a high school classroom being used as a meeting place for a battered-women's support group called "Stop Partnership in Violence"—SPiV. I swallowed hard and made myself amend my thinking right then and there. They were *victims of domestic violence. I* was here. *I* had a dick. Domestic violence wasn't just for women. I knew enough to know it never had been.

They were staring at me, and I shot a tight smile at the group's leader, who happened to be the nurse, Alice, from the hospital.

"First off I want to welcome Yasha." All eyes turned toward me. It was far worse than I'd imagined. Those women gazed at me with varying levels of pity and mistrust and outright hostility. Only one had unreadable eyes. She watched me shyly, with a hint of curiosity, and then glanced away. She must have been in her midfifties, and she was pretty and fragile looking. She wore a lightweight cotton skirt and a T-shirt that read *Miss Indepen-*

dence Pies under a soft pink cardigan. She had pearls around her neck. Her hair was trimmed in a pretty bob and held back with some sort of sparkly headband. When her eyes returned to mine, I smiled at her, and she smiled back timidly.

"Yasha?" Alice asked, and I realized I had been watching the pie lady and not listening. "You want to tell us a little about why you're here?"

Technically that question was my number one reason for not wanting to be there in the first place. That Alice asked it right out of the gate was almost perfectly ironic. The only thing worse would have been if they'd given me a button that read, *Beat me now, ask me how.*

"I—" My mouth went dry.

"It's all right if you don't feel like sharing today."

I rose to my feet so fast that my chair tipped over. It clattered noisily to the floor, going off like a bomb in the quiet room, and I had to dive to pick it up. "I don't belong here."

Alice rose, probably to forestall me. "At first it may seem like that, Yasha, but—"

I took a deep breath. "The thing is, I'm not a victim, see? I knew what was going to happen. I picked the worst possible time to argue. I had the flu, and I couldn't..." I decided it would have been a good thing if I'd stopped babbling a few minutes earlier. "I don't belong here." I took off out the door and headed toward the parking lot. I was making my way past the metal gates when I heard the feminine sound of *clackety* heels tapping after me.

"Hey, stop!"

I turned, fully expecting to see Alice following me. Instead, I was surprised to find my pie lady there, her sandals scrabbling along the pebbly blacktop as she chased after me. I slowed, afraid she'd hurt herself.

"Yes?"

She was chewing her lip. I could see that she'd come on a

whim and now that she'd caught me she had no idea what to do with me.

"I heard what you said. Back there. And I wanted to…I'm not a damned victim either."

I was surprised and ashamed. "I'm sorry if you think I meant…That is to say, I meant no disrespect."

"Yeah. No. That's not what's important here. Nobody wants to be seen as a victim. And if we all had to go in there and tell everyone what big fools we were and how we'd been bullied and abused, well…I don't suppose that some of us would ever go."

"I don't suppose so."

"My name is Mary Catherine." She held out her hand.

I took it. I murmured, "Yasha," while we shook hands, but I don't know why I said that name. Probably because I'd been introduced that way by Alice.

"Can I buy you a cup of coffee?"

"I don't have a car, and I don't live here. Someone brought me to the meeting." I looked around at the school parking lot, suddenly as tired as if I'd run a marathon. "I don't know what I'm doing."

"That's all right," Mary Catherine told me gently, taking me by the arm. "I live here, I have a car, and I know exactly what to do."

I DROPPED two sugars and two creams into my coffee and gave it a stir. No matter what I did, it would still taste like Denny's coffee, so I wasn't in a hurry to drink it.

"Are you all right?" asked Mary Catherine.

"Yes." I refused to fidget under her probing gaze. "I'm used to better coffee."

"How'd you end up in St. Nacho's?"

I laughed, and it probably sounded every bit as bitter as it felt. "I got thrown off the bus."

"What?" Mary Catherine had dimples when she laughed, and it held a light silvery sound, as though she were crystal and laughter made her ring. "That's got to be a personal low, huh?"

"I wish it were." I didn't meet her eyes. "I had a bad cold. I think they were paranoid about this new flu that's going around."

"I see."

"Anyway, they stopped by the SeaView and just told me to get off."

"My son stayed at the SeaView when he first came to town."

I stirred my coffee. There didn't seem to be too much to say to that. Mary Catherine sipped her coffee in silence. I worried that she was just waiting me out. As if I would crack and my entire story would come pouring forth like so much word vomit. And maybe if she waited long enough that's exactly what would happen. If I didn't say something soon, we'd both start looking anywhere but at each other, and things would go from bad to worse.

When she removed her cardigan, I realized that the name of the pie shop was part of a larger image, probably inspired by those World War II posters of women rolling up their sleeves to do a man's job for the war effort.

"So. Is there a real Miss Independence Pies? Or is that just like one of those fruit-crate-label things—vintage sign on a shirt."

"It's my company. I'm Miss Independence Pies. My son thought of the name."

"Cool." It made me warm to her. It was probably the connection to pie, which seemed a homely and generic sort of thing. Done right, it showed off a baker's skill, and done wrong, it was barely palatable. My mother had been a fine pie baker. She'd always let me roll out the trimmings and sprinkle them with sugar and cinnamon to bake along with the pie as a treat.

Mary Catherine grinned. “I caught you.”

I didn’t understand. “What?”

“There’s a certain look that some people get when you mention pie.”

“Really? Like what?” I took a sip of coffee.

“I don’t know. But you had it. Do you have fond memories of pie?”

I put my cup down, surprised. “Are you part of the Psychic Pie Bakers Network?”

She gave a ladylike snort. “Yeah, sure.”

“My mom used to give me the trimmings to make pseudo-cookies.”

“That’s just what I’m talking about.” She dimpled at me. “Some people have pie memories.”

“Me more than most, probably,” I told her. “Since I’m a pastry chef.”

Her eyes widened. “For real?”

“Yes.” For some reason I had trouble meeting her eyes. She reminded me very much of my own mother, from whom it had been impossible to hide anything. I don’t know what, specifically, I thought she’d see in me, but I worried that to her I was as transparent as glass.

Apparently I was.

“You know, Yasha”—she put her hand over mine where I fidgeted with a creamer pod—“I’m hardly in a position to judge you, even if I were so inclined.”

I knew what she meant by that, and it was worse somehow. The thought of someone harming her—she was so delicate—bothered me more than I could express.

“Are you still…? I mean…” I remembered the old joke, or trick really, of asking a man if he’d stopped beating his wife. There was no good answer to that, and equally there was no good way to ask if Miss Independence was now safe from her abuser.

"I left my husband to rot when my son moved here to St. Nacho's," she answered my unspoken question. "I probably never would have left, except Jordan got carjacked at the SeaView, and I wanted to make sure he was all right."

"Jordan's your son?"

She smiled. "Yes."

"The SeaView doesn't exactly seem like a hub of criminal activity. Was he all right?"

"He's fine now, or he will be when he gets his driver's license back. He had a concussion and a seizure, and California has a mandatory-reporting law."

"That sucks."

"St. Nacho's is a small place, and he can walk most everywhere. His partner, Ken, takes him when he has somewhere he needs to drive."

"I see." Partner? Maybe that was a business partner, or maybe it meant her son was gay. I didn't pursue it.

There was a protracted silence into which I projected a number of things. Mostly how Mary Catherine must have seen me. I was a mass of healing cuts and bruises. Alice had just removed the stitches on my cheek. My eye was still a little swollen. I said nothing but imagined what she was thinking until she surprised me again.

"I know you're looking at me and seeing what? Some fragile old lady who got beat up by her husband for years? You have sympathy for me. Empathy. You wish you could have been there to help me."

How did this woman see everything I was thinking? It was unnerving and made me want to take off. Before I could gather my thoughts and rise from the booth, she grabbed my hand again.

"I want you to show yourself the same compassion. No

more, no less, because that's just the beginning."

"But I—"

"I want you to tell yourself that shit happens, today is different, and you're going to find out what you don't know about our respective situations, even if you don't want to come back to the group."

I felt pinned in place like an insect under a microscope. "It's different for me."

"Why, because you're a man?" She gave me a sour look. "If it was just about strength, my husband, for one, would be dead. I'm way tougher than him."

"I don't doubt it for a second," I told her. "The person who did this to me won't get the chance again." It was more than I'd ever planned on saying, but I thought it might shut her up.

I was wrong.

"That's half the battle right there. Good for you." She took a sip of her coffee. Shoot. She *was* tough. "If you want to know how the rest will play out, you'll have to keep coming back."

I WAS WAVING at the taillights of Miss Independence's pie van as she drove away from the high school when JT arrived to take me back to the motel. She'd given me a lot to think about. I pulled myself up into the passenger seat and buckled the lap belt.

"How did it go?"

I was an abysmal failure. "Okay."

Jason glanced at me out of the corner of his eye. "That's good, then."

"Did you know Nurse Alice from the hospital would be in charge?"

"Yes, I did." He chuckled. "Did you know that she has me on speed dial?"

Busted. I looked at my hands.

"She might have mentioned you fled the group early on."

"I'm sorry." I meant that. "I know you mean well, but that group didn't seem like a really good fit for me."

"I see."

"I don't think the ladies want to talk in front of a guy anyway."

"What if I tell you I think that's horseshit?"

I tensed up at this. "You weren't there, okay? Anyway, I doubt it's the same."

"I'm sorry." JT backed down. "I guess that sometimes I see things on the job, and I wish I could do something about them. So when I get the chance, I go for it. There's not much I can do to prevent a major heart attack once it happens."

"Your heart's in the right place, JT, but you can't force someone into something like that. Especially if you don't know the situation. And you don't. No matter what you think, you don't know my situation."

"I'm sorry," JT murmured. "You're right, and I'm sorry." To my surprise he pulled the truck into the parking lot next to a lonely-looking wooden pier. "Suppose you tell me what your situation was."

I rolled down the window but remained silent. The wind from the sea was nothing to the faint teasing scent I remembered from JT's skin. The ocean air lacked the depth of something organic and living and male. Something that drew me in like the fragrance of great food or fine wine. A top note of beach, a middle of citrus and smoke, and a darker, earthier *something* that made my eyes close and my spine arch as though that *something* licked along my dick.

"I'm on your side, Yasha."

"I know," I told him. He was. I could feel it. His attention seemed to wrap me in something warm whenever I saw him. I wanted to get to know him. I guess I decided to believe he wanted to know me too, so I started with something innocuous. "I'm a pastry chef."

"Yeah?" JT smiled. "I have a legendary sweet tooth."

"When I moved to LA, I got a job at this Italian place, Il Ghiotto, and I joined the gym down the street. I met a guy there who liked to eat. I love to cook." I shrugged.

"Match made in heaven."

I snorted. "Not exactly. He stuck around because I fed him, and I let him because…"

After a while he prompted me. "You were lonely."

I looked down at my hands. "Yeah. I guess. It was okay for a while. Then he started juicing, and sometimes it made him irrational."

He watched the waves as they foamed onto the shore. "That's a nice way of saying he suffered from 'roid rage."

"Yeah."

"*Jeez.*"

I closed my eyes and leaned my head back. "I already feel stupid."

"Is that what you think?" he asked. "That I want you to feel stupid?"

"Isn't it?"

"No."

I looked over and saw JT's jaw tighten. "I'm sorry."

"Didn't it kill his libido?"

"After a while he required a lot more stimulation to get the job done. I found him in bed with three guys."

"Shit." JT squeezed the steering wheel. "That's cold. You need to get tested for STDs."

The way he said that made me feel ten times worse. "At least give me a *little* credit. After I realized what a dog he was, I didn't so much as scratch his back without gloving up."

"But—"

"I get tested regularly. So far so good."

The silence dragged out between us for a while.

"Mind taking a walk for a few minutes? I have to get back, but I think I'd like to take a break out here."

"Sure." I rolled up the window before I got out of the car, then followed JT onto the sand.

"I don't know why, but things always seem to make more sense when I'm on the beach."

I smiled, thinking the same thing. "I grew up in New York City, and we used to go to Sandy Hook with my grandfather in the summertime."

"I've lived here all my life. I went to school at UC Santa Cruz."

His hair whipped across his forehead, and I resisted the urge to brush it back. "A beach boy."

His eyelashes swept down. "I guess so."

"You don't have to answer this, but did your mom and dad have...domestic issues?"

"*My* parents?" JT laughed "Hell no. They were perfect together. They watched *Masterpiece Mystery*! and danced around the living room to the theme song. Every Saturday evening in the summer my mom and dad left the motel with the night clerk and biked down to the beach for picnics. My dad was devastated when she died, and now...he seems to be marking time."

"I'm sorry. I thought maybe—"

"My parents had the kind of marriage you see on the Hallmark Channel." He said this wistfully, as though he wanted one like it. I wanted to know but didn't ask. He swallowed hard. "The only thing they seemed to regret was that after me, she couldn't have more children."

"What about grandchildren?"

"There aren't any yet."

I frowned. Did that mean he felt responsible for providing them? "Do you—"

His pager went off, and he looked down. "Hey, sorry. I really have to go."

"Is it a call?"

"Yeah." He looked at me helplessly and pulled out his keys. "I can be back at the station in three minutes from here if I run, but my partner will pick me up on the street before that. Will you take my truck back to the motel, and I'll come for it later? Do you have a license?"

"Yeah, but I'm not insured."

"Truck's insured, and there's no one on the street once you're past Nacho's Bar."

"If you're sure."

"I trust you. All you have to do is adjust the choke. You'll see. Drive safe." He dimpled at me before taking off at a dead run.

I headed for the parking lot, heart racing at the thought of being allowed to drive JT's truck. I let myself in and sat in the driver's seat for a minute just looking around. I'm not really a car guy, but for some reason this truck was different. Powerful, strong, and cool. Solid. Dependable. It's possible I anthropomorphized that truck a little, seeing in it the same things I was seeing in its owner. It's possible I caught a faint whiff of JT's essence, that earthy note that made my belly clench. It's possible that St. Nacho's, the truck, and JT all combined to form a spiderweb of hope that clung to me, gluing me a little more firmly to the tiny town with each passing hour.

I'm not ashamed to say I took the opportunity to explore, opening the pristine ashtray and the nearly empty—except for a first-aid kit, a tire-pressure gauge, and a flashlight—glove box. I pulled down the sunshade just to see if it worked as smoothly as everything else, and a tiny piece of paper fluttered down.

I held it up to the miserably ineffective dome light and saw that it was cut from the flyer of some Jewish singles' group. I recognized the words from the Bible, the Song of Songs, "Tell me, O thou whom my soul loveth, where thou feedest, where thou makest thy flock to rest at noon; for why should I be as one that veileth herself beside the flocks of thy companions?"

Holding that paper, reading it, made me feel like I'd intruded on something unutterably private. That I'd violated JT in some real and thoughtless way. I carefully replaced it where I'd found it and pushed the flap back out of the way.

Maybe there was more to JT than met the eye. Certainly the way he'd treated me when I was sick showed a great deal of empathy. Maybe behind a tough job and a cool truck there was a man who felt things deeply, who longed for something lasting and real like the love he believed his parents had had. I wondered if he longed for someone to share his life with and that's why it was so easy for him to spot the loneliness that led to my own failed instinct for self-preservation.

I started the truck and adjusted the choke, giving it a little nudge with the gas pedal. I was able to figure out the gearshift, so we eased out of the parking space in reverse, and then I took a couple of trips around the parking lot to get used to how she handled. I rubbed my hands over the steering wheel and reveled in the feel of it beneath my fingers before I got on the road, but I drove directly—even though I wanted to keep going all night—to the motel. When I pulled into the parking space outside my room, I half expected Carl to come out and ask me why I had JT's truck. I didn't suppose I had an answer for that.

Even I didn't really know.

It was kind of an anticlimax when I closed the door behind me to face the silence of my motel room alone. I poured myself a drink of water and got ready for bed, but before I could even finish watching the news, someone was knocking at the door. When I opened it, JT was standing there, and I could see his EMS rig pulling away from the curb just past the office.

"Hi." He stood there with his hands in his pockets.

"That was quick."

"It was a first-time mother with a barking kid. Croup. We didn't need to transport."

"No?"

"No. It's always scary for people when they hear a croupy kid for the first time. They panic because the kids are scared. The airway narrows, and the situation can become urgent fast. This time it wasn't."

I nodded.

He continued, "Moist air helps. Half the time the kids are fine when they get to the hospital just because of the fog here on the coastline." He waited patiently. "I guess I should go."

"You'll need your keys…" I left him standing at the door while I went to get them, but when I turned around, he'd entered and closed the door behind him.

"Did you enjoy driving my truck?"

"Yes." I thought I ought to cover my face so he wouldn't see the pure naked pleasure I had experienced, but instead I shrugged. "But I only drove it from the pier here. I promise."

"You could have taken it farther than that." When I handed over the keys, he took my hand with them. I looked up at him. He didn't do anything else. He just held my hand and said, "I trust you."

I wondered, briefly, if he was still talking about the truck. He licked his lips and leaned closer. It wasn't really close enough that I believed he was coming in for a kiss, so I stayed rooted where I was.

JT shook his head and dropped my hand. "Can I tell you something that will sound weird?"

I nodded.

"My dad told me when he first saw St. Nacho's, he was here because the truck broke down. It was raining hard that day, and as he walked to a coffee shop to wait while they fixed it, he saw a girl without an umbrella. He ran over and held his over her head and asked her where she was going. He said he didn't think about it or anything. He just..."

I grinned. "Let me guess. That was your mom."

"Yeah." JT smiled and looked down at the keys in his hand. "I've heard the story a thousand times. He told me she looked up at him to thank him, and hers was the most 'familiar face he'd never seen.'"

"That's cool," I said. Nicer still to know their story had a happily ever after, at least as long as she'd lived.

"Dad said that in his whole life he never did anything more important than hold that umbrella over her head."

I felt something tighten my throat. "That's probably an exaggeration."

JT put his keys into his pocket and reached for me, gripping both my shoulders with strong, careful hands. "Maybe that's how I feel about making sure that you're all right though."

I held my breath.

"Maybe that's why I want you to go to a support group."

I sighed. "I doubt that your dad was saying he only wanted to keep the rain off her."

"I know," he whispered and drew me close enough to kiss. Instead he pressed his cheek to mine and slipped his arms around me, hugging me close. I felt his breath ruffle my hair.

"Are you looking for someone without an umbrella?"

"I'm looking for..." Gently, he pushed away. "I don't know what I'm looking for."

My hands were shaking, so I clamped them under my arms where he couldn't see them tremble. "I hope you find it."

He took a deep, shuddering breath. "In the meantime, I'd like to see to it that you don't end up back in the ER. At least not because some guy—"

"I'm stuck here in St. Nacho's for a few days," I told him. "I'll use the time to think, all right?"

JT nodded. "What are you doing for breakfast? If you stop by the firehouse at around seven, we can eat together as long as there's no call."

At last I was on safe ground again. "My friend, by that time I'll have been working for nearly three hours."

"You what?"

"It seems that my unplanned arrival in St. Nacho's is good for something. You're looking at the newest employee of Miss Independence Pies."

JT snorted through his nose. "Ms. Jensen's?"

"Yes. She followed me from the meeting, and we had coffee."

"I see."

"I told her why I didn't want to go to the group. She was very nice. It turns out that she could use some help at the bakery, and I—"

"That will be good." He laughed. "I'm sorry. I have to go back to work."

"What's so funny?"

"Nothing." JT appeared to get a grip. "I guess nothing."

"Look…" I opened the door to let him out. I felt like I needed to say something further but didn't know exactly what. "Thanks. You're a nice guy for trying to help."

Something flickered in his eyes. It looked like sadness, but it was gone in a second. "That's me, Mr. Nice Guy."

CHAPTER SIX

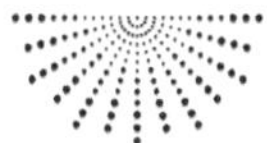

The moment I entered Miss Independence Pies at three a.m., I realized I'd been played. Not in the nyah-nyah-now-I-gotcha way or anything, but as sure as I was standing there, so were five damn women from the domestic violence support group, everyone except Alice, and they all waited in silence as I walked through the door. They watched me with wary eyes, and I had the uncomfortable feeling it wasn't me they were monitoring but my Y chromosome as if they thought at any moment it would cause me to leap at one of them and tug out her hair.

"I guess I should introduce myself to *the group*." I folded my arms. "My name is Jacob Livingston, and I'm a pastry chef."

A young woman, really no more than a girl, laughed from behind a wall formed by two taller women.

"Welcome, *Jacob*," she said in a tone of voice that left no doubt she was teasing me. Shoulders parted as she pushed her way forward. She had black hair that hung in her lined eyes and several piercings, including two prominent ones on her lower lip and a nasal septum piercing. Ordinarily I didn't find piercings attractive, but on her they looked perfect. They made her look like a marmoset with a spiked collar. I tried not to laugh.

"You're the one who called us victims last night."

I cleared my throat. "Well, technically all I said was that I wasn't—"

"*Muse*." Miss Independence herself, Mary Catherine, walked toward me from where she'd been standing by the walk-in freezer. "I thought we talked about letting Yasha get a foot in the door before we alienate him."

"What kind of a name is Yasha?" One woman frowned. "That's not a name. It's a cartoon show."

I laughed. "I may have given the impression yesterday that I didn't have a great deal of respect for the—"

"Damn right you did." A tall blonde woman edged forward. "I, for one, found your insinuation very insulting. Unlike some of the people in that group—"

"Oh, here we go," said the woman next to the girl called Muse. She had lovely dark hair, and she rippled with indignation. She stood poised with her hands on her hips and her head cocked to the side, an elegant, dark-eyed beauty with a great face and a body that, if I swung that way, would have made my dick hard.

The blonde woman turned on her. "What did you just say?"

"*Candace*, I know we don't gotta hear all about you being married to an above-it-all physician again, 'cause I know for a fact that your nose was reengineered three times, first by your med-school boyfriend and twice by that worthless, wife-beating psycho plastic surgeon you married, and only once in the OR, so don't tell me I gotta hear it when I'm working."

"I'm volunteering my time here, Bianca, and if I want to tell Mr. Livingston that not everyone here is—"

"Is what? You're not immune." The dark-haired woman called Bianca raised her brows. "Two words, honey: *Nip/Tuck*. Good thing your husband can fix what he breaks."

Candace narrowed her eyes. "He's not my husband anymore. And of course I'm not immune. But neither do I have to take this Neanderthal's inference that I'm some sort of—"

I tried. I tried so fucking hard, but the misuse of *infer* and *imply* is my biggest pet peeve besides...drunk driving or something. "Implication."

She glared at me. "What?"

I didn't even mind that she had called me a Neanderthal. "The word is *implication.* People switch *imply* and *infer* all the time, but in that sentence you need to use *imply.* But I wasn't, by the way."

"Wasn't what?"

"I wasn't implying that you were victims or anything of the sort, and we got off on the wrong foot altogether." I held out my hand for her to shake, and she took it. "I admit it's true that my lover beat the hell out of me. That looks really bad, but it isn't like it happens all the time. I usually don't let it get that far. I was sick. I couldn't stop the fight once it escalated, and I think it was just as hard on him as it was on me."

Even in my own head that sounded completely lame.

Bianca hissed out a breath. "Honey, did you hear yourself just now?"

"*Ladies,*" Mary Catherine quietly warned her off.

"I'm a veteran," I told them. It was oh-dark-thirty in the morning, and I was gazing at five pairs of eyes that held nothing but sadness and pain. *On my behalf.* "I can take care of myself."

Muse pushed her way forward. She only came up to my shoulder, and as prickly and spiky as she looked, I still wanted to get her a pretty little rhinestone leash and take her for a walk in the park.

"Dude." She wrapped tattooed arms around my waist and held on. "It's okay, man. I can take care of myself too. That doesn't have anything to do with the power you give away to the people you love."

Muse smelled exactly like a pumpkin muffin, and whether I liked it or not, in that very same moment she became one of the people I loved most in the world. I let her give me a squeeze like a python.

"Thanks, Muse. I do know that."

Muse looked around in the small kitchen space and gave a couple of the ladies a hard stare. One of them, who hadn't spoken at all, seemed to realize I was looking at her, and she dashed through the doors behind the worktables.

"*Play nice,*" Muse told them. I simply shook my head when her attitude subdued even my toughest critics.

IT TURNED out that Mary Catherine had an eye on expanding her pie empire to include savory pies. While I was there, we drew up a plan based on what she'd need, and my training came in handy as I worked with the ladies for the better part of the morning baking pies.

In the early afternoon, we loaded up the van for Mary Catherine to make deliveries. I found out she supplied all the local restaurants and on the weekends took two sets of deliveries out, some as far as Santa Barbara. Eventually she wanted to open a retail store, maybe even a tiny restaurant that would serve baked goods, soups, and sandwiches. It was a safe bet that I could streamline her operation and expand her horizons if I spent any time in St. Nacho's. When I left by the back door amid a flurry of heartfelt well-wishes, it was also even money she'd expanded mine a little as well.

Because there seemed to be nothing more than the cold comfort of my empty motel room waiting for me back at the SeaView, I decided to explore St. Nacho's. Moist air came in off the sea, and I could smell it all around me. I discovered if I closed my eyes, I could hear familiar sounds. Not the surf necessarily, but the gulls and other seabirds and the song of the wind over sand.

I began walking until I knew I was heading in the right direction based on the beach parking signs and the way that the small-town businesses gave way to convenience stores advertising umbrellas, camp chairs, sunglasses, towels, and sunscreen. Each little *tienda* advertised beer and firewood in prominent letters on store windows as spring turned into summer.

I was heading for the pier I could finally see in the distance when I heard a voice behind me call out, "*Yasha*. I thought that was you."

I discovered I'd headed down the street where the fire station was located, and some of the men of the Santo Ignacio Fire Department were scrubbing down one of the trucks in the driveway of the big garage.

"Hi." I walked across to one I thought looked familiar. "I can't help being envious of all your wonderful toys."

JT shoved a toolbox into the cargo compartment on the little EMS rig and slammed the door shut. He picked up a clipboard and hugged it to his chest as he leaned back against the rear fender of his unit. "I am living the dream," he teased. "What are you up to?"

"I thought I'd look around. What do you suggest I look at?"

"The beach is great this time of year. And Nacho's Bar is known for its Sunday brunch, but it's a nice place to get a drink and unwind anytime. A group of us will be heading over there after our shift at around six. Do you want to—"

"Who's your friend, JT?" A muscular giant of a firefighter wrapped a beefy arm around JT's shoulders, causing him to give up a soft *oomph*.

"This is Yasha." JT performed the introductions from a choke hold. "Yasha, Cameron."

"Ow." Cameron winced when he got a good look at my face. "Did our boy wizard pull you out of a wreck or something?"

"Or something." I extended my hand, and he let go of JT long enough to give it a pump.

"Yasha was sick—"

"And you saved the day," Cameron said, not unkindly. He ruffled JT's hair. "Good boy."

"Thanks." JT yanked his head out of the way of Cameron's heavy hand.

Cameron looked at me. "So did I hear we're going for drinks at Nacho's?"

"Sure," I said.

"Cool." Cameron shot me a look that didn't take an Enigma machine to decrypt, and I might have returned it in kind. He was bigger than big and handsome, and I couldn't help but notice that he'd lingered a bit longer on our handshake than was strictly necessary. JT looked oblivious, and I thought that was telling. I had wondered about JT's interest in me, whether it was simply follow-up care or something more. His indifference to the way Cameron hustled me back, leaning an arm on the truck behind me and hemming me in, subtle as it might have been for straights, seemed significant.

Cameron lowered his voice as he leaned over me, his big hand flat against the rig next to my head. It was such a powerful move, it shifted something inside me and made me shiver a little. Which was also significant. Why the fuck did I always respond like that with guys who could crush me? "So. How long will you be in town?"

With his arm raised like that, the short sleeve of his unbuttoned shirt strained to contain his bicep. A quick glance up into his eyes told me that Cameron was enjoying the interest it generated.

"Not long. I'm going up to Santa Cruz to visit my brother." I was pleased that my words came out measured and even.

"Well." Cameron's eyes were warm and blue and held a hint of teasing. "Maybe we can entice you to stay on for a while."

"Maybe," I told him. I was probably staring at the way his tight undershirt caressed his massive chest when I felt a tug on my arm.

"Have you seen the beach yet?" JT asked.

"No." I let JT pull me out to the street and waited to see why he'd done it, if he'd tell me or if he was simply going to pretend he hadn't just dragged me out from under a good-looking guy who was flirting with me. I hoped he couldn't read my mind. *Eeny, meeny, miney, moe. Catch a fireman by the toe...*

Apparently I had a *thing.*

"The pier is down the boardwalk at one end of town, and when you walk back, Nacho's Bar is at the other. You can't miss it. That's where we'll be meeting for drinks."

"Sure. Six, you say?"

"Six." JT's eyes held nothing but sincerity. He was warmth personified, and I began to think that maybe he really was just concerned for my well-being. "I don't want to..." He frowned, letting his words trail off.

"What?"

JT looked behind him. "I don't want to presume or anything. Cam's a really nice guy, but he's kind of a player—"

"JT, can you stop? The rescue is over. I can take care of myself."

"It's not about that." JT looked anywhere but at me. "Well. Yes, it is actually. He's known for being a bit of a brawler when he drinks, and a guy like you—"

"What do you mean a guy like me?"

"Well, someone who..." JT's face both froze and pinkened. "I'm sorry. I didn't mean anything by it."

"All you know about me is what you learned during what was arguably the worst week of my life."

"I see." JT's face shuttered closed. "I'm sorry."

"No—" I put my hand on his arm. He'd been nothing but kind, and I didn't want to give him the idea that I wasn't grateful. "I'm really glad you're looking out for me. But I've been taking care of myself for a long time. Even though you've seen every evidence to the contrary, I'm pretty good at it."

"I'm sorry. Never mind. I know that. I forget sometimes that people are more than the problems they have that bring me on the scene."

"Thanks again, though, yeah?"

JT shot me an "it's cool" grin and turned to go inside.

I was glad to see him smile, but I had felt something tenuous that had been building between us dissolve, something that had felt—at one point—like more than friendship.

Probably, all things considered, it wasn't really an actual loss. But it felt a little disconcerting. At least while I was sick and thought he was my grandfather, I'd felt allowed in. Deeply cared for. Worth a risk. Now I was less certain of that, and I felt something else altogether. Disappointment maybe.

I was surprised to find it hurt a little.

I FOLLOWED HIS INSTRUCTIONS, first toward the boardwalk and then to the pier. The tide was out, and I could see the pilings clearly, crusted with barnacles and what looked like mussels, rippling with algae, draped with seaweed and flotsam.

I tried to let go of everything that had happened to me when I sank into the sand, which I found to be rougher and more pebbly than the sugary sand beaches in LA where I lived. It was dusty brown and resisted the efforts of the sea to pulverize it into homogenous pieces. The shore too was a little rocky, and I wondered if anyone surfed here or if there were boulders under the waves that made it too dangerous.

The sand was warm on my back, the breeze light. Ocean waves and the cries of seabirds drew me easily into a relaxing doze. Soon I was caught up, carried away by it, and I felt as if my body were rising and falling on the crest of each crash of the waves as they broke against the shore.

Unexpectedly a shadow fell over my face, and when I opened my eyes, I found Muse standing over me with a paper parasol.

"You're going to get really sunburned." She kept the shade over my face while she sat down daintily beside me. "I fell asleep right there once, and even though it seemed a little cloudy at the time, I woke up with a bad burn, and my face peeled for a week."

"Good point." I sat up, and she held her little umbrella over both of us with some difficulty as gusts of wind caught it and threatened to tear it from her grasp.

She studied me like I'd washed up from the sea and she'd found me there dead. "What are you doing out here?"

"I thought I'd just look around St. Nacho's." I crossed my legs and leaned back on my hands, completely relaxed for the first time in days. "I like it here. It's the town that time forgot."

"I was born here."

"Yeah?" I asked. "You've never lived anywhere else?"

"No." She rolled her eyes. "St. Nacho's is really small and all, but I think I belong here. The place is an ancient source of power actually, although not everybody knows that."

"Right." I rolled my eyes.

"Laugh all you want, but Minerva at Rune Nation says that the local Indian tribe put a spell on this land so people would pass it by."

"Ruination?" Muse charmed me, but it was hard to keep up.

"*Rune Nation*," she repeated. "It's my favorite bookstore. They sell books and crystals and herbs. Stuff like that."

"I see. And this Minerva?"

"She owns the store. Anyway, she says that unless St. Nacho's wants you here, you won't even see it."

"Ah." I rolled over onto my stomach and rested my head in my hands so I could just watch the waves. It's funny how when you're doing that, you realize you don't do it nearly enough. "That's kind of cool. How old are you, Muse?"

"I'm nineteen."

"That seems very young to me."

"Does it? I guess so." Muse sat for a while in silence, but I thought it was killing her. She didn't seem the type. "How old are you?"

"I'm thirty-two. Well. I'll be thirty-two in August." I probed that spot in my psyche and didn't discover any issues. Thirty hadn't been hard on me, not like some of the guys I knew from clubs who built their lives around being young and cool.

"What about your guy?" she asked, staring straight ahead.

"What about him?"

Muse met my eyes. "Where is he? How'd you end up here? What's going to happen? Will you go back?" I think even she was surprised by the barrage of questions once she'd asked them, because she went back to staring at the water.

"I don't know the answers to any of those questions." I thought about it. "I know how I ended up here. I got kicked off the bus."

"That must mean St. Nacho's wants you."

"I'm sure it does," I said dryly. "Everyone wants me."

"Are you going to go back to your guy? When you leave, I mean."

"No," I told her. "I'm pretty sure that ship sailed a long time ago, but I just didn't notice. I'm not standing on the dock waving."

"Did you love him?"

"No."

"Oh." Her voice was small.

"What about your…?" Before I finished that sentence, I realized it probably wasn't any of my business.

"I went out with this guy in high school, and it was one of those dark, passionate teen things. I guess I'm drawn to that."

"No kidding," I teased. When I realized maybe it hit a little too close to home, I added, "Me too, really."

"I see." She gave that some thought. "I think maybe we just hit the trifecta. My dad beat on my mom, his dad hit his stepmom and all the kids, and we were kind of alienated socially at school. We found each other, and it was like coming home."

"You never think it's going to happen to you, do you?"

"Nope."

"I remember lying awake at night, chanting over and over again that I'd never be like that. At the time I thought the worst thing in the world would be to be like my dad. It never once occurred to me I'd be like my mom..."

Muse nodded. "I used to hear them screaming at each other and think, just hit him *the fuck* back. Show him you won't take that shit lying down. That'll stop it."

I glanced at Muse's profile. "Did you try it?"

She looked down. "Yep."

"Did that work?"

"Nope."

"Shit."

"One good thing was that the first time I came home with a black eye, my mom packed our things and moved us out of my dad's house. They're divorced now."

"It took you getting hit by *your* boyfriend?"

"That it did. And now she runs the group."

"Alice is your mom?" I grinned.

"Yes. Not being a doormat is now the family business. What about your family?"

"The only one left is my brother, Daniel. He lives in Santa Cruz. He's a mover and shaker."

"Family's good." She returned her attention to a group of gulls at the water's edge. It was nice sitting with her. Maybe she was a little dark, but she sort of sparkled with it. It gave her a resilience and a patina I found refreshing.

I remembered a different time and a different ocean. I remembered looking out at the water off New Jersey's Sandy Hook. My zeyde borrowed a car from one of the men he worked with at the appliance store and drove us down to New Jersey for a day on the beach, although at the time, I didn't know why. It was the off-season and cold, and he'd picked us up from school in the early morning, before lunch even.

None of those things made sense to Daniel or me, and we sat in the back of that big car—probably a Cadillac Eldorado or a Lincoln Town Car—trying to figure out what all of it meant. Daniel had a black eye and a cracked rib that day, but at fourteen he felt triumphant. He'd stopped our dad from hitting our mother, taken the punishment himself, and the two of us were flying high—him from fighting back for a change and me from hero worship.

Zeyde wore his usual navy-blue wool sport coat over a white shirt and a thin blue cardigan sweater with gray slacks. He'd had on an understated silk tie and wore his ubiquitous Borsalino wool felt hat. I thought at the time he was the epitome of sophistication, and apparently women thought so too, because wherever he took us, he attracted ladies like a magnet.

We arrived at the beach, and Zeyde told us to go have some fun, that we'd earned a day off school and a chance to enjoy ourselves. He gave us money for treats and took us to lunch and dinner. He chatted the waitress up and left her a show-off tip that made her pink and happy.

When we got home, my father was gone, along with every last trace that he'd ever existed. His clothes, his equipment, photographs, records, tools, letters, paperwork—all gone.

Neither Daniel nor I ever forgave ourselves.

"Yeah." I remembered Muse was there, and she'd said something about family being good. "Family's good."

"Are you okay?"

I spoke hoarsely. "Sometimes the way the light glitters on the water hurts my eyes."

She gave me a shove with her hand. "Mine too. Especially when I'm crying."

CHAPTER SEVEN

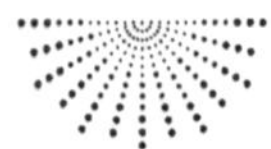

Muse and I said goodbye when it was time, and I made my way over to Nacho's Bar. At first glance it was exactly the kind of place I liked. Food service and a full bar. A game on the television. Nothing that spoke of pretension or desperation. It was a neighborhood place, and an assortment of people made themselves at home at its sturdy, dark bar or clumped casually around tables on the Saltillo tile floor. I found my firefighters out on the patio, mostly dressed now in jeans and T-shirts that read SIFD *Sparks*. They were relaxed and enjoying some beer. Cameron smoked, holding his cigarette in one hand and an ashtray in the other.

When he saw me, he put them both down on the table and pulled me over, grabbing a chair and placing it next to his. Apparently he didn't doubt his charm. I waved at JT, and he acknowledged me with his eyes as he took a long pull of beer. The way his lips looked wrapped around the neck of the bottle was so hot, I stumbled a little while I was in the process of sitting down. Cam gripped my forearm to steady me.

"Whoa there, cowboy." He let me go and lifted his hand—a signal to one of the guys to bring more beer. "You okay?"

"I fell asleep on the beach for a minute," I told him. "I guess I'm still a little out of it."

"The motion of the ocean." He peered at my face. "You look a little flushed."

"I got a sunburn."

"*Aw.*" Even though we were both seated, Cam was nearly a head taller than me, and he loomed over me again. "And here I was hoping you liked me."

I glanced back at JT, who was frowning now. Someone brought me a longneck, and I twisted off the cap.

"So what's it like being a firefighter in St. Nacho's?" I asked if only to get the conversational ball rolling. Cam was the only one who was close enough to hear me.

"I guess it's like anywhere else. We fight fires. Lots of ocean rescues for the EMTs. Lots of accidents on the highway." He took a drag and then mashed his cigarette out, politely blowing his smoke in the other direction.

"Do you get called for the wildfires?"

"Only when they need units to defend structures on the edge of a residential area being threatened. We're not wildlanders. There are some units around here that are. We mostly fight structure fires and respond to traffic emergencies."

A ripple of excitement flowed from inside the bar, and I heard a violinist tuning up.

"What's up?" I asked Cam, who turned to listen.

"They have a guy here who plays the violin. He's really popular, and right around this time of day the place fills up with people coming to listen. Lots of people stop in here on their way home."

I nodded. "My brother told me about him."

"Your brother lives around here?"

"He's up the coast in Santa Cruz. I'll be heading up there pretty soon for a visit. I thought I'd stay here for a few days first." I didn't mention that I didn't have much of a choice.

"St. Nacho's is a good place. The people here can be real friendly." The look in his eyes told me he was in the mood to prove that. I shifted uncomfortably in my chair. As attractive as Cam was, I couldn't get JT's warning out of my head. Contrary to what JT probably believed about me, I wasn't about to get involved—and especially not with a guy like Cam. His personality was already forceful enough to negate mine completely. I was done with being the moon to someone else's sun.

Suddenly I felt tired all over. Not just sleepy but bone weary. The kind of exhaustion that comes over you when you've run your race flat-out, it's over, and you can't take another step. Even lifting the beer bottle to my lips seemed like too much.

"Yasha?"

I must have been looking at the floor for quite a while, because I didn't have a clue when JT had moved to the chair next to mine, opposite Cam.

"Sorry, what?"

"Are you tired?" JT asked.

Cam leaned over to peer at my face again. "You look like you're about to pass out."

I shook my head. "No, I just—"

JT put his hand firmly beneath my elbow. It felt solid and sure there, and I realized what I'd known all along. His touch felt right to me. Familiar because of the night his dad had called emergency services to help me but not at all the impersonal, casual touch of an EMT for a patient. It never had been. That was why I'd reacted so strongly to it. Something strong and gentle inside him flowed into my skin every time he touched me, and I wasn't about to mess that up by hooking up with Cam.

"I can take you home." JT's eyes looked…hopeful, maybe, but confused as if he hadn't planned for the words to leave his mouth. "You need…"

I don't know what he was going to say right then, because a

dark-haired girl came up from behind him and wrapped her hands around his head and over his eyes.

"Guess who," she commanded as she pressed her mouth to his neck, leaving a stain of peachy lip goo on his skin.

He gave a guilty start and turned to her, lifting one of her hands to his lips. She shrugged that off and wrapped her arms around him and brought him in for a rather hot kiss. "Hi, baby."

I sat there in silent shock, wondering who the girl was and what she had to do with JT. His attention was focused on her, so I turned to Cam.

"Surprised?" Cam's eyes danced with mischief.

"No..." I shook my head. "Yes."

JT pulled her arms off him. "Linda? Meet Yasha. Yasha, Linda."

Cam motioned like he was showing the prize on *The Price Is Right*. I sensed that he knew exactly what I was feeling when he said, "JT's got a hot date."

My gaze found JT's. He closed his eyes immediately, his lashes lowering so I couldn't see what he was thinking at all. Linda held her hand out, and I took it. "You must be the man staying at Carl's motel. JT told me all about you. I was so glad when I heard you're going to be all right."

I inclined my head. "Thanks to JT."

"He's my hero." She pulled him to his feet, and he went with her, aiming a shrug in my direction. Like, *what can you do?* "You owe me a quiet dinner with no firefighters, mister."

JT's eyes met mine again, and I smiled and shrugged back, letting another fish off the hook. When he started to protest that he'd promised me a ride home, I waved it away. "No worries. It's not far to walk."

Cam offered to take me home, but I declined, worried that he'd had a bit too much to drink. In the end JT took me to the SeaView in his truck, and Linda followed us in a little silver Prius.

I thought it might be awkward to say good night, but JT made it easy, slipping an arm around Linda's waist after she got out of her car, even as we waved goodbye. He left his truck in the parking lot and took off in her car. I felt a strange kinship to Mithril the Truck, left behind like that. Abandoned.

I didn't have a reason in the world to have assumed he had any interest in me besides the usual concern a caring professional has for his patient. I had been an idiot to read more into it than that, but I felt sucker punched all the same.

All I could think of was the way I'd kissed his palm when I'd thought he was my grandfather and how he had allowed it. How he had understood it. How it had connected me to him from that moment on. A connection I thought went both ways.

I didn't have a hard time sleeping, especially after I took my pain meds. When I woke up, I lay in bed for a long time, both tempted to go to the window to see if JT's truck was still there and disgusted by the impulse.

Surely it didn't matter to me one way or the other if JT spent the night with a girl. He was securely out of my reach whether he'd stayed over at her place or gone home early to bed, alone.

Eventually, when I had to leave the safety of my motel room to go to Miss Independence Pies, I couldn't put it off any longer.

I told myself if the truck was there, that was a good thing, because that meant JT was getting a little action and of course I could wish that for a friend.

I told myself that if his truck wasn't there, that didn't mean he didn't get lucky, only that he hadn't spent the night.

I told myself it was none of my damned business, but that didn't make it any easier to open that door.

When I emerged from my room into the still, dark parking lot, JT's cool, cherrylicious truck was gone. I walked to Miss Independence Pies as if nothing had happened. My step was a little slower, though, than it had been the day before.

Muse was the first person I saw when I entered the bakery. She shot me a perky smile that lit things up for me a little. Candace worked quietly, rolling dough alongside the woman who had been there the day before but never said a word to me. Every time I had even approached her, she drifted into the background like smoke. I was determined to meet her that day and to let her know she didn't have to be afraid of me.

"Muse." I nudged her. "Who's the woman with the gray hair?"

"Her?" Muse leaned closer to me.

"Yeah. Every time she saw me coming her way yesterday, she drifted away. Is she scared of me?"

"She's scared of everybody." Muse spoke quietly, pushing me off to the side where we could talk privately. "That's Analise. The guy she was married to stabbed her, like, sixteen times. He went to jail for it. It's a miracle she lived. She doesn't talk to people anymore except Mary Catherine and my mom."

"Oh *shit.*" I wondered if Analise was JT's patient from the run that upset him so badly when he was a rookie.

"It's been especially bad because everyone's getting ready for his parole hearing, which is coming up in three weeks, and my mom, Mary Catherine, and Analise will be traveling to Soledad to speak. She's extremely jumpy right now because he threatened to kill her so many times when he first went to prison."

"Damn. Surely they wouldn't let him out if he's still a danger to her?"

"The prisons are overcrowded, and he's supposedly been a model prisoner. He says he's Buddhist now or something."

I sympathized with her. "Jeez. Having to see him again, even to tell her story so he stays put, must truly suck."

"That's why Mom and Mary Catherine are going. Mom's

armed with a boatload of statistics, and Mary Catherine…well, she just floats along on a tide of 'feel good,' doesn't she?"

"That she does."

"Analise comes here to work in the early mornings but has another job in the afternoons. She's got PTSD. Sometimes she's messed up." Muse pressed her lips together like she wanted to say more but couldn't. "Seeing her husband again is going to be terrible for her."

I watched Analise for a minute. She must have had an instinct, though, that told her there were eyes on her, because she backed away from us into the room where Mary Catherine kept supplies.

"It's hard to let something like that go. You feel it, you know? Like it's happening again, and it's not a memory, it's more like…"

"A hallucination?"

"No. Even more real than that," I told her. "Sometimes you feel it in your body. Adrenaline surges. Fight or flight kicks in. You hear the noise of glass breaking, and you smell the burning buildings. It's real but not real. You lose your ability to trust your senses."

Muse looked at me thoughtfully.

"Jacob," Mary Catherine called to me from the big commercial range. "I've been making the empanada fillings like you said —the one with beef and the one with chicken and green chilies. Can you come and try them?"

I took one last look at the supply room where Analise had gone and headed for the kitchen.

Soon Mary Catherine and I were experimenting with several different empanada doughs, trying several types of flour and fat until we found one that had a texture we liked. Filling recipes were plentiful, from the Cuban spicy beef picadillo with green olives to the Chilean beef with raisins to chicken and cheese to sweet fillings starring fresh and dried fruit.

Mary Catherine started with four: two beef, sweet and savory; one chicken with green chilies and soft cheese; and one I invented on the fly using chunks of roasted sweet potato and brown sugar with spices and just a hint of chili for a little zing. That one turned out to be an instant favorite among the ladies, and we made up batches of each to shop around to her restaurant clients.

Once we had enough, we put three of each type, twelve all told, onto foil-covered baking sheets uncooked, and froze them. Mary Catherine planned to deliver a tray of the new offerings to each of her current customers to be baked on-site. We did some experimentation with times and temperatures. The day fairly flew by. Soon it was noon, and we loaded up the van to make deliveries.

A man I'd never seen before came into the bakery and cornered Mary Catherine for a big hug. He was tall and handsome, built like an athlete, but he carried a cane and walked with a pronounced limp.

"Hi, Ken!" Mary Catherine gave him a squeeze and kissed his cheek. "I didn't expect you today." I watched as he soaked up her attention. He awkwardly moved out of the way of the girls who were loading the pies into boxes and taking them out to the truck. "Ken, I want you to meet the newest Miss Independence employee, Jacob. We all call him Yasha."

I held out my hand, then noticed it was covered with flour and pulled it back to wipe it on my apron.

"Nice to meet you," I told him.

"Likewise," Ken answered, barely glancing my way. He looked like a man on a mission. "I have a huge surprise for you. Can you come with me?"

"Yasha and I are in the middle of—"

"I found it," Ken interrupted her excitedly. "It's *perfect*, and don't say you're not ready, because you are."

I didn't have a clue what he was talking about, but as I stood there and watched Mary Catherine, I could swear all the blood drained from her face, and she wilted enough that I was convinced I needed to be ready to catch her.

"Where?" she asked him.

"Roger's Appliance is going out of business. My real-estate agent told me the owner is retiring. The building stands alone, and there's an alley with a loading dock. It's right there on Iglesias Road, in a great location two blocks in from the pier. If you sold ice cream, you'd have lines in the summer."

"That's a huge commitment, Ken. I'm not—"

"You're ready," he said implacably.

For some reason that I couldn't understand, my blood was racing a little at the prospect of expanding Mary Catherine's pie empire. Maybe Ken's enthusiasm was just that contagious. Maybe it was the way Mary Catherine held herself—as though she was excited and elated but didn't dare show it—that made me say something.

"You could just go take a look. Where's the harm in that?"

Ken glanced at me again, and this time he appraised me differently. "He's right. You can't turn it down without looking.

"But…" Mary Catherine gripped my arm. "Would you come? You know about these things, right?"

I started to worry a little. "I've never owned a bakery. I work in a restaurant. It's not like I'm an expert."

"But you work in a successful restaurant, right? Have you worked in a bakery?"

"Yes," I admitted. "I've worked in several, here and abroad."

It was Ken who asked, "So you would know if the building would work?"

"Well, that depends. Are you moving your entire operation? Do you lease this place? Will you be doing your baking here and using the other place as a retail space? Will—"

"*You* are coming with us," Mary Catherine told me as she pulled off her work apron and went to wash her hands. She kept talking, and I thought it was mostly to herself. "You're a godsend. You seem to have some idea of what you're doing. I don't have the faintest..." She trailed off, and I thought she was about to argue again.

"You need a business plan. Then you need to work on an idea of what your retail space should look like. I can probably help with that. What are your goals? You can break them up into short-term, midrange, and long-term goals. But first and foremost you need to decide what you're going to sell and where it's going to come from."

"What do you mean 'what we're going to sell'?" Mary Catherine asked. "We're going to sell pies."

"And ice cream." Ken smiled. He met my eyes then, and I realized he was happy that he'd found an ally. This time when I held out my hand, he took it between both of his, warmly, as if he was genuinely glad to meet me. "I'm Ken Ashton, and I'm MC's son-in-law. Sort of."

CHAPTER EIGHT

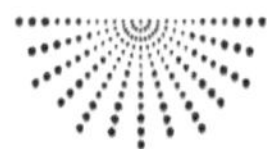

Wouldn't you know, the damned appliance store sat right next to the firehouse.

As soon as I got out of Ken's car, I spotted Cam out front wiping down one of the engines. He glistened in the weak afternoon light, his biceps bulged, and his huge legs bunched as he crouched to get a low spot. It was like porn, watching him. I half expected him to tear his T-shirt down the middle and shake like a wet dog.

I think Ken must have seen something on my face, because he laughed at me, and Mary Catherine stopped in midstride to mutter, "Location, location, location."

The real-estate agent came up and saw what we were looking at. "Yes, indeed. The view from the front window of this store is one of the finest anywhere along the California coastline. My name is Debra, and Ken tells me he's pretty anxious to have you check this place out."

Mary Catherine took her hand and shook it. "Well. It's not really…I mean…"

I put my hand on the small of her back and propelled her

forward a little. "It's just an exploration at this point, Mary Catherine. You aren't making any promises."

Ken shot me a grateful look. "I worried that I wouldn't be able to talk her into coming," he said quietly after Mary Catherine and Debra had strode off together and were out of earshot.

"How long has she been in business?"

"Six months," Ken answered. "But she's only doing sales to restaurants right now, and I know she'd like to have a retail business. This place is big enough to house both facets of her business—retail and delivery."

"Doesn't she have a lease on the other place? Surely she has some time before it's up?"

"No. She's leasing month to month." Ken grinned. "Actually she's leasing from me. I bought the building where she is now with her in mind, but it's a good investment even if she's not there. I'm sure I can find a tenant eventually. It's not a good spot for a retail bakery though. She needs somewhere with the kind of foot traffic this place has. Originally I thought we'd find somewhere small and continue the baking operation where she is, but when this place came up, I saw the possibility immediately."

As I watched, Cam shouted something to someone in the firehouse, and JT came out. He waved and made his way over to where we were standing.

"Yasha, how are you doing?" He looked from me to Ken with mild curiosity on his face.

"Fine, I guess."

JT continued to gaze at me, and I couldn't stop myself from filling the silence. "Mary Catherine is looking at this property for a possible bakery. This is Ken. Do you know each other?"

JT held his hand out. "Ken Ashton is St. Nacho's secret weapon." JT grinned like it was a private joke.

Ken nodded. "That's what they call me."

I suppose I must have looked blank, because JT filled me in. "The St. Nacho's police and fire departments draw lots to see who gets him on their team for softball games."

I guess this information surprised me, because Ken didn't seem like he could be much of a ballplayer. Ken confided, "They want the bat. Heaven forbid I should have to run."

"Last time you hit a game-winning double and beat the tag, Ashton. Well, partly because of my sucky glove, I guess."

"The pitcher threw you a dirt ball." Ken turned to me. "How do you know JT?"

"He had to rescue me when I got into town. I was sick." I turned to JT. "What do you think? Can you see a bakery here?"

JT looked at the appliance store as if he was picturing it. "Well, MC'll for sure have everyone from the fire station, plus St. Nacho's finest, in there all the time."

"That's what I thought," Ken said.

"She's going to need a lot of capital," I warned. "And the statistics for restaurants are disheartening in the best of times."

"But she's got a great product," Ken reminded me. "It's more specialized than a restaurant really. And she's quite the entrepreneur. Hardworking. Determined. Creative."

"She inspires loyalty," I thought aloud. I felt JT's gaze on me and looked up. "What?" He glanced away.

"Didn't MC tell me you lost your job?" Ken asked.

"Well, no. I mean, I don't know yet whether my job will still be there when I head home."

"If you're looking for work, I think we could find you something. Mary Catherine will need to come up with a business plan. She'll need a bank loan. It won't be a simple thing to borrow money given the economic climate."

"How are her numbers now?" I asked. "Is she mostly in the black? Covering the cost of the equipment and the lease, the delivery expenses? Taxes and insurance? Employee benefits?"

Ken considered this. "Yes. Although I admit she gets free

labor from me and Jordan—a lot of it. Some other folks in town help out when she needs them."

"So it's a true family business?"

"Yeah." Ken seemed happy with the arrangement. I could see that. "We're fully committed to seeing Mary Catherine's business flourish."

"Maybe we can figure out a way to help her expand her menu so that she has something no one else in town does."

Ken seemed to have worked everything out in his mind already, and he was smiling. "Maybe what she needs is a real pastry chef."

"O-oh, well..." I stammered. "No. Not for the kinds of pies she makes."

Ken continued grinning. "You said yourself she should have something no one else has. I think a real pastry chef is exactly the kind of thing you were talking about. As far as I know, there isn't one in St. Nacho's. There are two bakeries in town, but neither is what I would consider...How good are you?"

I felt the heat creep up my face. What a question. If I answered honestly, it would sound..."I'm good," I said simply. I was good. Very, very good, although I hadn't had a chance to really shine in quite some time.

"Think about it," Ken said simply.

"I will," I assured him.

JT didn't seem as pleased as Ken was, and I wondered why. He clapped me on the back and slid his hand to rest on my shoulder, then pulled me off to the side so we could speak privately.

"That means you might stay in St. Nacho's awhile?"

"Maybe." I didn't have much more to say, but he seemed to be waiting, moving from foot to foot, so I finally asked, "What?"

"Can I talk to you? Buy you a cup of coffee?"

I glanced to where Ken stood looking at a binder that Debra was showing him and said, "When I'm finished here, I'm free."

"Come by the firehouse. I'm off shift, but I stopped by to mooch lunch. I'll be in charge of washing dishes, and then we can take a walk."

"Sure," I told him.

As JT was leaving, a police cruiser drove up and parked at the curb near where we stood, and a uniformed officer got out. Ken and Mary Catherine came over, and we all stood waiting while he made his way toward us. When he got close enough, I read his name: *A. Callahan.*

"Andy." Mary Catherine hugged him, and Ken offered his hand. "Meet Yasha. He's helping me out at Miss Independence for a bit."

Andy didn't look like he was there for a social visit. "I'm glad I saw you. I was going to head over to your place. I got some news today, and I thought I should pass it on."

Ken and Mary Catherine looked at one another. "What happened?"

"Analise Salvador's ex-husband tried to kill one of the prison guards yesterday." Andy didn't mince words. "Knifed him with some kind of homemade blade. She might have seen that. It's been all over the news. He can say goodbye to his parole hearing now. I doubt he'll leave the prison alive."

Mary Catherine blinked in shock.

"What could have made him do that? He was so close to that hearing, he—"

"No one knows. It's being investigated."

"*Jeez.*" She laid her hand over her heart. "Is it a terrible thing that I'm so relieved?"

"No. He should never get out. You need to tell Analise, if she hasn't heard. I'll keep her informed of things as the investigation progresses."

"Thanks for stopping."

"My pleasure. I arrested that bastard for what he did to Analise, and the longer he stays off the streets, the better." Andy nodded to all of us before getting back into his cruiser and taking off.

After that Debra took Mary Catherine, Ken, and me inside to look around the appliance store. I had to admit that Ken was much better at picturing the building's possibilities. He enthused over the space, painting word pictures, gesturing with his arms, and dragging Mary Catherine and me along until we could all imagine what he had in mind for the place. Eventually Debra left, and the three of us stayed in the parking lot talking for a while longer. As excited as Mary Catherine was about the possibility of a retail space, she was having a hard time getting her mind off Analise.

Mary Catherine bit her lip. "I wonder if I shouldn't stop by her place and see if she's heard."

Ken said, "We could do that right now. I can take you there before I drop you off at Miss Independence."

Mary Catherine turned to me. "Do you need a ride back?"

I couldn't help glancing over to the firehouse. "I think I'll stay here for a bit. I'll see you tomorrow?"

"Fine." Mary Catherine waved. "I'll see you then."

"Nice meeting you." Ken put his hand out again, and I shook it. He had a warm, firm grip and gave a little pump before letting my hand go. "I think we'll be seeing a lot of each other if this works out."

"I look forward to it." I really did. I watched them drive away with a heart that felt—if not hopeful exactly—a little bit lighter.

THE COLD MORNING mist that moved in from the ocean like a blanket had never burned off completely, and this close to the water, visibility was limited. I stepped inside the firehouse and found Cam and his buddies playing cards.

He winked up at me, ready to throw down his hand and see

what I wanted, but I shook my head and asked where I could find JT.

"He's in the kitchen cleaning up. Are you sure you don't want me?"

Everyone laughed as I passed and headed for the kitchen without answering. Things must be vastly different in St. Nacho's if you could joke like that at the firehouse.

I found JT loading the dishwasher. Something smelled mouthwatering, and I peeked into a nearly empty pot on the stove.

"Not chili, I take it. I thought firefighters always ate chili."

"That's a myth." JT closed the dishwasher door and turned on the wash cycle.

"Like red suspenders?"

"No. That one's true." He had the same teasing light in his eyes that I'd originally thought might be flirtatious. Now I guessed it was just his way.

"Good to know."

"Want to get some coffee?"

"You don't have coffee here?" I looked around and found a full pot sitting on the counter.

"I want to take a walk." He looked away. "I want to talk to you."

"Oh." I felt the first stirring of apprehension. "What about?"

He jerked his head, indicating I should follow, and I did, walking alongside him, passing Cam's card game, back out to the street.

"You warm enough to be out here?" he asked, hunching his own shoulders. He wore street clothes—jeans and a long-sleeve henley shirt. He glanced back at the fire station. "I could probably find you a sweatshirt."

"No, I'm fine." I followed him when he headed for the beach. At one point the walk was narrow because of a row of hedges, and he went ahead. I had to tell myself not to watch him, not to look at the way his jeans fit him perfectly, hanging low on his lean hips, or the way his shirt pulled across his back when he moved. I had to tell myself he was straight and off-limits.

I had to remind myself more than once.

"Why are we here?" I finally asked when he got to the pier and stepped out onto the old timber boards to look over the water.

JT looked oddly nervous, despite how he stood with his hands draped casually on the weathered wood railing. "I think I may have given you the wrong idea," he began, looking anywhere but at me. "I feel bad about that. I should have told you I had a date last night."

"Why didn't you?" I asked, then thought better of it. "No. Never mind. That's stupid. Why would you?"

"I saw the way you looked at me...I think..."

He was embarrassed for me. *Great.* "I'm a big boy. I know sometimes you like someone and they don't like you back. Not that way...Straight or gay, sometimes it's just not in the cards. No harm, no foul."

The ocean rushed beneath us. I looked out over the railing to the foamy water. It wasn't unexpected—this moment between JT and me. He was just another fish to let off the hook. Nothing a tincture of time and a lot of hard work wouldn't cure. I could look forward to both those things.

He didn't turn toward me, and for the first time I was afraid he didn't want to hang around with a guy who liked him like that. Maybe he had a problem with the idea that I found him attractive. Maybe it made him nervous, or he had a little streak of homophobia that manifested when confronted with a man who wanted him.

"I'll understand completely if it makes you uncomfortable," I told him quickly. "If it changes how you—"

"Jeez, you don't get it at all, do you?" He turned unhappy eyes my way. "I don't *want* you like that."

"I get it." I stepped back, a little stunned by his vehemence. "No shit. No problem." I turned to walk back the way we had come, away from the pier, away from him, but he gripped my arm so hard his fingers bit into my skin.

"I don't want you," he growled, but then he hooked his other hand around the back of my neck and pulled me in for a kiss.

It was a tentative kiss but enticing and electric. One of those kisses that begins like a cream puff, all bland and maybe a little soggy, and then slowly, surely, when I broke into it, opened it up, and dived in, it changed into an un-fucking-believably satisfying, meltingly delicious, velvety, wet treat. He tasted rich and heady, felt all slick and smooth…

Oh *fuck*.

JT pushed me into the railing with his hips. I hung there, clinging to him, scared that I'd fall, sure that he'd let me go, but I was driven by a breathless excitement to see what would come next. I could hear the waves crashing below me as he stepped between my legs. There was nothing between me and a death drop into the icy-cold, churning water but thirty feet of air and the hold I had on his shoulders. He slid his hands down my back and around somehow, slipping over my hips, burning a path to my ass. He lingered there and squeezed, kneading the muscles until my knees went weak. His cock dug into mine, and he allowed them to rub together for the brief time it took for me to realize it wasn't an accident, and then I felt his entire body shudder.

He whispered my name and then, "No. *Stop*."

I brought my hands up instinctively between us to break his hold on me and shoved him none too gently away. "What the *hell*?"

He stood rigid, simply staring at me for a minute. He lifted his wrist as though he needed to wipe his mouth, but then stopped himself. "I'm sorry."

I still had my hands up like he was a wild animal. I wasn't about to make any sudden moves. "What the fuck was that?"

"I..." His eyes were wide, and the whites showed around the irises.

I started walking back the way we'd come. "Never mind. I *know* what that was."

He came after me. "*I* don't know what that was."

As he fell into step beside me, his breath contributed to the mist. He panted as if he'd been running a long way. He held one of his hands flat on his chest as if he was trying to keep his heart inside.

I stopped and asked, "Are you scared?" Because damn, he *looked* scared. He looked like he'd been in an accident. Dazed, sort of. I leaned toward him. "Maybe you should sit down."

He held his hand up as if to ward me off. "I can't believe I did that."

"It was only a kiss." I told the lie with as straight a face as I've ever shown to anyone.

He put his fingers on his lips. Like he could still feel the kiss there. I knew I still felt it on mine. I could feel it everywhere. He'd branded me. I doubted that the memory of that kiss would ever fade.

"It just...It felt..." He wrapped his arms around himself. I thought he meant to catch his breath. Maybe I'd walked faster than I thought. I tended to move quickly when things got ugly. His beautiful jade green eyes held nothing but pain. After that he took off running, and I let him go.

St. Nacho's sits poised on the most awesome crest of land overlooking the endless sea. Once what little sun there had been set and the breeze dissipated the fog, the moon rose high in the sky, peeking every now and again from behind a veil of swiftly moving clouds. I don't know how long it took—hours maybe—until I stepped down from the pier into the sand. I could hear the music from Nacho's Bar in the distance, and I made my way toward it. Cars were parked everywhere on the streets around the brightly lit building. The violin music of dinnertime had given way to the heavy, rhythmic *thump, thump* of dance music.

The first thing I noticed when I got close was the number of people milling around outside. Some were chatting away from the noise. Some had left the building to smoke. Most were openly affectionate gay couples. They had to be coming from outlying areas, towns and cities stretched along the coastline, north and south. As I got closer, I saw people I recognized from walking around town. Apparently Nacho's Bar was the official place to see and be seen. There were straight couples too. When I entered, I recognized Candace at a table with a man I'd never seen before. She smiled politely at me, and I waved back.

At the bar I ordered a draft beer and a shot of bourbon. It had been a day since I'd taken the pills they'd given me for pain. I was no longer sick. I knew if I felt like it, I could drink safely. There was no one to answer to and nowhere to go but back to my motel room on foot.

"Here you go," said the bartender. "Bourbon, beer back. Eight bucks."

"Thanks." I slapped a ten down on the bar and said, "Keep it." The music was loud but not painfully so. The mix was good—dance tunes with a romantic ballad thrown in every few songs for the gropers. I ordered a plate of nachos, and they were damn good, cheesy and hot, with plump tomato bits and shredded chicken, topped with avocado slices and jalapeño discs. Someone reached over my shoulder for one of my chips, and I looked up to see Cam grinning at me.

Why is it always so easy to hook up with the one who doesn't make your heart race?

"Whatcha up to?" he asked, taking a big bite of one of the few remaining chips. He got sour cream on his lip, and I thought then that if it had been JT, I'd have licked it off and promised to follow up on that anywhere else he...

"What?" he said, surprising me. "What's that look for?"

I shook my head. "Nothing. I thought you were working?"

Cam rolled his eyes. "What does it say about me that I hang around the firehouse even when I'm off shift? There's always something to do, and resources are a little thin. Plus, it's easy money playing poker with the boys."

I pushed my nachos toward him, indicating he could eat as much as he liked, not that he wouldn't have eaten them anyway.

"Come dance with me." Cam pulled me off the bar stool and asked the man sitting next to me to watch my food.

"You're not supposed to do that." I pulled away and sat back down, wedging him in between me and the other guy. "I don't leave my drinks unattended."

"That's 'cause you live in the wicked city," he told me, already grooving, waiting for me to finish my beer but dancing so close he was practically humping my leg. "Here you can leave your stuff. It's safe." At the risk of seeming paranoid, I finished my beer and put it down on the bar.

Cam sashayed backward as he pulled me into the throng. We danced for a few minutes, and I became fully aware that I was in no shape to be doing it. I was a little loose from the booze, although not yet drunk, but I was tired and grateful when they played a slow song that I didn't recognize. Cam was a man you could grab onto, and he'd hold you up if you needed it. I appreciated the hell out of that when he pulled me close. The song was a twangy country ballad, but full of rich, lovely harmonies. The lyrics were something about God and a broken road.

It felt good to dance with Cam. It felt natural to lean up against him, to feel those thickly muscled arms band tightly across my lower back. He was tall enough that our cocks didn't rub together, but he more than made up for that by shifting me so I could ride his massive thigh while he ground against my hip.

My mouth went dry before the song was over, and I would have done just about anything to stay like that, but the next song was a techno dance tune that worked as quickly as a slap to bring me back to reality.

Cam wanted to stay on the dance floor, and I excused myself. Last I saw, he was in the middle of a rowdy bunch of equally massive men having the time of his life. I fought my way back to the bar, and when I got there, I saw JT's girlfriend, Linda, searching the crowd. She talked to a couple of the firefighters and eventually found Cam. She didn't see me, mostly because I took the coward's way out and ducked toward the men's room.

Maybe I did have to pee. It's not like I was actively avoiding her.

Well. Yeah, I was.

But apparently so was JT, because when I finally opened the door to the can, there he was.

CHAPTER NINE

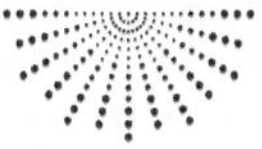

JT took me by the arm and yanked me inside, allowing the door to close behind us.

"What the hell?"

"I need to talk to you. Is Linda still out there?"

"Yeah, she's looking for you. Are you in high school? What are you hiding for?"

He raked a hand through his hair. "I don't know."

I turned to leave. "Well, good luck with that."

"*Wait.*" He reached for me again, and I backed away.

"Stop grabbing me," I told him. "That shit ends now."

"I'm sorry." He stood before me with quiet dignity, confusion and desperation written clearly on his face. "I don't know what to do."

"Here's the deal. First you man up and go talk to your girlfriend."

"Linda's not my girlfriend. She's just a girl I go out with sometimes. One of them. We're not—we just date." Troubled jade green eyes met mine. "That's the problem."

"That doesn't sound like a problem. That sounds like a rich and vibrant social life."

JT rolled his eyes. "I'm an unmarried man with a job. I'm a first responder. In a Jewish singles' group, at least among the nonprofessionals, I'm the Holy Grail—you should pardon the expression."

"So far nothing you've said sounds remotely like a problem."

"I wanted to kiss *you*. That's the problem. I did it. I actually—What the hell does that mean?"

"There's a whole bar full of men out there who can answer your question," I told him. "Just ask them."

"I don't want to ask them. I don't want to know. It's not right."

"What?"

"What, what? How can you be a Jew and not know it's not right?"

"I guess I'm not that kind of Jew." I frowned. Was he saying…?

"What kind are you?" he asked. "Either you keep God's laws or you don't."

I blinked in surprise. "Well, I guess I don't. And you don't either, fully, or you wouldn't speak—"

"That's a pretty big no-no, being homosexual."

"Yeah, well, I can't exactly change what I am."

"You can change what you choose," he said.

I admit to rolling my eyes.

"Yeah. *No.*" I turned to leave the bathroom, and he very nearly grabbed for me again but pulled back at the last minute.

"Yasha, I don't have to act on all my impulses."

"I don't either. You should be grateful for that right now as a matter of fact."

"What does that mean?"

JT seriously didn't get it. *Jeez.* "I'm not going to tell you how to live your life, JT. Don't tell me how to live mine." I left, and either he had to follow me and face his "girlfriend" or stay where he was. *Good luck with that.*

On the way out I waved to Cam, and he waved back, a sloppy, one-handed thing that barely rose above the pile of men he was dancing with. He looked happy enough, and I was definitely done for the night.

I began the walk home in more of a mood than I realized—a little tense, a little angry. A car going too fast swerved around the corner behind the bar. The tires screeched, a terrifying, sharp whine in my ears, and I jumped back. It unnerved me, but I waved off the driver's hand motion of apology.

Still, my heart was racing, and I relived a few of the worst moments of my life until I could get my breathing back under control. Sometimes it was hard to remember where I was. Loud noises, cars backfiring, even breaking glass—a common enough occurrence in restaurants—all reminded me of things I preferred not to remember.

Oddly enough, walking toward the SeaView Motel through a sleepy St. Nacho's effectively soothed me through the aftereffects and drained me of the turmoil that often lasted for hours. I could almost feel the push-pull of the surf tugging my anxiety out to sea.

As I headed toward a residential part of town and the sound of dance music receded into the background, I became aware of the occasional barking dog or the volume of a television turned up too loud. It really was a small town, with a main drag that was basically commercial, that had grown inland behind the two landmarks: St. Nacho's Bar and the pier. It had been built in concentric layers like a shell. The SeaView was close to the farthest southern edge of the first layer, by the highway, which was maybe three miles away. I was used to walking, and the distance gave me time to think.

Maybe I belonged in a place like St. Nacho's. I'd had enough of big cities. I'd left the States to make aliyah at the behest of my grandfather and lived in Israel for six years. When he died, I returned to be with my mother in New York for a year until she passed away suddenly of a stroke.

I traveled to France for cooking school and then to Los Angeles. Wherever I lived, I always felt like I remained half-packed, always in transit, always one more plane ticket or bus fare away from the next destination.

I'd originally chosen Los Angeles because it was near my brother but not in his pocket. I knew his wife wouldn't countenance a close relationship, but I felt close enough here on the West Coast, a few hundred miles away. Living there had always held the possibility, however remote, of our closing the gap between us and recapturing the bond we'd shared as children.

I'd loved him so much. Looked up to him. Laughed and cried with him. He'd taken more than one beating for me, and we'd taken on our dad together, united in our determination to protect our mom. I knew the vibrant yet invisible tie that bound us couldn't be broken ever, not by time, not by distance, and not at the hands of a woman who didn't approve of it.

I'd heard it in his voice, even as recently as the last time I'd called, when he'd waffled so completely about coming to get me. Daniel would be strong. He'd be a lion in his determination to take care of me if I asked it of him. He'd be torn to ribbons by it, but he'd be there for me if I only asked, and that was precisely why I never would.

Knowing was enough. It nurtured me in ways I would never be able to put into words. Like having a home to go to, even if I never did. The way Zeyde felt about Israel, choosing in the twilight years to make his way back to his spiritual beginnings, to spend his final days in contemplation and prayer on the same earth where the prophets walked.

For me, although I never told him, there was no real connection. I went because Zeyde was my safe place. I did my service for his country, protecting his homeland. I would have been perfectly at home wherever he chose to be.

I'd never really felt at home anywhere since. Until now maybe.

When I finally reached the SeaView, the little light in the office still glowed in that welcoming way motels have. I had a notion to say hello to Carl, maybe born of my longing for my grandfather. They were similar in the way they studied and teased me. They had a dry wit in common. Maybe it was meeting Carl that had made me dream of Zeyde. Whatever it was, I felt it here—that connection to home in this town that time forgot.

Muse had told me that no one could see St. Nacho's if the place didn't choose to allow it. Right then, in that brisk, chilly darkness, I believed she was right, and I felt absurdly grateful that for some reason St. Nacho's had chosen me.

I was chuckling when I opened the door and walked into the office, trying to shake off my mood.

Carl sat behind the desktop computer, and he took his time looking up. "I'll be with you in a minute."

I smiled. I thought it possible he hadn't planned a life running a motel in St. Nacho's, and every time he made a customer wait, it was a minor rebellion against fate. Hadn't he said just that when I remarked that he must have liked it here to stay so long? He'd answered, *"Not exactly, no. But it didn't let me go."*

How odd, in retrospect, because already I felt the town's tentacles beginning to latch on to me.

Carl finally looked up from his work. "Hello, Yasha. Where are you headed so late? Nacho's Bar?"

"I've just come from there actually."

"Did you see JT? He's often there, I think."

Did I ever. I saw him, touched him, kissed him. Shit. "Yes. He was there when I left. I imagine he'll spend the evening with Linda."

"Oh, Linda. She's a nice girl. He's quite a Romeo. He can never seem to date just one girl at a time."

"A player." I forced myself to smile. "He mentioned he's in a Jewish singles' group."

"Yes. And the girls are fairly determined. I'm sure I don't have to tell you! They're nothing like girls were when I was young. They're like alien predators from the movies these days."

"Well, I'm not—"

"I know. You're not in the market for a girlfriend, but does that stop them?"

I thought about the women I'd met in LA. "Not really, no. I can't say that it's a bad thing though. For those who swing that way."

Carl laughed. "You want a beer? I have some in the fridge, and I doubt we'll get any more traffic through here tonight."

"Okay. Yeah, my buzz wore off on the walk home."

Carl took off his reading glasses and placed them in his shirt pocket. The act itself was like a sigh. As if when it was complete, he was technically off the clock. His aging features relaxed, and he put a hand through hair that was still full and soft looking. Badly cut. He had on a button-down shirt and a pair of Dockers. Over that he wore a Fred Rogers sweater. He pulled up the part of the counter that lifted like a bridge, and allowed me back behind the desk, then led me into the office's inner sanctum. It was a small room jumbled with books and papers. It looked like the break room in a department store—calendar on the wall, a place for mail, and a time clock. There was a door at the back I thought must lead to a private exit.

"You punch a clock?" I said, surprised.

"Nah. That was in the old days. My father-in-law used to make my wife, Margaret, and her sister, Mary, clock in and out when they worked. At the time they were teenagers, and he thought he'd give them some of what he called 'real business experience.'"

"I'm having a hard time picturing Jewish girls. Margaret maybe. But Margaret and Mary? I can only imagine nuns."

"They were Irish Catholics. The girls went to a parochial school in a town just south of here. I can assure you, my Margaret had probably never dated a Jew before I came along. It didn't go over real well with her folks."

"What about yours?"

Carl opened the door to a dorm-sized refrigerator and pulled out two Coors bottles. He handed one to me, and I twisted off the cap. "Mine expected me to take over the farm with a nice Jewish girl. They weren't happy either. What about your parents, Yasha? What did they expect?"

"I can't really say. My father left when I was a kid, and my mom passed away pretty suddenly after I came back from Israel. I guess in the long run she expected me to bring home a girl and have a family."

"Did she ever know that wasn't in the cards?"

"Yes," I answered, worried that the conversation would head —however obliquely—toward JT. "She wasn't happy, but it wasn't something I could change."

"No, I don't suppose so." Carl took a long pull of his beer. "How old were you when you knew?"

"For sure? I think"—I tried to remember back—"maybe twelve?"

Carl shook his head. "That's got to be tough. I had a cousin... He never said, but we all thought maybe...It was harder back then. Nobody ever said anything."

"It's never been easy. Even though the world is more open, people have expectations."

"I didn't mean that it was easy now. No. I can see...What about religion? Did you worry about that? Did it make you feel like a sinner?"

I was starting to feel the beer in my toes, like a wave of warmth flooding beneath my skin, relaxing me. "I don't know. We weren't such great Jews. We went to Hebrew school and synagogue, and my brother and I celebrated our bar mitzvahs, but…" I fingered the label on my beer, scratching it off while I thought about what I wanted to say. "For me religion had more to do with family. We all looked to Zeyde. If my zeyde said something was good, it was good. He didn't keep kosher, and that was that. We ate bacon because he liked it. My mother tried a Christmas tree one year to see what it felt like, and we started having it every year because it was pretty. We took pictures with Santa Claus. We knew what real Jews did. We just weren't that bothered by what we did that was different."

"That's interesting." Carl nodded as if he understood. "I think it was like that for us too. Of course, there weren't that many of us in town so our culture wasn't exactly reinforced."

I nodded. "I grew up in New York, and we were definitely the oddballs in a predominantly Jewish neighborhood. People were fairly strict, and they thought we ran wild to no good end. But when Zeyde got old, he wanted to make aliyah, and once we were in Israel, he grew more fundamental in his beliefs. He started talking about dietary laws and the ancestors. Maybe he was trying to live up to their standards because…" I trailed off. It was still hard for me to believe that my zeyde was gone.

"Because he was looking forward to joining them," Carl finished for me.

"Yes."

"JT worries about religion too much. We were never observant, and because my wife was Catholic, he wasn't even really considered a Jew by Jewish law. He had to go through a formal conversion process. I don't get that really, where that drive came from to belong. We didn't go to synagogue. We never had a Passover seder. In fact, he often went to St. Ignatius for Mass with his grandmother. I don't know where he gets his determination to study the Torah and join groups."

"Some people have a more spiritual nature. I think it helps them. I don't."

"Me neither." Carl grinned behind his beer before he put it

to his lips and finished it off. He tossed it into the trash. "But JT's been trying to get me to join one of the groups to meet ladies."

I grinned. "Watch out. A guy like you: handsome, still young, a business owner. It'll be open season once the ladies get a load of you. Prepare yourself for the chicken-soup brigade."

"There are a lot of ladies out there. I can see why JT hasn't settled down."

So can I. "Well." I put my beer bottle into the same bin where Carl had put his, and then I rose. "I have to get up early to bake pies. I'm helping Mary Catherine Jensen until Friday when—I hope—my brother comes to get me."

"It's been a pleasure. I hope you'll stop by anytime you feel like it until you leave."

"I will. Thank you." I held out my hand, and he shook it warmly. "You remind me of my zeyde."

Carl shook his head. "From what JT tells me, there's a lot of that going around."

I laughed. "I probably have him on my mind because...St. Nacho's feels like home. That's weird, huh?"

"Not really," Carl said as he pulled up the counter, and I passed through. I opened the door, and he was right behind me to lock it when I left the office. He turned the sign from OPEN to CLOSED, which had a phone number to call if he was needed, then walked back behind the counter again.

I rounded the corner to head for my room and was unsurprised to see JT's truck there. Some things you just know. I knew that Linda wanted a husband. I knew that Carl wanted someone to talk to. And when I approached JT's attractive old Flareside truck—before he saw me coming—I saw him drumming his fingers impatiently on the steering wheel and I knew he wanted *me*.

CHAPTER TEN

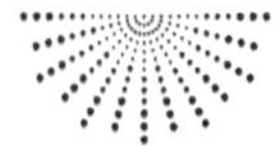

Sometimes I sit on a decision, maybe waiting for some kind of confirmation, maybe thinking things through. Sometimes I savor the anticipation of something fine, or I take a minute out to worry about remorse or regret. I stopped when I saw JT's truck. I simply stopped and let time pass for a second or two as I allowed what I knew was about to happen wash over me. I put my hands in my pockets and felt for my motel key.

Was this what I wanted? A guy who needed to experiment? Someone who didn't want me but sat in his car waiting for me just the same, beating time on the steering wheel because he was nervous as hell?

I could tell he was scared by the way those soft white hands stilled when he saw me, then gripped the wheel tight, until the knuckles looked pale against the rest of his skin in the dashboard light. It looked like it took a conscious effort for him to let go as if he were dropping a lifeline and swimming into shark-infested waters.

Such drama.

The first time I had sex with a man, I was fifteen. It was wrong, and we both knew it. I remember exactly the way shadows played over his face beneath the light of the mercury vapor lamp in his church parking lot. I remember the feel of his skin, the pebbles of his nipples in the cold autumn air. I remember gooseflesh and whiskers and the deep and heady knowledge that he wanted me more than I wanted him. I made his hands shake and his breath come in gasps and groans. Sometimes he uttered explosive grunts of pleasure as if he was helpless against me. He despised my religion, and he deplored my nature—our nature—but I owned him.

Even so, he was gentle and careful and kind, and I liked him despite the fact that now, if I caught him with a kid brother or a younger cousin, I'd have to kill him. I don't know where he is, and I don't care. Maybe that's not consistent, but maybe I'd swum with some sharks of my own.

I watched JT as he got out of the car, wringing his keys. I thought maybe I was his first man, and it scared him. It scared me too. While I stood with my hands in my pockets, the fast-moving clouds revealed the moon, and light limned JT's face. He wanted me, and he hated me for it. I was no stranger to those twins: desire and distaste. JT looked reckless enough to throw them both at me. Plenty of men I knew had been beaten by one twin after they'd slept with its brother.

I trusted—in that moment—the gentle hand I'd kissed in my worst, most vulnerable memory and moved forward.

JT let out the breath he was holding.

When I passed him to open the door of my room, he slipped his hands around my waist and clasped just above my belt buckle. JT hadn't come for a grope of the quick and raunchy variety. There was no grab for my balls or scrabble to get my zipper down. He twined his arms around me and held on, unaware that I could probably handle the situation better if I couldn't feel his cheek pressed against my shoulder.

His breath sighed against my hair, and he finally said, "Hello," with his lips pressed to my skin.

I thought then that JT was a man with no sense of self-preservation. His father owned the motel. He could see us from his office if he was looking out the window. JT's family, his friends, his girlfriends—anyone—could drive by and see him clinging to me like a limpet. They'd see that remarkably unique truck outside my door from the street and the highway.

I ushered him into the room and closed the door behind us. The silence seemed complete. Neither of us dared to breathe. I think I cocked my head to the side, asking without words *Are you certain*? He held his hands out to his sides, palms up. His keys dangled from his fingers, and as if it was a signal—*I surrender*—he let them fall to the ground. I took that as my cue to reach for him. He stood still as I unbuttoned his shirt, his breath accelerating when I placed the tip of my finger on his bare skin.

"What do you want, JT?" I guess whatever he wanted right then, I wanted to give it to him. Whatever it was. *Whatever it cost me.*

"I don't know," he whispered.

I let my fingers graze and circle his nipple, then I pressed down and gave it a squeeze. "Am I the first?"

JT nodded.

My hand traveled higher, over his collarbone and to his throat. I brushed his Adam's apple with my thumb, and my fingers curved around the back of his neck. "The first you've wanted?" I asked incredulously. *Couldn't be*. I knew I couldn't be the first he'd wanted. I felt that Adam's apple bob when he swallowed. His eyelashes brushed downward as he shook his head.

"You're the first I've wanted *enough*. The first I couldn't talk myself out of. Maybe I'm just getting too fucking desperate to hide it."

I agreed. "Maybe."

Our lips met, closed and teasing. Tender and in no hurry. He still held his arms to the sides, like…a gift. His hesitant lips, his shortened breathing, the tenderness with which he nuzzled his face against mine built my desire for him until it was like he'd poured rocket fuel and lit it with a match. He was beautiful. Perfect. I slipped my hands around his waist and pulled him to me until he clung, at last reaching for me. I slipped his shirt off his shoulders, but it hung there on his biceps because his arms were so tense. I cupped his face between my hands.

He unfastened the first buttons on my shirt, watching me as closely as I watched him. He mirrored my movements, so when I dropped my shirt, his hit the floor. When I toed off my shoes, he did likewise. It almost felt like a game, like I should feint and pretend to see if he would drop his jeans before I did mine. That silly notion led to a feeling so genuinely breathless with anticipation that I thought my heart stopped, waiting to see him, wanting that last piece of clothing to come off so it could beat again. So I could look him over in all his naked glory, and when it happened, I wasn't disappointed one bit.

Once again he held his hands out, and I took one and led him to the bed. I coaxed him to lie on it so I could look my fill. He was tan, and I was surprised. I expected to find that the rich, sun-kissed skin stopped where his sleeves ended, but it didn't. The golden velvet stretched everywhere except for a line that I guessed meant he swam in a Speedo. He had the build of a swimmer, compact and streamlined but wiry and strong, broad in the shoulders with full thighs and calves but lean in the hips. His ass was round but firm, like you could crack an egg on it, and he had the most delicious curve to his spine, which enhanced it.

He rolled over and clutched the pillow, suddenly shy.

"You can stop me anytime," I told him.

He looked up at me and batted his eyelashes. "If I get scared, will you only put it in halfway?"

"You've been sleeping with too many girls."

JT nipped at me playfully, but when I looked at him, his eyes were serious. "Yes," he said gravely. "I have."

I kissed him then to make him forget them. I wanted to surround him with sinew and sweat and spunk so the women he'd had would barely be a memory. I coaxed him to his side, rising over him to press my advantage, rolling with him until he was on his back. It was awkward at first, fitting our mouths together, breathing and tasting. Finding a place for our noses, while our lips and teeth and tongues brushed and nibbled one another's.

I found a spot just beneath his jaw on the right side that made him shiver, and he gripped my upper arms as tightly to hold me as I suspected he would later grab them to push me away. I nuzzled behind his ear, finding the skin there sweet with the scent of his aftershave. It was redolent with herbs and citrus, making the man underneath smell tasty and fine. I sipped at the skin there, and it was salty and sweet over the musky flavor of a thoroughly aroused human male.

Fuck, I wanted more of that. I traveled lower, teasing JT's skin and biting his nipples gently, testing and trying and measuring his response. He wanted that zing of gentle teeth after the sensuous lick of a tongue. He arched for me every time I did it, urging me on, pulling my head close so I could hardly mistake his need. I slipped my tongue into his belly button, and he moaned, his legs falling open. I moved surely along a trail of light hair to the similarly hued thatch above his cock.

The hands on my upper arms gripped me harder, and I looked up. His eyes held apprehension and something I didn't recognize, but I worried might be doubt.

"Say the word no and this doesn't go any further," I told him, although I think it would have killed me if he had. "Tell me to stop now, and you never did any of it."

"Please."

Thank fuck. Thank *fuck,* because I didn't know if I could

have stopped, that close, just inches from his dick. The tip of his cock glistened wetly, and he smelled musky from arousal. I didn't know if I could have turned away without tasting him.

I buried my face in his groin, pressing my nose against his skin, and inhaled. After that I took his balls into my mouth one at a time and stretched the delicate skin there, tugging and letting them go with a little *pop* that both surprised and aroused him further. He tasted like salt and sweat and man—briny, bitter, and sweet—all at the same time when I took him into my mouth. I looked up and saw he was uncertain. Maybe his girlfriends didn't do this much—or as willingly—and he had doubts.

I let him know that I liked what I was doing by pressing my aching dick against his hairy leg. I let him hear how much it aroused me by vocalizing the nonsense of my pleasure against his skin. I came just from blowing him, and I wasn't ashamed of it at all. Even as the sticky warmth of my cum hit his skin, tangling, pulling, and tactile, he shot down my throat, clutching my head and murmuring soft curses up at the ceiling.

I wanted to stay right where I was, but he dragged me up by my shoulders, and we shared the taste of him in kisses that seemed to last forever, long enough for me to think we might go again, until he fell asleep in my arms. Exhausted? Yes. Content? I hoped so.

I held him, but sleep was a long time coming for me.

LATER I WOKE up with a bad case of beard burn in an empty bed.

JT was long gone. There ought to be a law that a guy has to leave a rose on your pillow to let you know he enjoyed the labor you put into his walk of shame.

CHAPTER ELEVEN

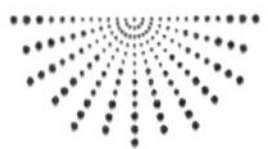

I had to get showered and dressed before I went to Mary Catherine's bakery. I wondered what she'd decided about moving. She probably slept better than I did even though she had some big decisions to make.

When I arrived, Muse caught me by the arm and dragged me out the door. "In the name of all that's holy, do you have a damned fork? I need to *stick it in my eye*."

She looked so outraged I had to laugh. "What's going on?"

"Candace had a date last night, and she's holding court." Muse rolled her eyes. "It's making everyone crazy."

"I saw her at Nacho's Bar. She seemed happy."

"That's just it. She does this every time she goes on a date. She's in there talking about everything they did." Her eyes grew wide. "Everything."

"Hot stuff, was it?" I opened the door and invited her to lead the way. When I entered, the girls were arguing as usual. I noticed Analise right away, as if she'd made some dramatic change, although it was hard to tell what it could be. She seemed more... visible somehow. While she showed no obvious signs of lipstick or blush, somehow she gave the impression of being more colorful that day. I wondered if it was possible she had heard about her ex-husband and was simply relieved that he wasn't getting out of jail.

I walked past her, and she even gave me a sweet, tentative smile. I grinned back at her. "I promised Mary Catherine I'd help her write up her thoughts on a possible retail space."

Muse followed me as far as the dough sheeter. "You don't have a fork? I'd settle for a mechanical pencil."

"She's happy, Muse. That's okay, isn't it?"

Muse hissed, "She's talking about the implications of frottage versus full-on oral sex for a second date. Considering she's bipolar, this is like the forward motion of a rocket ship that's destined to plummet to earth."

"Hi, Yasha." Candace beamed from where she was filling pie shells with custard. "Did you see my guy last night?"

"I did," I said. "You make an excellent couple."

"He was hot, huh? Good looking? Tell the girls how cute he was."

"He seemed nice—"

"I mean, you think he looked nice, right? And you should know too, right? You look at guys all the time."

I coughed to hide my embarrassment and shrugged.

Bianca made a seppuku motion behind Candace's back with a wooden spoon. "Miss Mary Catherine is in the back." She jerked her chin toward a storage room.

"Yasha"—Candace turned hopeful eyes my way—"is it really true men give the best blowjobs?"

Muse pushed in front of me like she was going to take a bullet. "Candace."

"I don't have anything…to-to base a comparison on," I stammered. "Really."

"Well, maybe you could just—"

Muse growled, "*Candace.*"

"All *right.*" Candace pulled her sweater tighter around her shoulders. "I'm just asking. We could all use a little—"

"Yasha," Mary Catherine called from the doorway to the storage room. "I thought I heard your voice."

"I'm here, Mary Catherine." I left Muse to deal with Candace. When I got to the back room, Mary Catherine had a cup of coffee waiting for me.

"I brought my laptop. I think we should start by making notes about goals, okay?"

"That sounds great." I took the coffee gratefully and added a sugar to it.

We sat on metal folding chairs with some boxes pulled between us. She put her computer down and opened it. I saw that her desktop wallpaper was a picture of Ken, whom I'd met the day before, and a man close to my age. I angled the screen so I could look closer. They were dressed for camping. Ken wore a bucket hat and a backpack. He held trekking poles. The other man had on a floppy-brimmed hat and carried his own pack. They made peace signs at the camera. "Hey, he has your eyes."

"That's Jordan, my son."

"They seem good together. It looks like they have fun. Do they camp often?"

"When they can. My son works full-time at a gym, and Ken is getting his real estate license."

"Yeah?" That made sense. Ken seemed to be interested in investing in property.

"That's how he found out about the appliance store. He's a real go-getter. Originally it was Ken who gave me the courage to go into this business."

I watched her computer screen while she brought up a spreadsheet program. The numbers looked good. I could see that Miss Independence Pies was doing better than most start-ups could expect.

"What do you envision when you imagine your retail space?"

Mary Catherine looked at her hands. "I don't know if I'm so good at imagining things," she said quietly.

I thought about that. "Me neither really."

"My husband used to say I was full of crazy ideas."

"Did he?"

"Maybe he was right. What do I know about—"

"Where is he now?"

"In Wisconsin. We're divorced."

She continued to look at her hands. I took them in my own, and they looked very small by comparison. "It's hard to let that kind of thing go, isn't it?"

"Yes." She swallowed.

"Can I tell you a secret?"

"Of course, Yasha."

"It probably doesn't matter what your husband thinks anymore." I guess she expected something more profound. Her lips curved into a small rosebud of a smile.

"How many years did you let him tell you that your ideas were worthless?"

"Thirty."

"Did you try to stick up for yourself?"

She snorted. "What do you think?"

"I think if you're anything like my mother, after you had to explain your first few black eyes to the neighbors, you didn't talk back," I told her. "And that didn't exactly stop him. So you stopped letting the neighbors see you."

She closed her eyes, and I thought I might have gone too far.

I gave her hand a squeeze. "So. You owe yourself."

She nodded and opened her eyes again. They shimmered a little but looked hopeful. "I think—"

"Don't tell me. Let me guess. You want to decorate in pink flamingos."

"No." She laughed a little.

"Clowns?"

"No." She gave me a playful push and began to describe her ideal store. We made a few drawings, wrote down some ideas. Then we talked about the menu, about starting small at first, doing a short list of things really well, then expanding the range when she saw what worked. We talked about how important keeping her restaurant-delivery contacts would be when she branched out. And how she might be able to expand her business with wedding cakes and catering. How it might be possible to turn it into a full-service bakery business eventually, rather than a pie shop. My thought was that one of her employees, maybe the silent Analise or even Muse, would attend baking courses at the local junior college or a baking school. The way she described what she wanted reminded me of a Parisian bakery/bistro, and I could tell she'd thought about it for a long time.

"Have you ever been to France?" I asked.

"No, but I've seen pictures of the cafés."

"Is that what you want? A French café in St. Nacho's?"

"Yes." She closed the laptop and put her pencil down on the yellow legal tablet we'd been doodling on. "I do."

"That's probably an achievable goal." I thought of the hard work in front of her but knew she was up to it and had plenty of help. "I have faith in you."

"You do?"

"I do."

"I wish…" She bit her lip.

"What?"

"I wish I could talk you into staying here and sharing it with me."

That shouldn't have surprised me, but it did. "*What?*"

"I need a pastry chef to give the place class and credibility. From what I understand, you need a job. Will you at least think about it?"

"Mary Catherine, I'm just here until my brother can pick me

up tomorrow night. I have an apartment in Los Angeles. A life..." I guess what I was thinking—*but I'm stuck making fucking cannoli*—showed on my face.

"Are you happy there?"

"I don't know. What's happy?" I got up, thinking I'd go see if the girls needed help with the pies. If they'd exhausted the topic of Candace's hot date. "I have a life there is all."

"Just promise me you'll think about it, all right?"

"All right. I will think about it."

Her smile trembled when she held her hand out. I took it and saw the hope in her eyes. Suddenly the idea didn't seem so ridiculous. It grew roots in my heart and sprouted wings in my head.

I had to get out of there, away from the contagious optimism of the look that Mary Catherine sent my way. I heard the girls arguing—Candace offering expert advice in her haughtiest voice, Muse barking back like an angry Pekingese. It was easy to picture Bianca's outrage and Analise melting out for a cigarette. I'd been thrown out of better places.

I said nothing but planned to keep my options open.

AFTER WORK I went home and slept for a few hours. Getting up so early for work and then staying up half the night was taking its toll. After I woke up, I decided it might be fun to make my way to the pier. And yes, I was in full possession of the knowledge that the firehouse was on the way. It wasn't an awfully long way to go and provided the possibility that I could ask JT if he wanted to go for a beer after work like any normal guy. Except JT wasn't a normal guy, and it wasn't a normal situation.

I had no illusions that he'd greet me with a kiss.

I'd had some time to do a little thinking about waking up alone. Over the course of the day I'd begun to believe it was a *bad thing*. Not, like, an aliens-experimenting-on-your-brain bad thing, but not like waking up in bed with the guy you'd had sex with either.

Sometimes that happened, but it usually ended with a guy coming back through the door with coffee and bagels. I had dated a man who always went out for the paper at the crack of dawn. When I woke up later, he'd be back, reading it in bed. Otherwise pretty much everyone mostly said goodbye and made nice before hitting the road.

And I couldn't help wondering if the fact that JT didn't was a *very bad sign.*

THE WIND off the ocean was a little gusty; it blew leaves and bits of papers along the pavement and caused the flag on the pole out in front of the firehouse to whip and snap percussively overhead. It made my heart race, and my instinct to dive to the ground and cover my head was virtually impossible to ignore. I had to remind myself where I was, consciously telling myself I could hear the Pacific Ocean and I was safe.

The air burst with a freshness that brought all kinds of scents with it: the briny tang of ocean water and decay, of fish, wood smoke, and ozone. The engine wasn't in the garage, nor was the EMS rig that was JT's purview. The large space echoed with the absence of the life that usually inhabited it as if ghosts carried on the business of the living there.

I was walking toward the pier when I heard the unmistakable growl of the big fire engine rumbling toward me, followed by the smaller paramedic's truck except JT wasn't in it. He must not have been working that shift. I waved at the firefighters and saw Cam smile warmly from inside the truck. He waved back. I waited for a while until they regrouped after their call. I stood in the shade of an avocado tree and listened to them unwind.

What seemed like aeons ago, I'd been a soldier, and often I missed the everyday chatter of men, the camaraderie and teasing and tough justice of life as part of a team. Hard jobs sometimes make hard men, yet these firefighters had never seemed anything but diligent, genuine, and dedicated. I'd seen them in action firsthand and been rescued by one. I admired them more than I could say.

Cam ambled over to where I stood. He put his big hand on a branch above my head, hanging there a little, his biceps bulging at right about eye level. I smothered a laugh. He knew exactly the effect he had on me—on everyone—and he enjoyed it tremendously.

"Whatcha doing?" he asked. The branch gave a little, and his head lolled dangerously close to mine. "Come to see me?"

I felt bad that I hadn't. He was a big, goofy kid. The sixth grader who shows off and pantomimes gagging behind the teacher's back. I liked him a lot. "No." I shrugged apologetically. "Sorry, I came to see JT."

"Well, I'd say you're outta luck there, because he's off shift and he's got a hot date."

I colored. "Has he?"

"Yeah, he's probably home right now getting prettified." Cam looked at me with a remarkable sensitivity I wouldn't have given him credit for. "It's probably best if you don't hang your hopes on him, Yasha."

Disappointment melted me. I thought I hid it pretty well until Cam took my upper arm and told me he was buying me a drink.

CHAPTER TWELVE

Once inside Nacho's Bar, Cam and I decided to have dinner together, something that seemed natural since the kitchen was still humming, and the violinist played dinner-time music from table to table, taking requests. From my experience, eventually the kitchen would close except for appetizers and snacks, and the tables would be cleared to make room for a dance floor. After ten most of the patrons were gay men with a few straight couples thrown in, looking blown off course but not surprised or disappointed to find themselves around an affectionate same-sex couple or ten. I noticed a knot of younger patrons using sign language; either they were deaf or they were learning and wanted to practice.

All in all, it was a remarkably eclectic and easygoing crowd, and that night was no exception. Cam filled me in on the people he knew, pointing out the owner, Jim, and his partner, Alfred, some firefighters I hadn't met, one or two of the St. Nacho's police officers dining with their wives, and the violinist, a pierced and tatted, bad boy-looking guy named Cooper, who played with a skill and sweetness I hadn't heard anywhere, ever.

He was so jaw-droppingly brilliant I wondered how he could have ended up in such an impossibly tiny place.

"I'm not an expert or anything, but he's—" I tried to think of a word as I hissed my disbelief in Cam's ear. "He's fantastic. Unreal."

"Yeah. He's amazing. He just pulled up here one day on a Harley and never left. Jim told me he asked if he could play his violin for tips, so he offered him the use of the studio upstairs. He worked in the kitchen for a while. Still does when they're shorthanded. He should be playing with the symphony in a major city, but he met someone who lives here in St. Nacho's, and they clicked right away. He likes it here, I guess."

"Unbelievable." I watched, riveted as he played a piece I knew, the theme from an old film called *Laura*. The way he imbued it with everything he had, the way he dipped and swayed made it seem as if he was more than just a man making music. It was intensely personal for him. He interacted with the music in a way I'd never seen before.

I gave him a few bucks and asked him to play the theme from *Schindler's List*, a piece of music I knew my mother had loved when she was alive. He was brilliant. I had tears in my eyes when he stepped away, both from the beauty of his playing and also from the futile wish that my mother and my zeyde could have been there to hear it.

Cam stared at me but said nothing. I gained a new appreciation for him based on his patience.

"Muse told me that people end up here because it's a place of intense spiritual energy," I murmured. "Like *Buffy's* Hellmouth, only not in the demons-jump-out-at-you way."

"Muse?"

"Yeah, one of my cohorts in pie. Actually she told me that you can't see St. Nacho's unless it wants you." I expected him to refute this, to call it crazy or laugh. He didn't.

"I won't say it's invisible or anything, but it does seem to be the case that it's stayed relatively unremarkable."

I took a sip of my beer. "Except that everything about St. Nacho's, from its tranquil beauty, to this bar and its amazing violinist, to Mary Catherine and her band of merry, pie-baking handmaidens is completely unique. And why that's unremarkable remains a mystery."

Cam shrugged his beefy shoulders in a way that indicated that he hadn't thought much about it. Yet from the glimpses I'd gotten of him that night, I wondered if maybe he had been giving thought to a lot of things and simply wasn't letting on. Given his penchant for playing the clown, for enjoying his massive muscles and the attention he got from his physical perfection, it seemed likely that he played down his brains and sensitivity. I had to think there was more going on inside his head than anyone gave him credit for.

He must have seen a look of speculation on my face, because he leaned in with a leer. "What's that look for?"

Before I could ask him what had drawn him to St. Nacho's, there was a bit of a commotion at the door, and JT walked in with a girl on his arm. She was gorgeous, sort of a kosher Kim Kardashian, thin as a rail with tits like angels had piped them there in frosting, high and firm. *Perky*. She was tiny but perfectly formed and had ankles like fine-crystal wine stems poised on shoes with heels so high and lethal they ought to be registered as weapons.

"Wow. Flashy. She looks like a professional cheerleader, doesn't she? Right on cue," Cam muttered. "Sorry."

I didn't have time to wonder what Cam meant by that because I was watching JT and his girl make their way across the room, smiling and shaking hands with friends. Eventually they fetched up on our table, a happenstance so seemingly casual, so perfectly calculated to appear random it had to be anything but.

I whispered to Cam, "What happened to Linda?"

Cam only shrugged.

"Hi, Jacob." JT held his hand out to me. Those were the fingers I'd licked and sucked the night before, the palm I'd kissed when I'd thought he was my zeyde.

He was nothing like my zeyde.

I took it and gave it a firm pump, pasting a smile on my face. *Howdy do. Howdy doody do.*

"This is Elaine."

Tension must have crackled in the air around me, because Miss Girlfriend didn't reach over when I glanced her way to see if she'd shake. Some girls have a sense of self-preservation around gay men and feel the threat of a curse hanging in the air, whether there is one or not. I wasn't above thinking evil thoughts, but I didn't let her see them.

"Lovely to see you again, *Jason*. Elaine." I inclined my head.

JT's gaze swept over toward me but slid away like a shadow when mine—probably overbright and accusatory—met it.

"Well, we're for dinner, then," JT said.

I couldn't help it. "Chef must have forgotten to write that on the specials menu."

Next to me Cam snorted.

"Nice to see you." JT put his hand on the small of Elaine's back, and it belonged there, his fingertips stretching across her body like the webbing of a corset.

It fit perfectly.

I didn't speak before he walked away, but once he was out of range, I couldn't help giving voice to my thoughts. "Yes, and so expedient too. Imagine the inconvenience of having to look for me, even in a town this small, to make your point."

Cam said, "I'm sorry, Yasha."

"For what?" I could at least hope he didn't see how *Jason's* date had affected me.

"Guys like that—they can't help but follow up with a pretty

girl. Drive the point home with a few big public displays of affection."

"What?"

"I saw his truck at the motel last night." Cam looked down at his beer. "I'm sorry. It was late, and I kind of figured you and he had something going. Then he's here like this today and calling you Jacob. It doesn't take a rocket scientist."

"He's done something like that before?" Please, please don't tell me he's a liar as well as a motherfucking straight coward down-low prick.

"Not that I know of actually." Cam shrugged. "He's looked plenty. Like a kid in a toy-shop window if you know what I mean."

I nodded miserably.

"But so far he's stayed so deep in the closet they're going to crown him king of Narnia." Cam drank the rest of his beer in one pull and signaled the waiter over to order two more of the same and a couple of shots of Patrón.

I asked, "You're not driving, are you?"

"Nope, I'm off work and on foot. I'll just find somewhere to sleep it off. Unless...I'll walk you home if you want."

"I'll be fine," I told him. "But I'm in the mood to drink, so keep it coming."

Yeah, well...shit.

We ordered carnitas, and they came in a heaping plateful with delicate corn tortillas that tasted handmade. We got rice and beans on the side and a bowl of pico de gallo and one of red hot salsa, chopped extra fine but not quite pureed, smoky with chipotle and maybe a hit of habanero, but bright with fresh tomatoes, cilantro, and sweet red onion.

Cam could eat, and I liked that on a guy since I'm somewhat handy in the kitchen. I often expressed myself with food, and

Cam—he could really put it away. He grinned around great mouthfuls, bluff and hearty, but still boyish and maybe a little impudent in his worn cowboy boots and formfitting jeans. He dared me to drink three shots in succession—the time-honored way with a lick of salt and a bite of lime—and eyed me with the kind of intent that made the hot sauce seem tepid by comparison. At least four times I sat there silently wishing that Cam were *the one*. That my focus didn't stray to the quiet corner of the bar where JT sat with his homecoming queen, hand on his chin, hanging on her every word. At least that many times I begged the Fates to turn me around, to cause my heart to quicken when I looked at Cam the way it did when I caught sight of JT lifting his wineglass to his lips.

All the same, while I chatted and ate, I felt JT's gaze on *me* as if he was as drawn to me as I was to him, and I felt sorry for him.

Cam's appeal was in-your-face, and JT's was as subtle as a whisper. JT lacked Cam's cowboy charm. He lacked Cam's humor and bravado, yet I couldn't keep from looking over at him again and again, until JT and Elaine shared a dessert and then paid their tab and got up to leave. By that time I'd had plenty to drink, and his presence seemed funny if a little sad. My own pathetic state didn't bear thinking on.

"So then"—Cam was telling the story of a dramatic 911 call that involved downed electrical wires and rain—"we have to rescue this guy in a pickup truck, and we discover that he's been riding around, naked from the waist down, flashing truckers. Started the whole damned thing."

"What a mess," I agreed, grinning now because JT was finally gone and I could breathe again. "It's a nightmare when you're doing something dumb and you need to be rescued."

"What dumb thing have you done?"

"Me?" I remembered a time when I was about twenty-three. "I was in a bar getting shitfaced, and a bomb went off outside the disco next door. It just decimated the crowd waiting to get in, blew out all the windows on the block."

"What were you doing that was so stupid?" Cam asked, frowning.

"When the blast went off it was total chaos. I'd been trying to forget whatever was bothering me at the time by getting drunk, and the end result was that when the chips were down, I couldn't *help* anyone. There were these kids from Ukraine who were there on a school trip going to the disco as a big treat and a way to blow off steam. Big chunks of metal, ball bearings, and screws had flown from the source of the detonation, blowing holes in all that flesh." My hand shook, so I put down my beer. "I got a couple of people comfortable, but fortunately EMS was there in a heartbeat. First they shoved me out of the way to get to the worst injured, and then they patched me up, monitored me for shock. I didn't even realize I'd been hit."

"Shit," Cam hissed.

"I managed *supplies* in the Tzahal. I didn't see much action while I wore the uniform, but I was nearly killed off duty. Go figure."

"No shit." Cam leaned in a little sloppily. I suppose he'd already seen more carnage from car accidents than I would probably ever see in my lifetime.

"Twenty-two stitches. That was a tough year there, 2001."

"Here too." Cam raised his most recent shot glass.

I muttered a curse. "Yes, indeed. *Hell yes*. Here especially." I tapped my beer against his shot glass and vowed to talk about more upbeat things.

"Are you sorry you left Israel?"

"No, my grandfather was dead. All the family I had left was here."

"Must be strange, though," he mused. "To move there, serve in the military, and then return here."

"I'm not really political or religious. I only went to be with my zeyde. Israel filled a void in my grandfather's heart, and I'm glad we went, but I don't have the same desire to belong there, I guess."

"I miss my family a lot." Cam swallowed hard. "But I got tired of explaining that I couldn't just pick out a nice girl and settle down if I really wanted to badly enough."

"I'm sorry," I told him. I *was* sorry. A sad Cam was unbearable. It felt like a crime against nature.

"Nah. My family threw me out. They made it impossible to live in the town where I grew up, so I moved on. I came up here to St. Nacho's from New Mexico when I saw an Internet ad for an experienced firefighter, and here I've been ever since."

"It feels good here. It's a good place."

"You need to think about staying. I heard JT saying Mary Catherine Jensen wants you for a business partner."

"She's not looking for a partner really. Just a baker. I could do that." I tried the image on: staying in St. Nacho's, finding a small place to live, walking to and from wherever Mary Catherine baked her pies every day. I could be part of the St. Nacho's unofficial domestic-violence work-study program and let the ladies set me straight when I made a mistake. They would call me out for pining over JT when I was having one of the best evenings I'd had all year with Cam.

Still, I dangled over the precipice. So many moves. So many times I'd relocated thinking the next place would be better, that I'd put down roots and start to build—if not a family—a sort of tribe where I belonged. I'd already adopted Muse and Mary Catherine. There's nothing I wouldn't have done for those two. I had strong and inappropriate feelings for JT, sure, but I loved his dad. I really, really liked Cam, which made me sad in a way, because if I'd been smart, I'd have taken him up on the encounter that his eyes and that slow, country-boy smile had been promising me all night.

I was thinking about all these things when Cam got right

next to my ear and said, "You and me isn't going to happen, is it?"

Ah shit. "No," I told him honestly. "I want it to be different, but I can't get JT off my mind. I'm damned if I know why. I'm not a guy who goes after straight men."

"JT's not straight." Cam pursed his lips in distaste. "He's a fucking coward. His loss. Is this the first time that's happened to you? You hook up with a guy, and you're invisible the next time you meet?"

"I'm nearly thirty-two. What do you think?"

"I think it sucks to be alone," Cam said. "Tonight, stay and dance with me. At least drink. Be out and proud and forget the JTs of the world."

I only had to think about it for a minute. "All right."

CHAPTER THIRTEEN

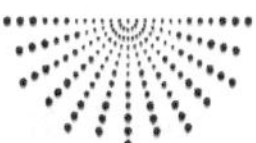

Cam threw a couple of twenties on the table, and I paid my half. I vowed to eat there again and see if the rest of the menu was as good. By the time we got up, some of the waiters were pushing back the tables, so we decided to take a walk to get some air before going back to dance.

The minute I stepped outside, my head cleared enough to appreciate the beauty of the place. I wanted to walk on the sand close to the water. Cam followed along, pulling off his boots and socks, making a remark that he'd be sorry later when he was dancing with sand between his toes. I toed off my Vans and socks as well, rolling up my pant legs as I'd seen him do, and we left our things lying where the dry sand gave way to the wet and the shore dropped steeply off.

Water foamed around our feet as we walked in silence. I watched it, not really seeing it except to avoid sharp shells and rocks and bits of trash. Cam took my hand, and I knew he intended it to be more of a comfort than a pass. I gave it a squeeze and let go, then threw an arm around his waist, inviting him to put his around my shoulder.

Clouds moved overhead fast, almost like time-lapse photography, drifting over the stars and the moon in an inky black sky. Thicker, darker clouds were headed our way, ominous with moisture. It looked like we'd get more rain if they stood still long enough over St. Nacho's to drop it.

At some point we reached the pier and stopped walking. We sat down on the damp sand and simply watched as the waves rolled gently into the shore.

"Yasha?"

"Mmhmm?" I rested my head on Cam's thick biceps, sorry once again that I could offer nothing more than friendship.

"Do you ever feel like the only time you exist is when others are watching?"

"What do you mean? Like if a tree falls and there's no ear to hear it, does it still make a sound?"

"Yeah. Exactly. Am I really here if there's no one to see and remember? No one to care that it's me?"

"I don't know. You're taxing my brain after too many drinks. Here. Look. If you push your finger in the sand like this"—I demonstrated—"you don't just move the grains of sand you push. You move sand all around. See?"

"Yeah." He watched my finger as I did it again.

"You can't know which ones either. You change things up close and farther away whether you like it or not. A guy like you —a guy who rolls out on a fire truck when there's an accident on the highway—you've got to be changing things you'll never even know about. Touching lives you can't imagine."

"That's right." He grinned down at me during a break between clouds, and the moon glazed his face with a silvery light. "Cool."

"I don't like to be alone, Cam, but I'm getting older—too old for recreational sex and one-night stands. I'm getting tired of Mr. Right Now. The last guy nearly killed me. I'm pretty sure I have sucktastic taste in men."

Cam laughed at that, and I laughed with him. "You must

have, or we'd be hitting it like rabbits right now. Come on. Free ride on the Camshaft..."

I rolled my eyes. "As enticing as that sounds, do you honestly think that's a good idea? I'm not your type."

Cam looked thoughtful. "I'm still trying to decide if I have a type. Whether you're it or not. Mostly I figure breathing is good." He grinned, and I knew we'd gotten past a particularly tricky land mine. "So far that's been my type."

"Yeah, well, you ought to probably narrow it down from there if you want anything to last."

"You know what? You're probably right," he teased, getting up and dusting his ass off. "I'll get right on that tomorrow. Right now, I want to hop into a pile of flesh and dance until I'm creaming my jeans."

I looked back at Nacho's up the beach. Cars were already starting to park on the streets around it. In the distance the headlights looked like strings of Christmas lights.

"Gonna be a busy night," Cam said, starting back toward our shoes.

Suddenly I felt so tired. "Yeah, you know what? I think if you don't mind, I'm just going to head back to the motel."

"Really?"

"Yeah, I keep baker's hours, and all that booze made me tired."

"It's the ocean. Very relaxing."

"If I don't head home, I'll fall asleep here on the beach."

"It's fine. You need me to walk you back? No strings."

"I'll be fine."

When we found our shoes again, we could smell the cigarette smoke from the patrons outside the bar. I couldn't say I'd miss that. People stood two and three deep outside, smoking and waiting for others to show, cooling off from the dance floor in the night air.

I shook my socks out and regretted the necessity of putting

them on again, but it was a long walk back to the hotel. My Vans slid easily back on my feet, and in no time Cam and I stood at the corner of the street where we would part company for the night.

"I had a good time. You're a great guy. When you find out what you want, I know you'll get it. You deserve all the good stuff."

Cam jerked his chin in my direction and said, "Likewise," before giving me a bone-crushing hug. "I'll be seeing you around. Beware of counterfeit."

I knew what he meant—not money but emotions. Look out for guys like JT who were all hot and bothered in the dark but didn't know you when the sun came up. "I will."

I didn't want to tell him I'd be heading home if Dan came to get me the next day, and I didn't know if I'd be back.

"See you." He turned and walked away. I half expected him to get a running start and then just plow into the knots of hot guys standing around like some juggernaut of love, leaping naked into a pile of willing flesh. I wondered what it would take to slow him down. Not me. I knew that. Still, he made me smile.

I turned on the main drag again, finding my way along quiet streets to the motel. It would be useful to have a car here, not that I'd really need it, but on one of the few big rain days it might be nice to stay dry. There was no public transportation whatsoever in St. Nacho's. JT'd told me there weren't even cabs. The town stretched out farther on the other side of the highway, past the motel, and I hadn't begun to explore it. That's where the high school was and where Ken Ashton lived with his partner, according to Mary Catherine.

I liked the apartments near the beach, and I'd seen a FOR RENT sign or two. I didn't doubt I could make it work. I could give up my lease on the apartment in LA when it came time. Move here. Work somewhere.

Did St. Nacho's want me?

St. Nacho's certainly called to me. Maybe it did want me. And maybe I was ready to settle down with a place if not with a person.

My thoughts continued like that until I became aware of an engine on the street, doing the curbside crawl next to the sidewalk where I ambled along. I knew it was JT before I looked up. The purr of his engine seemed as familiar to me now as his face.

I kept walking. I knew he'd have to lean way over or even stop the truck and put it in park before he could crank down the window on the passenger side to talk to me.

"Sucks to be you," I muttered.

Eventually, after trying and failing to get my attention, he parked the old Ford and got out, sort of speed walking to catch up to me.

"Wait," he called. "Yasha. Wait."

I wasn't exactly afraid of what he'd have to say to me or in any way surprised when he said, "About what happened in the bar—"

"Dude—"

"No, listen. I'm sorry about that. Really sorry."

"Cool. Okay, thanks, *Jason*." I began walking again. He could follow me to the motel for all I cared. He'd just have to walk back and get his damned truck.

"I asked Elaine out weeks ago. *Yasha*, will you hear me out?"

I spun around to face him. "Sure. But what do you have to tell me that I don't already know?"

JT looked blank.

"I thought so." I turned back and started walking again.

"Well, *hell*. I panicked, all right?"

"Sure."

"I woke up in the middle of the night, and I thought, oh *fuck me*. I'm gay."

"So. Did Elaine the Minisupermodel help you decide otherwise?"

"I—"

"What if I say, being an expert in the field, that you're not gay? What if I swear to it? Would that make you feel better? You're bi-curious and tempted by something you've never tried. Go forth and be free forever. I'm leaving. I need my beauty sleep."

"No, stop." He followed me. "*Yasha.*"

I faced him again, wanting to start a brawl, wanting to wipe the misery off his face if I had to do it with my fist, knowing it was that kind of thinking that had brought me here to St. Nacho's in the first place.

It had to stop somewhere.

"Look. I'm really sorry I don't have anything to say to you, but I don't. You need to stop following me. You need to get in your car and go home to wherever it is you live and forget about me, all right? Because I don't do this. I don't want this. I date *out gay men*. Period."

"But you want me. I know you do." He glanced my way, and even though I felt it, I didn't look up.

I rolled my eyes. "I *want* a pony and a personal aircraft. I'll live with my disappointment."

JT looked dispirited when he got back into his truck and drove off.

ODDLY ENOUGH I was neither surprised nor particularly unhappy to find that very same truck sitting outside the door of my motel room when I arrived, angry, tired, and sweating, a mile and a half later.

I didn't stop this time to speak. I simply pulled out my keys and unlocked my door. I didn't bother to turn on the light in the small room. Instead, I waited for him to follow me inside and took him by complete surprise. I spun him around forcibly and pressed his body into the door after I closed it. His face was wedged against the wood, but he let out a chuckle like he knew I was playing with him.

Which I was. There was no way in hell I was going to hurt him.

"JT." I wanted to bite the skin of his neck, just below his hairline, where he smelled of cologne and nervous sweat. "Here's the deal. Maybe we got off on the wrong foot. I understand curiosity, but if you don't leave now, I'm going to bend you over that cheap desk and fuck your ass until you can't sit down for a week."

"Shhhhiiit..." he hissed, pressing his ass back against my cock. *"No."*

The sibilant whisper made the hairs rise on the backs of my hands where they held him fast. "No? JT, if you keep chasing after me, I'm going to own you. No way you can chick-date yourself out of that."

He huffed another sound of surprise and ground out, *"No."*

"'Cause this here is what happens to little boys who don't know what they want. I *will* leave marks all over your body that you won't be able to explain away. I *will* out your ass every time I see you in public, and take it—whenever I want, however I want, short of rape—when we're alone."

Frankly I planned no such thing, but it was my own version of *Scared Straight!* and had worked more than once to back a bi-curious boy off the deal.

JT caught my hand and pressed it to his heart. "Can you feel that?"

"Yes." It beat frantically, erratically.

"Then you know I'm as excited right now as you are." He nearly whimpered when I leaned against him, my cock wedged firmly between his ass cheeks against the seam of his tight jeans.

"Or you're scared."

"Hell yes, I'm scared." He pushed back enough so that I let

him up, but all he did was turn and pull me into his arms—his legs splayed—holding me between them. “You know I’m scared.”

“Then don’t put yourself through it. They don’t make a girl pretty enough to pretend that away.”

JT laughed. “You should have seen your face.” The little pisher mocked me. *“Lovely to see you again, Jason.”*

Silence stretched taut between us, and I could swear I felt his heartbeat inside my own chest.

“That hurt. Seeing you there like that.” I swallowed hard. “I don’t know why really.”

JT put those gentle, delicate hands of his on my face, cupping it tenderly and bringing me in close. “I’m so sorry,” he whispered between kisses. “I’m sorry, Yasha. I saw that I hurt you, and I am so, *so* sorry.”

CHAPTER FOURTEEN

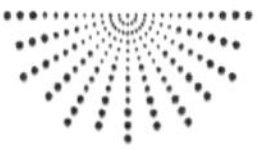

JT dropped his fingers to my shoulders and tightened there, and I recalled the stupid threats I'd made. That I'd bend him over and hurt him or out him to his friends. We both knew I'd do neither of those things. The fact was that we were attracted to each other. I could feel it in my gut each time he looked at me like I was melting ice cream he wanted to lick. My resolve oozed and gushed and ran in rivulets whenever he was around, and no matter how much I hated the thought of being the guy he came to after he dropped off his pretty girlfriends, I wanted him.

I planned to leave town with Dan the next day, and so I just gave in to it. I'm not entirely proud of that, but I didn't beat myself up over it at the time.

Our clothes hit the floor with no ceremony whatsoever. Just a whisper of fabric, the scratch of a zipper, and the *ping* of one button torn off in someone's impatience.

I did push him down over that desk, though, for show, because I'd said I would. But when I got him there, I wanted to worship him, not debase him. I started by nuzzling the skin of his neck in the warm corner where it met his shoulder. It seemed sensitive. He squirmed and begged while I did it, while I kept my hand flat on his shoulder and ground my cock into the crack of his ass.

He clutched the surface of the desk. His fingers clawed, but they found nothing to hold on to until I covered his hand with my own, gripping it tight. He caught it and laced our fingers together, squeezing until my hand stung where his nails bit into my skin.

I wanted skin on skin: pressure, friction, lips, and sweat and the desire that builds when the train leaves the station and you're trying to burn out the brakes, gaining speed, pulling back just enough to incinerate anything that could stop it before it reaches its destination. Somewhere along the way JT started making these amazing sounds, like tiny grunts but needy, like it wasn't enough, and I ran my finger across the tender, puckered hole between his ass cheeks. Cum splattered audibly against the drawers of the desk.

Fuck, if that wasn't the hottest thing.

"*Yasha.*" His legs began to quiver and shake beneath me. It felt like an earthquake at first until I realized he was still shuddering from the force of his climax. I kept his hand as I led him to the bed, where I yanked back the bedspread and pulled down the covers. He stumbled there, falling into the pillows, and I climbed in after him, rolling him facedown. Then I stretched out all along the hills and valleys of his back.

JT's skin was damp with sweat, and I could glide my body over it, keeping my cock in motion, pressing him into the bedding. At that point I didn't know what to think, whether I'd get off like that, from the friction, or whether he'd consider allowing me to penetrate him, part his ass and—ostensibly—pop his cherry right there in his old man's motel. The briefest touch of my finger against the sensitive skin of his hole had caused him to come like a rocket, but I wasn't sure he was ready to be taken that way, no matter what either of us said.

His body hair tickled me, tangling with mine, scraping my skin, crackling and sparking what felt like little electric shocks all along my legs and arms. I slipped my hands beneath him, cupping his pecs, fingering his nipples, finding the buds pebbled, and pinching them hard. I couldn't help arching against him, nipping and fondling. I was everywhere at once until I could feel him let go of his brain in favor of his balls. I pumped my hips, my dick riding the crack of his ass on a slick trail of pre-ejaculate, and he gasped out my name and writhed beneath me.

"Do it." He gasped. *As if I'd just stick it in.* "Just...do it. I want it."

"Turn," I told him, slipping off.

When he complied, I could tell he was leveling off. His breathing had slowed, and he'd pulled back from the frantic, desperate edge I'd driven him to moments before.

I crawled between his legs and slipped down, parting them, unable to stop myself from burying my face in the nest of damp hair above his cock to breathe in the scent of man and spunk. "You smell so damned good."

"Wait. Stop."

"What?" I froze.

"*Jeez*."

He put a hand to his face, over his eyes, and I found it endearing. Like a child who thinks you can't see them if they can't see you. I nuzzled down and licked his perineum from his balls down to his tightly puckered hole.

"I can't believe you do that."

"Don't you eat pussy?" I asked. I don't know if I expected him to answer. It might have been fun if he'd jerked with outrage. Instead he shrugged.

"*Yes*. That's a little crude though."

"Sorry," I told him, after mouthing his balls. "I love this. Love the damp skin. Love the spunk." I demonstrated by swiping a lick up his cock and suckling the tip, tasting the glistening fluid gathering there. "Love it sticky like this."

"That's—"

"I'm going to touch you again," I said, brushing my finger lightly around his hole. "Here."

"Oh hey. No," he said, closing his eyes and jumping a little when I did it. His dick twitched.

"Don't you touch yourself there?"

He moaned when I pressed harder. "Of course not."

"No?" *Liar.*

"No." He growled at that, lifting his head to shoot me a glare.

"Does it feel good?"

JT closed his eyes. "*Yes.*"

After a while I laughed a little. I couldn't help it. "It *does,* doesn't it?"

He shook his head but refused to meet my eyes.

"Why do you suppose that is?"

JT lifted his gaze. "Heroin feels good. I don't have to do everything that feels good."

"Sexual pleasure is hardly heroin, JT." I backed away. "Even if you're religious, you must have some notion that it's a gift from—"

"I understand *that.* I do. But there are things that are unnatural. Things that are forbidden."

I felt like waggling my eyebrows at the melodrama in what he was saying but refrained. I couldn't help using my Dracula voice, though, when I said, "The darker passions. The love that dares not speak its name…" I wasn't proud of it necessarily.

"Don't make fun of me."

I was contrite. "I'm sorry." I crawled along the bed to lie on my side next to him, leaving sex for the moment in favor of discovering boundaries. I managed a nonchalant pose, my elbow bent, my head resting on my hand as if I had all the time in the world. "What is it, exactly, that you want from me?"

He took my free hand in his. "I want to be close to you."

"How close?" I asked, leaning in a little. "This close?"

Instead of speaking, JT put his forehead into my neck, asking to be held. I wrapped my arms around him and pulled him against my chest. He clung to me.

"I'm embarrassed by what I want."

"You don't have to be. Never in front of me."

It took a long time for him to speak, and when he finally did, it was more of a whisper. "I have a small plug. Sometimes I…use that."

"Does it feel good?"

He closed his eyes. "*Yes.*"

After a while I laughed a little. I couldn't help it. "It *does*, doesn't it?"

He shook his head against my chest but refused to meet my eyes.

"Why do you suppose that is?"

He finally lifted his head. "If you're going to say that it feels good because the Creator intended for you to have a cock up your—"

"I don't pretend to know why it feels good, except for the physiological reasons. I was just wondering if you had any ideas."

He put his head back down. "Well, I don't."

"Did you know you can let your girlfriends peg you? Have you ever tried that?"

"*What*?" His eyes flew open. "No, of course not."

I stilled. What the fuck was I thinking? Suddenly I was going to be his marriage counselor? But I went on, undeterred. "Why not? You're obviously into anal play, and you date women all the time. You could get all the pleasure from the act without going to a man behind their—"

He shoved me off him so hard, I rolled until I hit the floor.

"Get the fuck off me, you shit." By the time I got up again, he was dressing.

"JT, I'm only trying to—"

"You are *such* a fucking jerk."

"I said I was sorry." I guessed I had touched a nerve. "I really didn't mean anything by it. You obviously date women. I thought…I don't know what I thought. I thought I could help."

He clamped his hands together after he got his pants on. "I want to just…smack you."

"Maybe I bring that out in people." I wanted to laugh, but given my background, it wasn't funny. "Probably I do."

He raked trembling fingers through his hair. "Yasha, you stupid motherfucker. It's you I want. Your dick and everything that goes with it. The laughter, the heart, the uncertainty, those eyes of yours watching me…Did you think I didn't know that *anyone* can fuck my ass? Including girls? That's my problem. I don't want girls. I wish I did."

"I'm sorry."

He'd worked himself up into a state and kept talking while he yanked his T-shirt on. "I've never told anyone I had those feelings. That I've…touched myself there. I've never let it past my lips that I might want that. It's such a source of *failure* for me. I can't stop wanting, I can't stop looking at men, and now it's worse than ever because it's all narrowed down and personified in one man. A man I like—someone who wants me—and now I can't stop thinking how it could be between us."

I shook my head. "I don't know what to say." I sat down on the bed and watched him.

"I don't need you to say anything. It's my problem."

"Not exclusively," I reminded him.

"I want what my parents had."

"But also to be fucked by a man?"

He muttered a curse. "I don't know why I'm bothering. You're rooted firmly in the basest, crudest terms of physical gratification." He searched around for his socks and his shoes and slipped them on.

"That didn't seem to bother you *at all* when I was sucking your dick." Now I was getting angry. "I see. I'm an animal, and you want a true marriage of two minds."

"I warned you not to make fun of me." As he tied his shoe, he yanked so hard he tore the lace. He pulled the other side hard enough to tear it too, then threw the ends down onto the carpet.

"I'm not making fun of you." But maybe I was. "I think you have unreasonable expectations, and I know you have conflicting desires. I know you want to love someone and be loved in return. I know you want the kind of marriage your parents had—"

"Exactly."

"I also can't help but notice that you're the one who's been following me home late at night and—"

"I wanted it to be *you* inside me. If it's not you, it doesn't mean shit. It's not worth letting go of my principles if it's not *real*. I guess it's not your fault that for you it can be just anyone." He turned and strode out the door, slamming it behind him.

Later, long after his truck had roared to life and rumbled out of the parking lot, I wondered if I'd alienated him on purpose. Probably I had. One time, while I was living with Sander just putting one foot in front of the other, I found some Nietzsche quote—"Whoever despises himself still esteems the despiser within himself"—and pinned it up on the bulletin board at Il Ghiotto. No matter how many times I looked at it, I'd still gotten on the bus after work and slogged home to Sander, whether he was there or not, allowing my life to unfold in an endless pattern of predictable disappointments.

Finally, spectacularly, and probably entirely by accident, I realized what it meant and let my mouth run faster than my brain. I'd so completely pissed off JT that there could be no going back. I didn't despise myself for being who I was, and I never would. I wouldn't allow anyone to make me feel bad about that. That was a line I could draw in the sand.

JT tugged at my heart like no one ever had. He seemed so young to me. Melodramatic on the one hand, yet on the other I admired his determination to be whole, to unify his physical and spiritual natures. I liked that he thought about things like integrity, when I mostly just fell into relationships without thinking at all.

I assumed that he'd find a nice Jewish girl, and I hoped he could make it work, hoped he could find the type of love his parents had found. I wanted him to have his happily-ever-after.

Maybe I'd find one too. I wanted exactly what he wanted. I *did* want a life with someone. But I wasn't about to go binge dating or joining singles' groups. I wasn't going to attempt any of the other oddly specific things he did to find love.

More important, I believed I could find what I wanted with a man. But if I couldn't, I didn't want it at all.

Anyway, JT was gone, and I would be leaving the following day with Dan.

SINCE I GOT no sleep the night before, I knew how I'd look in the cold, predawn fluorescent light outside of Miss Independence Pies before Muse even had a chance to utter her shriek, but the piercing sound drew every eye my way anyway.

"What the hell happened to you?" Bianca asked. "Don't you have a mirror?"

Candace looked picture perfect as usual, as cool and blonde as a runway model. "Bianca, give the man a break. He's healing from the injuries he sustained and a very serious illness."

"Nuh-uh, that face says rode hard and put away wet. It says I was at Nacho's Bar drinking, and I did not go home alone. Tell Mama the truth, honey. Was it worth it?"

"Bad night," I growled, and everyone but Muse backed off.

Candace was about to reply, but Mary Catherine drove up, her headlights blinding us temporarily as she sang out a cheery hello from the open driver's window. We stamped our feet and blew thick mist into the air as we waited for Mary Catherine to disembark and open the door.

"You need coffee?" Muse asked.

I didn't do anything more than glance at Muse, but she scurried inside ahead of me as though I'd given her backside a swat, and looked for me a few minutes later near the mixer with a mugful of hot and black, holding it out like an offering to a god.

"Thanks." I grinned ruefully, the scent of the coffee melting some of the frost from my sense of humor.

"You look like you got no sleep."

"I got some," I prevaricated. "A little."

"I take it you weren't sleepless for anything good."

"No."

"And you don't plan on talking about it."

I glanced at her. "What do you think?"

"I think if you wanted to talk about it, you could. It wouldn't go any farther than these four walls."

I blinked in disbelief and turned on the machine to start the dough. For once I wished this particular mixer didn't have a slow-start feature, making it so it wouldn't spew all over if you started it up fast. I'd have liked to make a mess. A mushroom cloud of flour and fat to mirror my mood.

"All right, I lied," she amended, pinkening up. "As soon as one of us left the building, we'd talk. No one would have to twist our arms or anything, and all your secrets would become public knowledge."

"I appreciate your honesty."

Muse grinned, sipping her coffee. "No point in lying."

And just like that, it became bearable to think about JT and the way I'd blown it the night before. It became funny in the face of all the other relationships I'd screwed up over the years. Letting go of my pride and my common sense, I told Muse obliquely that I'd advised JT to allow his girlfriends to fuck him up the ass.

"Well, aren't you just Mr. Romance?" Muse shuddered delicately. "I'm guessing you picked the worst possible moment to offer that advice?"

"When will I ever learn to keep my fucking mouth shut?" I turned off the mixer, added the mixture of water and apple cider that was the secret flavor enhancer of Miss Independence's piecrust, and started it up slowly again. I glanced around and caught sight of Analise talking to Bianca. Actually talking. And it wasn't my imagination, but that morning she was actually wearing lipstick. It was nude colored, but it gave her mouth a wet gloss that made it look plumper and more attractive.

"Wow." I nudged Muse.

"Oh, I know." She spoke softly. "She's blooming before our eyes."

Something about that made my heart kind of plump too. "It's fucked up being scared all the time. It takes a lot of energy."

"Yes, it does." She helped me pull the dough for its trip to the refrigerator.

We worked that way for most of the morning, my mood less sour as the day wore on. Ken stopped by to say that he had an appointment for another look at the building by the fire station and to press Mary Catherine into going with him. He had some rough numbers worked up. Apparently he'd spoken to some contractors about turning the place into the café she wanted.

"The drywall and decorating we can do for ourselves," Ken told us. "Jordan is good with his hands, and a lot of folks around here are willing to help out if we ask. Most of them will only expect a pie or two out of the deal."

"It must be amazing to live in a place like this."

"I've lived here all my life, and Jordan comes from a small town. It's just the way things are."

"I hope everything works out for you," I said sincerely.

He frowned. "Have you decided to leave, then?"

I stopped what I was doing, making a base for a special Mary Catherine type of pie: cooked tart apples covered by the custard and nuts of a traditional pecan pie. Half apple, half pecan, and all delicious.

"I'm going to go to my brother's place. He called to say he's coming to get me today."

"I thought you might be considering coming here to stay."

"Well, sure," I said. "I'm giving it some thought, but I still have things in LA. A place. People. Maybe a job, but I'll think about coming back."

"Did something happen?" Ken asked, fixing me with a curious stare.

"No. But I landed in this town all fucked-up, and I want to wait before I make any big decisions." I thought about it. "Or little ones even."

"I guess I can understand that."

I held out my hand for him. "Like I said, I wish you all the best, you and Mary Catherine, and I hope it's a huge success."

"Thanks." He shook my hand. "And I'm sure MC would welcome you anytime, so don't be a stranger. Please think about working with her here. She really likes you."

"Thanks."

I watched him leave with Mary Catherine in tow. She glanced back at us, surveying her little kingdom before she closed the door on it. My cohorts in pie and I picked up speed, and consequently there was time for Candace to run out and pick up a nice lunch from a Chinese place down the block a ways.

We were sitting around a patio table outside, eating out of cartons with chopsticks, when Dan drove up. He got out of his car and walked toward where we were sitting, and the first thing I noticed was the absence of a smile on his face. Ordinarily a detail like that, something so small and seemingly insignificant, wouldn't even stand out to me, but this was Dan, my brother, the hero of my childhood. The only person in the entire world from whom I was guaranteed a smile by the mere fact of my existence, and he wasn't smiling.

His step was measured and slow, and when he reached us, he barely said anything but led me a few feet away where we could talk privately.

"What's the matter?" I asked, wondering if he'd tell me. How long did the quid pro quo of privileged information exist between siblings after childhood? "Do not tell me BreeAnna's angry just because you wanted to do me a solid. How can it bother her if—"

"She's cheating on me. I left her."

I froze. "*What?*"

"She's seeing someone." Dan's lips tightened painfully. "I thought she was having an affair for a while…but…I finally got proof, and I couldn't ignore it anymore."

"What happened?" I couldn't imagine. True-blue Dan finding his skinny shiksa ice queen with another man.

"I found some things." He shook his head. "Letters. Videos."

"No. Fucking. Way."

That seemed to make him smile, and he met my eyes for the first time. "Way." A pale but legible copy of the boy I'd known as a child shot me a quirk of his lip. "You can check them out yourself, since I uploaded them to Xtube."

I was shocked—and completely delighted—by his anger. "You *didn't*."

"It seems I did."

"Good heavens." I gazed back at his car. *Probably not a good time for a happy family reunion*. "What are you planning to do?"

"I took a motel room in the place where you're staying. In fact, it was the owner who told me where I could find you."

"That was Carl. When you walked in, did he say 'just a minute' or put you off? Did he make you wait?"

"Yes, he was reading the paper, and he said, 'I see you. Give me a sec,' and finished the article."

I laughed. "I *love* that old man. What a piece of work."

"He reminded me of..." Dan pressed his lips together.

"Yeah." I agreed with the unspoken thought.

"Anyway, I could use a break. My lawyer is filing for divorce. I'll be giving Bree the house."

"That's shit! After what she did?"

"It's a small price to pay for my freedom, Jakey." He wrapped his arms around himself as if he was cold. "Honestly my first thought was what a fucking relief. I feel like an overfilled Macy's parade balloon that someone's just...cut loose. It's magnificent and terrifying at the same time."

"Sure it is." I realized that his lack of smile had more to do with uncertainty than unhappiness. I threw my arms around him and gave him a hard hug. "Can I buy you a beer?"

"Oh *fuck* yes." He relaxed, as though I'd said a word that made all his muscles go limp at once. Like he'd been unplugged. "And keep them coming until I'm passed out. We can take a cab back to the motel."

"No, we can't. But we can walk."

"You're kidding." He allowed himself to be pulled along toward the group of women we'd both felt staring at us for the entire length of our conversation.

"Family emergency, ladies. Duty calls. My brother needs me to get him drunk."

Muse was the first to laugh. "By all means. What should we tell Mary Catherine?"

"Tell her my family and liquor come first. You've got everything under control, right?"

Candace drew herself up. "Certainly we can do without you, but I'm not entirely sure it's wise to be complicit in—"

"Give it a rest, honey," Bianca told her. "Man needs a drink, let him have a damned drink."

Candace growled back at her, "For your information, *Bianca*, it can't be said that anyone necessarily *needs* a drink. While alcohol is certainly going to make him feel better for a moment as he loses his inhibitions, in the long run, its depressant properties are counter—"

"I know we don't gotta listen to you going on and on about alcohol, seeing as to how you were born with a silver toilet around your head. I've seen you drink, honey, and it's not as pretty a thing as you think it is."

Muse intervened, "What I think Bianca means is that it's unwise to—"

"I know exactly what Bianca means," Candace said icily. "She means it's not pretty to have flaws. Like when she has her legs locked around some stranger's neck simply because it's last call and—"

"Whoa!" I said. "Whoa, whoa, whoa. My brother just got here."

Candace and Bianca had the grace to blush.

"Save the catfights for when he knows you and can put money on them."

Bianca swatted me, and Candace offered the glacial raise of one perfect eyebrow.

"I'm going," I said, wrapping a hand around my brother's upper arm and shooting Muse a grin. "Anyone who wants to see us will have to show up at Nacho's later, but I make no claim that I'll be recognizable by then."

"You'll recognize me." My brother saluted the ladies. "I'll be the one holding up his fairy ass."

We walked to Dan's car, leaving a pocket of silence behind us.

I turned to him as we left the parking lot. "You did not just say that."

"Yes, I actually did."

I turned to him again, almost because I couldn't keep myself from checking to see if it was true. My brother was there, smiling and free. "Welcome back, Brother. I've missed you so much."

"Me too, man." Dan didn't look my way, but he shoved my shoulder hard enough to knock me into the passenger door. "Me too."

CHAPTER FIFTEEN

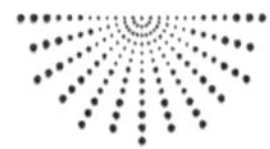

Since I'd just had lunch at Miss Independence and Dan had grabbed breakfast late, we helped each other through an enormous bowl of chips and salsa and lined up beer bottles on our table until the busboy finally took them away. Someone came by and told us it wouldn't be right not to have guacamole, so we ordered some and a couple of shots of Patrón, because by that point both those things seemed like a good idea.

By the time the late-afternoon sun slanted onto the patio, we were laughing at elephant jokes and making plans to become surf bums.

"That's where it's at. We could get an RV and follow the weather, go where it's warm. Surf when we feel like it." Dan spun the beer in his hands and then lifted it to hover in front of his lips. "You can take the Pan-American Highway to Chile. Once you get to South America, it runs all along the coast except for a small chunk of rain forest."

"Who are you, man?" I asked him. Dan's familiar face, his dark brown hair and eyes, his olive skin—all the features that were so very much like my own—zoomed in and out of focus, but his voice sounded familiar.

"I don't know, Jakey." He picked at the label from his beer. "I have no idea, and it's killing me."

I couldn't think what to say. When I'd gone to Israel with Zeyde, I was barely out of high school. Dan had been in graduate school. In the ensuing years he'd done everything right. Gotten his MBA, then his broker's license, and immediately began to work exclusively in the pricey Monterey Bay area, both selling real estate and investing in it, buying and flipping homes in Santa Cruz while it was still a viable way to earn heady cash, and also making independent loans, buying and selling mortgages. He'd done extremely well, and it looked for a while like the sky was the limit. But the past three years had been a swing of the pendulum in the other direction that had cost him and others like him a great deal of his accumulated wealth, which I calculated to have been—at one point—in the millions.

It looked like his marriage was ending too, and it was hard to know how to respond, because I'd never liked his wife. As he drank and talked, it became clear to me, at least for the moment, that he wasn't fatally depressed by his change in fortune. In some indefinable way he felt freed by it.

This Dan drinking with me was the same Dan who raised his arms to the sky in triumph on the day we celebrated our freedom from tyranny—the day my zeyde took us to the Jersey Shore so our dad could sneak away. That was a season of incredible highs and gut-wrenching lows. In the end, even counting the loss of our father, I don't think we had ever had a better day than that. Anything we dreamed seemed possible—even likely—then.

Dan smiled shyly behind his beer when the dinner crowd found its way into the bar. He began to hum with the music of Nacho's talented violinist.

"What the hell?" Dan craned his neck around to get a better look at the musician, who played a mariachi favorite.

"Isn't he something?"

"How come I've never been here before?"

"Probably because your wife doesn't eat," I snarked.

"This place is awesome. Is this the place with the brunch?"

"Yeah, I guess. If we get hungry enough, we can order dinner. Food's great. Later it turns into a gay bar."

His eyes widened. "No kidding?"

"No kidding." I caught familiar faces out of the corner of my eye, two of the local firefighters. Not Cam. I was pretty sure he was still on shift until the next day. They acknowledged me, and I lifted my chin in their direction.

"Looks like you already know some of the locals."

"Yeah, well, with my history, did you doubt it? It's either the cops or the EMTs." I took a sip.

Dan frowned. I could tell he was cataloging the traces of the fight I'd had with Sander, some of which were still faintly visible on my skin. "You going to go back? To him?"

"*No.*" I said it more forcefully than I had planned. "No way in hell."

"Good."

"I don't know if I still have a job at Il Ghiotto either."

Dan leaned back and gazed out toward the beach. "Aren't we a pair of fucking losers?"

"I'm not a loser. I don't feel like a loser."

"Because you're shitfaced." He rose. "I need a cigarette."

"You don't *smoke*."

He laughed as he pulled a pack and a lighter from the front pocket of his jeans, then sat back down. "Not in front of anyone who could tell Mom or BreeAnna. Mom's dead, and I don't give a fuck about my wife so…I can smoke here, right? We're outside."

"I think so. People do."

"Don't look at me like that." He lit the cigarette and took a deep drag. "If you don't have a job, what will you do?"

"I was thinking about moving again. There's nothing keeping me in LA."

"Yeah?"

"I've been thinking about moving here."

"This place?" Dan glanced around. "What's here?"

"There might be a job offer. Pastry chef for a new bakery. I've actually been working under the table at a pie place."

"Like a Marie Callender's?"

"No, this is a place that does pies for delivery to local restaurants and markets. The owner is thinking of opening a retail space, something like a French café. And she needs a pastry chef."

"If she's doing the pie business, that means you could do pastries, breads, and cakes. You could manage the retail space, and she'd be free to enlarge her delivery empire." He tapped his cigarette ash out on the patio floor. A busboy caught him and brought an ashtray. "Would you be partners?"

"Doesn't that cost money?"

"Everything costs money." He stubbed his cigarette out in the ashtray. "Some things are worth it though."

I knew he was thinking about BreeAnna and what it would cost to be rid of her.

"I can back you in a small business."

"Won't your finances be difficult to sort out until after the divorce?"

Dan chuckled and picked a stray bit of foil off his beer bottle. "Can you say prenup? We had an infidelity clause."

"Oh, you lucky *fuck*. What the hell was she thinking?"

"She wanted to keep *me* from cheating and make me pay if I did. Plus she thought I'd be an asshole." He grimaced. "Maybe she was right there for a while. I acted like one."

"Uncertain times make things hard between a husband and wife," I said. "It's pretty common to fight over money."

"She wasn't used to hearing the word no. It's been hard for

her. I don't want to fight with her, and I won't have to because that clause gives me the right to throw her out on the street. Most of what I had was acquired before we met, so legally it's mine anyway. She gets the house, a car, some spousal support. Things got bad when the market tanked, and I won't be doing as well, but she'll be happy I didn't toss her out, and that will buy me peace of mind."

I nodded. "Peace of mind is good."

"You can't buy that," he agreed dryly.

"But you just said—"

"Has any of this drinking and snacking given you an appetite?" He signaled the busboy over and asked him to send the waiter.

"Not really," I told him honestly.

He rolled his eyes. "Don't say that. For the first time in five years I'm in a restaurant where I can actually eat without apologizing."

I felt bad for not being hungry. "I didn't think of that."

"I am *free*." He lifted his beer bottle. "*Viva la revolución*, Yasha. It's Independence Day!"

A voice from behind echoed his enthusiasm.

"Viva! What are we celebrating?"

I turned an instant before Cam put his hand on my shoulder. I was beginning to wonder whether the firefighters' shifts were all part-time. "Hi, Cam. Do fires only occur between the hours of eight and five? You guys all seem to just knock off for the night."

Cam glanced back toward the bar. "Some guys are actually off shift. I just came for takeout. They're making paella at the station tonight, and I'm allergic to shellfish. If we get an alarm while I'm here, my pager goes off, and I have a minute and a half to get back to the station." He preened, showing his muscles. "I'm big *and* fast, so I can make it."

"Big, yes." I felt like teasing him. "But fast? I've yet to see this speed of yours."

"I'm big all the time." Cam gave me a predictable leer. "But I take my time with all the really important things. I'm only fast when lives need saving."

Dan spoke. "Why don't they just make it without shellfish?"

"What?" Cam turned his attention on my brother and did a double take. My brother was an older, more refined version of me. When we were kids, I always felt like he was James Bond and I was barely GI Joe. In a world where I could be said to have an appeal based on friendly, unassuming charm, Dan radiated something more elegant and cool. Something powerful that BreeAnna hadn't entirely eclipsed with her neediness and hauteur. She'd eroded the foundation of self-confidence I'd always admired in him, but it seemed to be back with a vengeance.

I wanted to sing the "Hallelujah Chorus."

"The paella—why don't they leave the shellfish out?" my brother clarified.

"Because they like it," Cam answered as if Dan were stupid. "It's not hard to run over here and pick up something, and it doesn't make sense to deprive them of something they like."

Dan grinned up at him, trotting out his lethal charm, and Cam did something completely uncharacteristic. He blushed and looked down at his hands.

"Okay, bye. I gotta go." He turned and headed back inside the restaurant, picking up speed, and didn't look back.

"Do you think his pager went off?"

"I don't know. I've never seen him like that. It's like you just...deflated him."

Dan smacked his forehead with his hand. "I'm in a *gay bar*."

"Yeah. But not everyone in here is gay. I don't think he thought anything if that's what you mean."

He was laughing, and I thought that was a good sign. "Thank goodness Sister BreeAnna Homophobius is no longer with us. She's like the fucking church lady when she gets going." He mimicked her unkindly, and I nearly spit my beer. "That's because your brother's unnatural, and when someone is unnatural, they've forgotten that they become the tool of a little homosexual guy we like to call Satan, the prince of darkness, the son of man, the devil, the beast, beeeeeelze-buuuuub..."

"*Dan*...what the hell?" I busted a gut laughing. I had no idea who this person—who looked and sounded exactly like my uptight, humorless brother—was, but I loved him. "Why did you marry someone like BreeAnna in the first place?"

"I dunno. I thought I loved her enough to make it work." I must have made a sound of denial, because he shook his head at me. "I really *thought* if I...Anyway, I don't know. It didn't take long to see the problems we'd have."

"I can't imagine how you stood it."

Dan leaned over the table toward me, cupping an empty beer bottle between hands, which were like a mirror image of my own. It was as if—suddenly—all the fight went out of him. "I'm not him."

"Who?"

"I'm not Dad. I didn't hurt her, and I didn't leave. Even when I wasn't happy."

Dan's loyalty to BreeAnna had always baffled me, but now I understood it was another of my father's strange legacies. Like a bill marked *payment due* from Dad's hand to ours.

Shit.

"*Dan*." I breathed.

"Never mind. It's not important anymore, and it could have been worse." He grinned. "I had to pass my own test. I had to prove I'm not Dad. I never will be. Best million I'll ever spend."

CHAPTER SIXTEEN

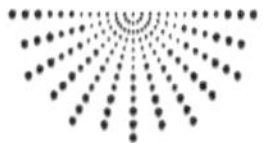

Why wasn't I the least bit surprised when JT showed up at the bar at around ten wearing his femme du jour on his arm?

For that matter, why was I still there? Dan and I had spent the entire day and into the night drinking and reminiscing. I'd long since lost count of the number of beers we'd drunk and baskets of chips we'd eaten. We'd stopped only long enough to order plates of tiny grilled fish tacos. They came—succulent mild whitefish topped with crunchy shredded cabbage, pico de gallo, soft Mexican cheese, and the hottest smoky hot sauce, which necessitated our switching to margaritas. Between the booze, the memories, and the terrific food, it was no wonder time had simply flown by.

I was heading back to the patio from the bathroom when I spotted JT. He milled through the throng and pressed the flesh of those locals he knew, tugging his date along like a puppy. I saw his face when he caught sight of my brother and stopped in his tracks.

Dan and I really do look alike. We were different enough in age that we'd never been mistaken for twins as children, but now it wouldn't stretch the imagination too far. Except for his hair, which was starting to go gray at the temples, and the bulk I'd gotten in the Tzahal which I'd kept by the hard work and heavy loads I often carried at Il Ghiotto, we could easily have been twins. I saw JT's gaze travel the crowd, and when he found me, he realized I knew he had been looking for me. He lowered his eyes and pushed his date toward the bar.

The shit.

I went back and found my brother had settled our tab and was getting up, ceding the table at last to a group of tired and sweaty kids who had been dancing.

"I thought we probably ought to go." He looked back at the table with longing as though he was reluctant to head home after a great vacation.

"I could use the walk." I was none too steady on my feet and ready to go.

Someone called from behind us as we slipped out of the club and into the cold sea air, "Yasha!"

Dan and I both snapped around. My brother looked like he was expecting a ghost. At least I wasn't the only one who heard the similarity in the way Zeyde and JT spoke my name.

"*Jeez,*" Dan whispered as he took in JT.

"I thought I saw you." JT squired his lady friend toward us. "Then I realized it had to be your brother." He held out his hand, and Dan took it. "JT, and this is Stephanie."

"Dan. Pleased to meet you." My brother took her hand as well.

"We were just leaving." I admit you can always count on me to point out the obvious.

"So early?"

I looked at Dan, and we started laughing, probably more than we would have if we'd been sober. "We've been here since lunchtime."

"Got our swerve on." Dan snorted through his nose and

demonstrated, swinging his arms and twisting like a speed skater.

"Some more than others." I stared at Dan. *Who was this person?* "Time for a walk, Danilo."

"We could drive you," JT offered.

Stephanie didn't think much of that idea. "We just got here, Jason."

"It will just take me a few minutes. Why don't I get you a drink and then run them home?"

If that wasn't the most spectacularly bad idea I'd ever heard, I didn't know what was.

"Jason." Stephanie frowned.

He leaned toward her. "Last week Yasha was half-dead. Now he's running around all over town. Let me take care of this so he's not overtaxing himself. I don't want to have to take him to Emergency again."

I rolled my eyes, and when they came down and back into focus, Stephanie was doing the same. "Fine, whatever. If you take too long, I'll go home with someone else," she warned.

JT flashed her a smile, unperturbed. "Thanks." To us he said, "I'll be out in a sec, once I have Steph situated." Then he dived back into the bar. I caught Dan by the arm and started walking.

"What the hell was that?" he asked.

"That?" I glanced back to the door where JT had disappeared. "That was genus *Homo*, species *whowantstofuckus*, subspecies *closeted headup hisassia*. Let us move on to the cages with the interesting animals."

"You're kidding me." Dan pulled his arm away and sauntered down the street like he owned it. He could be cooler than cool, for which I'd always envied him.

"How could I make that up?" I asked. "It's all 'I want you, but I hate myself' with guys like that."

"Not everyone has your courage." Dan looked at the ground.

"It's honesty, not courage. You don't drop your date off and stop by a guy's place for a blowjob after."

Dan's whole body tensed. "He does that?"

"Yeah, well. No. Not really." I could see I was making things worse. "That's Carl's son. The guy who owns the motel? He's got feelings he doesn't understand and a strong religious nature. He's scared, and he talks to me. I don't know why."

"Maybe because you understand. You went through a lot to be who you are. You took a load of crap in high school."

"This town is full of gay guys he could talk to."

"Is he Jewish? Maybe it's because you are."

I stopped moving. "Maybe. I never thought of it that way."

"You stood up to Mom when she went on and on about violating the laws."

"Zeyde was on my side."

"Neither of them approved."

"They said it wasn't what they had planned for me." I couldn't see the stars, even though I looked. The marine layer—the thick, chronic cloud cover that wasn't low enough to be called true fog—was too dense. It made distant sounds, like the highway noise and the rumbling of the waves more audible, but draped like a blanket over town, obscuring the sky. "They didn't make me feel wrong exactly."

"You're whitewashing it. You were getting beaten up at school and fighting all the time."

"It was a godsend that Zeyde wanted to go to Israel. I know Mom was relieved to be rid of me for a while. That distance made it so much easier for us to be together when I came back."

"Yeah." Dan snorted. "A godsend."

I didn't like the way he'd said it. "What do you mean by that?"

"Zeyde never planned to go until you were done with college."

"*What?*"

"You sped up his timetable by about six years, Jakey. Didn't you know?"

"No, I didn't know. Of course I didn't."

"Both Zeyde and Mom thought it would be easier for you in Israel."

"Easier?"

"Being gay."

"It was. Well. That *was* easier. Plus I was glad to stay with Zeyde." I continued walking and failed to notice that JT's truck crawled along next to us. It stopped when Dan acknowledged him and put a hand on my arm to pull me toward it.

"Here comes your guy."

"He's not my guy. I've never met anyone more confused in my life."

"Yeah, you have." Dan opened the door and jerked his chin to let me know I should go first. "You just don't know it yet."

I didn't have time to think about what he meant, because JT spoke right away.

"So, how are you finding St. Nacho's, Dan?"

"I keep a magnifying glass in the glove box of my car, JT, and I just use that."

For some reason I couldn't fathom, JT found that hilarious. He got control of himself by the next stoplight. "It is kind of a small town. I can't get over how much you two look alike."

"The similarities don't end there. We have the same parents, for example."

"Dan." I nudged him hard.

"Ow." No one said anything else until JT parked his truck in front of my motel room. My brother and I got out and leaned back in the door to say goodbye. JT's expression was unreadable. He shook Dan's hand and then mine.

"So I guess you'll be leaving tomorrow."

My brother hadn't surprised me in a long time, but when he

took his hand back from JT and said, "No such luck, Closet Lad. We're here to stay. Pick a team."

Well. Yes. *That* surprised me.

Then he shut the door of the truck and gave a little wiggly-fingered wave.

My heart slammed against my rib cage, and I remembered what it was like to be Daniel Livingston's baby brother. Like hitching a ride on the back of a comet without a space suit.

Here we go.

JT stepped down from the truck on the driver's side, and he came around, his arms folded and an expression on his face that mirrored my brother's. He resented the hell out of us right then.

"'Scuse me?"

For some reason Dan thought *that* was hilarious. "You're excused."

Maybe reckless mouthing off was a family trait?

I put my hand on my brother's arm. "Dan, go to your room. I'll call you first thing in the morning, and we'll go for breakfast."

Dan spoke to me but never took his eyes off JT. "I don't think so."

"Dan—"

"I don't know what your problem is." JT frowned. "All I'm here to do is give you a lift home."

"In that case, thank you very much. Jakey, go get some sleep."

"Jeez." I pulled my key from my pocket. "Dan, you're a rude pain in the ass. Take your own advice. Get some sleep. Mary Catherine doesn't expect me tomorrow, so I'm sleeping in."

I heard Dan mutter something like, "Sleep tight," but I opened my door and stepped inside, then locked it behind me.

I couldn't hear the rest of what they said, even with my ear pressed to the door, but eventually JT's truck engine fired up, and he pulled away. My brother's footsteps were heavy on the cement stairs at the end of the row of rooms.

My phone rang five minutes later.

"Hello?"

"I wanted to talk to you." JT's voice.

"Don't you have a girl waiting for you at Nacho's."

"Yes." I heard a percussive noise that sounded like a fist hitting a steering wheel.

"Isn't she expecting you to take her home?"

JT hissed a sigh. I wondered if he used a Bluetooth earpiece. "She's not expecting anything else."

"No?"

"No. I don't usually…It's a first date. I go on an awful lot of first dates, Yasha."

"Where the hell do you find all these girls in such a small town?"

"She doesn't live here. She's from Goleta."

"That's a hell of a drive."

"We met in the middle. Her car's parked at a diner off the 101."

I thought about that. "Why don't you man up and go out on a first date with me?" I asked. "If nothing else, I'm local, and I put out."

He gave a little halfhearted chuckle, and I felt for him. "Can I come over later after I drop her off?"

"For what? If I'm staying, no way I want to do a one-off with Closet Lad."

"Maybe we could talk?"

"I'm not convinced that would be a good thing after the things you said last night."

"I'm sorry about that. I was on what my dad calls my high horse."

"I'm not some indiscriminate loser."

"I know that. I regret saying anything that made you feel like that."

"Thank you for that."

"You've been very patient with me." He sighed audibly. "I'd like to make it up to you somehow."

I was silent for a while, but he didn't rush me. "Don't pull your truck up, or my brother will know you're here."

"Hey. Are you ashamed of me?"

I did that thing—that stupid thing—where I looked at the phone as though I could see through it to the person on the other side. "Are you fucking *kidding me*?"

"Yes. I am kidding. I'm sorry, Yasha. That was in bad taste."

My grip tightened on the phone, but I smiled. "It was pretty funny actually."

"Kinda."

"Yeah."

"See you later?"

"Later." I hung up.

CHAPTER SEVENTEEN

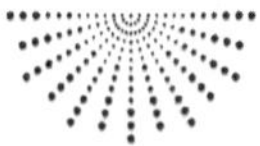

I admit to hitting the shower. I scrubbed behind my ears and between my toes and…everywhere. I slipped on a T-shirt and a loose, low, comfortable pair of jeans and watched the news and then some show on Biography about notorious serial killers.

It was pretty easy to imagine JT laughing and drinking with Stephanie, the girl of the day, just as it was easy to imagine he'd lost track of time, or he'd changed his mind, or worse still, he'd decided to take what Stephanie was offering before or *instead* of coming over.

And if he did?

It would be no different than what he'd been doing all along. At some point I had to admit that I was entertaining hopeless fantasies and JT was playing with me. It had been tried before, but—usually—unsuccessfully. If I hadn't met JT under such unusual circumstances, if he didn't remind me so much of the one person who had meant everything to me growing up, then he might have been unsuccessful as well.

I meant what I'd told him though.

If he spent the night with me, I wasn't about to hide my feelings for him. I worked with a number of shrewd, shrewd women at Miss Independence, and he wouldn't stand a chance.

I jumped about a mile into the air when JT knocked softly on the door. When I answered my heart was still pounding hard, but not because I was scared.

JT waited on the other side, holding two six-packs of Michelob AmberBock beer.

"Are you moving in?"

JT's face heated up predictably. "I just thought…" He pointed to the area next to the television. "You have a fridge. I thought you might like some beer, since you might be staying. Housewarming gift."

I watched as he pulled the bottles out one by one and stored them in the fridge. "Did you figure out what you want to talk about?" There was no reason to make it easy.

"Come on, Yasha." He took my hand in a tight grip. "You know what I want."

"Yeah." I pulled him to me, and there wasn't a need for words. It didn't matter to me how many prom queens he squired around town. I'm sure it didn't matter to him that my brother would kick his ass come morning. There was something compelling us together, something that caused me to tighten my arms around him and close my eyes and breathe him in like air. To soak him up like sunshine.

"I feel right when I'm with you, Yasha." He hid his face against the skin of my neck. "Nothing else seems to make a damn bit of sense."

"C'mere," I told him, pulling him down to the sheets. I was already fumbling with the buttons of his dress shirt, pulling it from the waistband of his gabardine trousers. He had on a nice, supple leather belt with a pretty, sleek gold buckle. It only took me a minute to pull it through the loops. I dropped it on the carpet while he unbuttoned his fly. As soon as he unzipped, I knew I'd mouth his dick through his shorts. They were tight briefs, gray, with a burgundy stripe on the elastic. It took some work to forget he'd worn them for his girl.

He toed off his shoes and slithered out of his trousers while I followed the thin line of hair from his navel to his balls. He fidgeted, and I became aware that he had no idea where to put his hands. When I looked up at him, his eyes glittered with unshed tears.

"What on earth?" I pulled him into my arms. "Talk to me?"

He shook his head and clasped his hands together.

"You came here, remember?"

"I know," he said hoarsely. "I want this. I do."

"One date, even one guy, doesn't make you gay, JT. Curiosity might be a natural thing for you. You aren't condemned by it."

"Shut up and kiss me." JT scrabbled at my clothes, first yanking my shirt over my head none too gently and then fidgeting with the fastenings of my jeans. "You promised. You said if I came back, you'd bend me over the desk and—"

"*Shh.*" His hands were shaking so badly that I caught them between my own. They were cold, and without thinking, I brought them to my mouth to warm them. "Will you just level off?" I rubbed his fingers. "We can go slow. We can take one thing at a time and decide yes or no. All right?"

"All right." He relaxed, and his hands warmed up. "Slow sounds good."

"I'll put your clothes here." I picked up his trousers and held my hand out for his shirt. He seemed to shrug off his residual anxiety and pulled his T-shirt over his head and handed both to me. I laid everything carefully over a chair and turned back to the bed.

"Need my shorts?" He looked down, red-faced but ready to pull them off.

"I think you can keep them for now. They look hot." I pulled off his socks, though, because as many times as I'd seen a guy in porn wearing nothing but socks, it never failed to make me laugh.

"Can I get rid of your jeans?" His hands hovered over my fly.

I held my hands at my sides. "You can do whatever you like."

"I want to touch you." He opened the button on my jeans gingerly. "I want to taste you."

I watched as he carefully lowered my zipper. Then I put my hand on his head, into the brush of brown hair there. It was cut precisely, long on the top and neat over the ears and tapered into the neck. It felt good, and I stroked it a little, petting him. He couldn't control his beard, heavy and coppery in the light, with that same precision. I loved its bristly, rough texture under my fingertips and stroked his cheeks to feel it more than once.

"You have these golden spots that feel like sandpaper," I pointed out, although to him it must have seemed a rather absurd observation. But they made him appear to glisten, and I thumbed the scratchiness over his mouth before he moved in to press his lips to my dick. I stayed still—and it killed me—while he lapped at my cock delicately, his first vague exploration. He nuzzled in and tasted, breathed in my scent. I found it excruciating. Embarrassing. But so fucking sexy that I nearly blew in his face as he gathered the fluid leaking from the tip onto his tongue.

He stayed there a minute and then pulled me down to share a deep, intimate kiss that brought my flavor back to me.

Holy cow!

What a mouth. He had a full upper lip with a defined, perfectly formed cupid's bow, and a lower lip that begged to be nipped between my teeth. He shifted back on the bed, and I crawled up to stay close to that fucking, fabulous mouth, and then I bit down gently. That tiny pinch of pain caused him to moan and shift beneath me. His legs fell open loosely, and his arms tightened around me, and the next thing I knew I was swinging a leg over his thighs—straddling him—to get closer.

I was determined to squeeze all the air from between us, and it made me want to press him down, to cover him and gather him up beneath me until we were flesh against flesh in the most primitive way.

"Fuck, Yasha." He moved his hand up to cup the back of my neck and kissed me with everything he had. I pressed my hips to his and felt the knob of his erection jutting against my own.

"What do you want? You want to fuck me?" I whispered. I was ready to give him whatever he needed, even though I ached with a few needs of my own.

He shook his head. "I want you to fuck me." His hips rocked frantically as he ground against me.

"Are you sure? We can wait. I can give you pleasure all kinds of ways without that."

"You don't want it?"

"Oh hell yes, I want it. I just don't want to move too fast for you."

"I want it too," he told me, fresh determination in his eyes. "I want to be with you like that."

I backed off slowly and watched his face for clues. After a while, during which I saw nothing but sincerity—no fear and no distaste—I helped him turn beneath me.

"All right, then. Here."

It was time for those briefs to hit the floor. I pulled at them, and they twisted in my hands until I got them off his feet, a tiny figure eight of fabric and elastic that smelled like him when I sent it sailing off the bed.

I positioned myself between his legs and kissed the curve of his spine, running my tongue all along the length of it, up and down, dipping lower and lower into the cleft between his ass cheeks each time. His body tensed and sizzled beneath my mouth, his skin trembling when I tickled it. I parted his thighs and brushed him with my lips, a brief, intimate kiss. He chuckled with embarrassment and nearly whined with need.

"Nightstand drawer." I pointed. "I have lube and condoms."

He reached over, lifting his body just enough for me to wedge a hand beneath him to fondle his balls. The rumbling, purring noise sounded so much like his truck, I nearly laughed. He handed me the supplies and pushed his hands under his chin, content to lie there while I familiarized myself with him.

"Might feel a little odd," I said, squeezing lube into my hand to warm it.

He turned and gazed at me with apprehensive green eyes. "I trust you."

"Do you?" I asked, slipping a slick finger along his perineum and circling his tightly puckered hole.

JT tipped his head and smiled, and it took my breath away. "Yes, Yasha. More than…anyone really."

"Just say the word, and I'll stop anytime, no matter what. You know that, right?"

"I know." JT shook his head. "Jeez, you'd think you'd never done this before."

I breached him with the tip of one finger, gently, and he flinched. I smoothed my hand over the muscles of his ass to soothe him. I remembered he had a plug, so I knew he wasn't completely unused to penetration. "Steady."

"I was just…" He put his forehead down on his arms. "Go ahead."

"I am." I circled and tapped the tight sphincter that guarded his channel until it gave way, and my finger slipped in.

"Ahh." JT breathed out. "Feels good."

"To me too." I loved the heat of him, the way he clenched around the invasion. I sucked on the tender skin on the inside of his thigh and felt him push against my finger as he tried to get me to go deeper. "More?"

"Yeah. *Yes. Please.*" JT panted. "*More.*"

"Better than a plug?"

"Shh…*shit,*" he hissed.

I added a second finger, and soon he was pushing back against me, begging me to fill him. I pulled him up to his knees, and he positioned himself on his elbows. He held his head hidden in his forearms, deep in the pillows, while he offered his ass to me like a gift.

I nudged my knees between his thighs and continued to work him, opening a condom with my teeth, rolling it on with my left hand, none too easily, as I'm better with my right. I fumbled it a little because my hands were shaking, and I knew if I couldn't have JT soon, I'd blow right there, all over his back, and how embarrassing would that be? He'd never let me have control again.

He made a strangled noise when I pulled my fingers away. I lined up my cock and pressed at his entrance, nudging my way into him as I cupped the skin of his back and his ass, finding it felt like stiff, hairy bread dough, something firm and dense like super-wheat, whole-grain *pain de champagne*, the baker in me kneading it, smoothing the knots in the tough muscles there.

Soon I was balls-deep in the incredible heat of his ass, and he was moaning with each push, grunting with each drag back. Vocal and flexible and taking as much pleasure as he could, pulling pleasure from my body in every way he could.

He grabbed for my hand and drew it to his cock, only semi-erect and dangling between his legs, and when I wrapped my fist around it, I felt it tighten and fill, slick at the tip, sweaty at the balls, and all mine to control, just as I controlled the pace in the heady, steady ebb and flow of our fucking.

Then, as if it were magic, he and I found a rhythm, a frantic rocking tempo that met both our needs, and it felt like we soared together. As if it were a foregone conclusion between us, I surged over him and he arched beneath me, and for the first time ever I wished I could see it, capture it on video, because it felt perfect and beautiful, not just my fucking him but his taking my desire, intensifying it, then passing it back.

"Fuck, *JT*."

"So hot." He dug in and pushed back. I met him fully extended, so far deep inside him I felt his heartbeat all along my cock. "Harder."

I slipped my hands under his arms and cupped his shoulders, pulling him toward me, spearing him on my dick over and over. "C'mon, baby," I chanted, wanting to feel him clench around me in release. "Give it to me."

"It's yours." He panted. "Whatever you want. *Take it*."

"I just want you," I whispered, nipping at the skin on his back. His muscles tightened with each thrust. "Come for me."

JT growled low in his throat, the sound a little chilling in the otherwise quiet room. "*Yasha*!"

I felt hot cum splash onto my hand where I stroked his shaft, even as his body tightened all around me. Mine shuddered and stopped at the apex of my pleasure, hanging on the precipice of the best orgasm of my life. "Fuck, *Jason. Fuck, fuck*."

"*Yasha*!" He pressed back until we were a single entity, flesh and bone and two hearts that rocketed in the exact same rhythm like trip-hammers. My muscles strained with his to stay connected, so that even when I softened and slid from the warmth of his body, we floated down to the bed together, and he stayed that way, wrapped in my arms and gripping my wrists as if he never wanted me to let him go. I pressed my lips to the back of his neck and breathed in the scent: jizz and sweat, and resignation, maybe. Eventually I got rid of the condom in a trash bin someone had thoughtfully placed next to the bed.

It didn't surprise me that he never let me turn him toward me. He kept his face buried in the pillow, even as he pressed back into my arms. I brushed my lips along the back of his neck and held on, knowing that what he felt wasn't personal. That it was as inevitable as my feigning sleep while he gently dislodged me so he could get up and dress. As inevitable as the regret I knew we both felt when I heard the door close behind him.

CHAPTER EIGHTEEN

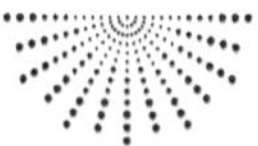

I didn't wake up until the phone rang at seven. Dan didn't bother with a preamble.

"Do you ever get the feeling that neither one of us is much of a judge of character?"

I ignored that. I knew what he meant. I'd ask him later how he knew that JT had come back. "Good morning," I said, sitting up. *Shit.* Sticky turns into stuck in the morning, and it's neither fun nor spanky. "I need a shower, and then I'll be ready for breakfast."

"Great. Thanks to Carl from the front desk, I've already been to pick up my car from Nacho's. I want to take a drive around. See what's here. See what could be here. This is an amazing little town."

"I want to stop by Miss Independence and introduce you to Mary Catherine."

"She's the one who's offered you a job?"

"Yeah. You could take a look at the place she's got her eye on. See what you think."

"Sure."

"I'll be ready in thirty." I hung up and blew out a deep breath.

If Dan really had seen JT leave last night, I'd have some explaining to do.

When I was dressed and ready to go, I left my room and found Dan outside my door, leaning against his Lexus, smoking a cigarette. He unlocked the doors, and we got in, taking our time fastening our seat belts. Dan keyed the ignition and turned to look at me while the wipers eradicated the condensation from the outside of the windshield and air defogged it from the inside.

"Thirty minutes. What a refreshing change from cooling my heels until lunchtime before I can go out to breakfast."

"Women care what they look like," I pointed out. "Clearly I don't share that."

"Your guys like what they see apparently."

"I guess."

Dan hesitated, grinding his cigarette out. "Look. Do we have to have a talk about self-respect?"

"No." It was cold, and I waited for the car to warm up. "We do not."

"Do I have to remind you that some guys will take what you have to offer and never, ever admit it publicly? Doesn't that bother you?"

"When the hell is the expiration date on those brotherly meddling minutes?"

"No time soon," he growled, putting the car in reverse and backing it out of the parking space. "When will you start looking out for yourself?"

"I do all right."

"That must be why a man in Los Angeles beat the crap out of you. That must be why you're happy to be Closet Lad's dirty little secret."

"You have enough shit to worry about. Don't you have a divorce to plan?"

Dan clenched his teeth.

"I'm sorry." I looked out the window on the foggy coastal morning as he left the parking lot at a crawl toward Miss Independence. You could hardly see fifty feet ahead, and he was being cautious. "I know I'm not doing myself any favors. I didn't expect to want to stay here. When JT showed up last night…I don't know. I wanted him. Surely that's happened to you?"

"Not for a while."

"You were never tempted? Nothing against BreeAnna, but she seemed kind of—"

"Cold?" Dan shook his head. "That was…maybe my fault. I thought loving a girl because she was bright and pretty would be enough."

"Enough for what?"

"To make up for not wanting her very much." He turned to me when I would have pursued that and held his hand up. I had my mouth open, ready to ask what the hell he meant by that, but that hand stopped me. "I don't want to talk about me right now."

"But—"

"Leave it. I just…don't."

I closed my lips over my questions for the moment, but my heart raced. *What the hell*? "Me neither."

"Fair enough. This fog is insane. Is that the place?" He pointed to the warehouse-style building that housed Miss Independence Pies.

"Yeah." It was impossible to see anything inside the glass front doors, but there were a couple of familiar cars in the parking lot. "Come in and meet the ladies."

"All right," he muttered as he parked. "Although I met some of *the ladies* yesterday, and it was like *Jerry Springer*."

"You don't know the half of it, but I think"—I hesitated. *What did I think*?—"I like them. I fit in here in some odd way."

"That should scare you." We exited the car, and he followed me up to the doors. I opened one and ushered him in.

Muse looked up from where she stood at the mixer with Mary Catherine, who peered closely at us.

Muse caught her expression. "I told you they looked just the same."

As one, my brother and I said, "We do not."

I was dressed in my normal scruffy jeans and a tight T-shirt, and my brother had on black microfiber trousers, engineered to fit his body perfectly, and a black cashmere sweater with a high neck that closed off center. I didn't make the connection when I'd first seen it, but it made him look like a heist-film cat burglar.

"Oh my." Mary Catherine eyed us. "Two of you."

"Oh come on," I complained.

Dan just laughed. "I'm Daniel Livingston. I understand you're thinking of opening a café here?"

"Yes." Mary Catherine held out her hand for him to shake. "And I'm trying to get your brother to stay on and help me run it."

Dan smoothly pulled her away from Muse and monopolized her attention. "I thought maybe we could talk about that. I have some thoughts about his future myself, and I wondered if I could see the space you're thinking about."

I watched him neatly usher her into the supply room she used as an office, even though he'd never been there before. The force was strong with Dan as far as the pursuit of business went. I didn't worry about it too much because I'd seen that Ken Ashton had the same kind of drive. That would be a clash of the titans if their interests weren't mutually beneficial. Just watching him charm her put me in mind of Zeyde and all the pretty blushing waitresses, store clerks, and bank tellers he'd left in his wake.

When I looked up, Muse didn't look happy. "What?"

"I wonder what St. Nacho's sees in *him*?"

"I beg your pardon." Well, at least one person didn't appreciate my brother's brand of charm.

"He doesn't seem like the kind of guy who would like it here. He seems like the kind of guy who will slap a high-rise hotel on the boardwalk between the pier and Nacho's, and the next thing you know, we're all living in western Dubai."

"I don't know about that, but your assessment of my brother is probably more accurate than you know."

"I've got to ask Minerva what she thinks."

"Minerva?"

"At Rune Nation."

Then I remembered. Rune Nation was Muse's favorite metaphysical bookstore. "If she's right about St. Nacho's, I doubt even my very industrious brother can do it much harm."

"I hope not."

"You're serious?"

"Of course I'm serious. How do you think this town has stayed off the radar of land moguls and developers who would build it up until it's unrecognizable?"

"No clue, but if St. Nacho's is a seat of sacred power, it can probably take my brother. Of course, he'll put up a fight. Maybe we can get front-row seats."

Muse tightened her expression and went back to her work.

"So." Candace spoke from where she was working, putting pie dough through a tabletop dough sheeter. "Your brother left his wife?"

"Yes," I said. "I'm afraid so."

"Do you think—"

Bianca made a rude noise, looking up from what she was doing, fitting dough rounds into pie tins. "Oh no. *No no no.* What happened to Dr. Magic from the other night at Nacho's? The one that we all had to hear sucked on your lame-ass toes in the hot tub of his big-ass house?"

"Him?" Color crept up Candace's neck. "Apparently he's

seeing a nurse from OB as well as one of the drug reps. Alice gave me the heads-up on him."

"Can't say I'm sorry to hear it. Man who sucks your toes has gotta be desperate or crazy."

"I beg your pardon. My toes are—"

"Man who sucks anyone's toes. What is wrong with you? Do you want a man so badly you'll just go off with any old toe-sucking bastard that comes along?"

"He was charming!" Candace argued. "And hot as hell. Ask Yasha if you don't believe me. He'll tell you."

All eyes were on me, even Analise's. "I can't say I saw him that clearly," I hedged. "He seemed nice. I'd probably have let him suck my toes."

"See?" Candace went back to the dough sheeter.

Muse snorted. "You'd let anyone suck your toes."

Under my breath I said, "Not Candace."

"I heard that, Yasha." Candace pierced me with her most intimidating stare. "And it goes without saying you'll never have to turn me down."

"Sorry."

She turned and stuck her tongue out at me from a position where Bianca couldn't see it. Suddenly I wondered how much she enjoyed pushing Bianca's buttons. How much of her supercilious classy act was a put-on?

Dan emerged from the back with Mary Catherine. Their talk had been brief, but she looked happy enough, ready to roll up her sleeves like Miss Independence's poster girl and get to work. We could do a lot worse things—Dan and me—than help Mary Catherine make her dreams come true.

"Ready for breakfast?" he asked me, and I thought I saw Candace shoot a hopeful glance his way.

"Sure." I followed him back to the door. Muse peered at him warily as we went past. I figured she'd throw salt or something, but I didn't see her do it. I walked with Dan back to his car and got in.

"So." He snapped his seat belt on. "Want to explain how you wound up working in a pie business that was originally funded by a loan from the Santo Ignacio City Council and intended to provide jobs for female victims of domestic violence, giving them a way to break free from financial dependence on their abusers?"

"I doubt anyone breaks free on what they make."

"With other programs, subsidized housing, Medicaid, and WIC, Miss Independence makes it a more realistic goal." Once we left the parking lot, he headed for the beach. "But you didn't answer the question."

"I mainly helped out because I was here in St. Nacho's anyway and I had the skills. Mary Catherine gives me a little cash at the end of the day so I can buy food. I would have done most of what I've done even if she hadn't paid me. Mary Catherine inspires a protective instinct."

"For me too, and it's odd because she's tough as nails. She sees right through my charm." I didn't think he'd said that about many people in his life. *Poor baby.*

"She sucked me in when I refused outright to go to that domestic-violence support group. Little did I realize that she'd shoved me in through the back door because those women *are* the support group."

"I like her a lot."

"Me too," I told him. "She's special."

"Have you met her son?"

"No, just his partner, Ken."

"Yeah. Ken Ashton. I have an appointment with him. I was hoping the three of us could work on some sort of partnership deal so you have a stake in the enterprise as well."

"But if it's a charity—"

"It's not only a charity. Mary Catherine needs to make a

living, and the better the business does, the more it can help the community. But regardless, if we're all on the same page, this retail space can be a separate enterprise from the original pie bakery, and that can stay very much the same as it is today."

"You mean we can operate both?"

"Yes. I think there's a market for both, but I'll have to do some serious research. I like it here. I think we should look for a more permanent place to stay."

At the stoplight he grinned at me in that I'm-going-to-take-over-your-life-so-try-not-to-struggle way, and my blood ran cold. I put my hand on his arm. "Look. You're probably at a loss right now. Since you're starting over, it makes sense for you to take your time and think very carefully about your next move. I don't see you as the kind of guy who'll be happy here in five years' time. Definitely not in ten years."

"I'm not saying I'll move here permanently, although the place has a lot of potential."

That was exactly what Muse was worrying about. "Too quiet for you. You'll be off to a bigger town in a matter of weeks. And I'll be fine here. I'm ready to slow down."

"Let's hope it's not too quiet, or you'll be baking for the seabirds."

"Where are we headed?" I asked him when he turned in the opposite direction from the motel.

"If you're serious about relocating to St. Nacho's, I thought we'd get breakfast and then figure out how to get your shit."

I realized I'd have to go back to LA to sort everything out and pack it up. I'd have to face my landladies to give notice. I knew I'd feel like I was letting them down in some fundamental way because they'd been so kind to me, but at the same time they scared me a little because they weren't quite sane. I needed to do everything else: turn off the utilities, forward the mail, and change the addresses on all my cards and documents. *Shit.*

I buried my head in my hands. "I'll have to go back to LA and finish up things there."

"Yeah. But you don't have to go alone."

"What about you? Have you moved out?"

Dan pulled into the parking lot of the Denny's, one of the few chain restaurants in town. He turned off the ignition and then sat there looking lost for a minute. "Bree and I have a housekeeper. She'll pack my things and send them. I'm only taking my clothing and toiletries. My electronics."

"You know..." I spoke because he seemed unhappy, quieter than he'd been since he'd arrived. "Bree is a religious woman, and you could appeal to your pastor. Maybe go to counseling. If you want to make it work with her, you could probably—"

"I don't want to go back." He fidgeted with his keys. "But I don't know how to move forward."

If I knew Dan, taking over my life would be the first thing he'd try. I didn't even mind so much at that point, knowing it was all for a worthy cause. We had an unspoken rule between us: only one of us got to fall apart at a time. Unfortunately for me, between Sander and illness and some really bad choices, it was definitely my turn.

He took a deep breath and opened the door to get out. "I'm seriously getting a children's menu so I can make notes of things you'll need as we think of them."

We entered Denny's, and the smiling hostess took us to our booth. I thought about what Dan's making lists on my behalf would mean to me. "Can't you use the memo function on your phone?"

"Sure." He smiled at me. "And I would if the list were for me. I'm making this list for you, and we need to come up with a timetable and some achievable short-term goals."

"Oh, thank you." I grimaced. *Thank. You.* "I've gotten nearly a half day's rest. I was getting bored."

"You'll thank me sincerely later." He tore off half his kid's menu, which wasn't blank anywhere but had a small amount of white space between the games and puzzles. "Write down everything you know about running a bakery business."

I picked up the small piece of paper and waved it. "All right. One good thing anyway. It's more than will fit on here."

"Just start." He ordered a cup of coffee and tried to get the waitress to leave the pot, which she wouldn't. Fortunately he was already thrumming with energy because he had a new project, and he was excited to get it started.

Unfortunately that project was me.

He shot me an enthusiastic smile. I took up my orange crayon and prepared to do as he'd asked.

CHAPTER NINETEEN

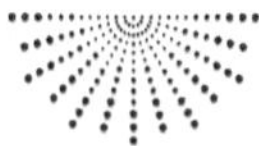

After breakfast I stopped by the SeaView to let Carl know I was keeping the room and that Dan and I had decided to head home to LA for the weekend. I told him I'd be back by nightfall Sunday, probably. I figured that I was telling JT, however obliquely, as well. Dan and I took off in his sporty little Lexus, armed with big to-go cups of coffee from a local coffee place and his GPS navigation system, which we ignored for the most part so we could follow the road where it hugged the coastline. We'd left at about noon and stopped for a late lunch of fish and chips in Ventura at a place right at the water's edge where the menu boasted seafood fresh from the boat.

Dan seemed oddly quiet, and I wasn't really feeling talkative myself. Before we hit Thousand Oaks, I called Phil at Il Ghiotto and asked about my place.

"I let Sander in to pack up everything he said was his and then he hit the road," Phil said over the noise of the restaurant.

Great. I could probably say goodbye to my Linkin Park CDs. "That's good anyway. That he's gone."

"I had the locks changed afterward. I don't think he'll bother you further."

"Thanks. That's a relief."

"I'm sorry if it turns out he took stuff that wasn't his. I had no way of knowing."

I decided to adopt my brother's attitude that it was worth the price to be rid of him. "I'm really grateful to you, Phil. I don't care what he took as long as I don't have to see him again." Over the clatter of pots and busy shuffling noise of the kitchen, I could hear Maurizio's smooth, accented baritone talking to one of the line cooks.

"Well"—Phil seemed distinctly uncomfortable—"as to that, he's moved into one of the other apartments in your building with some guy named Seth."

"No problem." I *knew* that at least one of Sander's fuck buddies had looked familiar. Seth. Right. *Seth*, who took my laundry out of the dryer while it was still wet so he could dry his. "As long as I don't have to deal with him."

"As far as I know he's still working nights, so you probably won't have to."

"I really appreciate everything you did for me. Has..." I heard a familiar, petulant voice barking orders in Italian in the background. "That answers my next question."

"I'm sorry, Jacob. Giorgio's at Il Ghiotto now and you know he's—"

"Not going anywhere," I replied. "Yes, I know."

"What are you going to do?"

"Actually I found a little town up north, and I'm thinking of working there for a while."

"Near your brother?"

"Yeah. He's maybe going through a relocation process himself. We might both end up here."

"That sounds nice." I could hear him muffle the sound of the phone while he directed kitchen traffic for a minute. "I'm sorry. I'm back."

"How's Hannah?"

"Ready to have that baby any minute. Maybe I'll relocate with you. It will save me from her temper. I've got to run, Jake. I'm being paged by a patron, damn it."

"Do I need to stop by there for my key?"

"No, I left it with *the ladies*."

"Oh shit," I said automatically. It was either that or make the sign of the cross and spit. "I owe you."

"Hell *yes*, you do." He hung up.

"What?" Dan turned to look at me briefly. "Who do you owe?"

"Phil left me a new key at my manager's office. He let Sander in to get his things."

"At least he's out of your life. Do I need to point out that you're on a disturbingly familiar road in St. Nacho's with this JT, who can't even be seen in public with you but sneaks out of your room at four in the morning?"

"Will it stop you if I say no?"

"No. Isn't it time you found someone who will stand by your side and not on either your neck or behind the big sign that says 'Door Number Three: I'm heterosexual/bi-curious/ashamed, but I don't mind getting my dick sucked'?"

"I hear you."

"Then *listen* for a change," Dan griped.

I bit back a hasty reply. He was right, of course, which made it suck much worse than if I could have told him to shove off.

"You have so much to give someone. I sometimes wonder if we haven't spent our lives trying to walk along an imaginary balance beam with Dad on one side and Mom on the other. It's not okay to spend our lives in the framework of their mistakes. Value yourself, Yasha. And for that matter, I need to trust myself. I'm not going to turn into Dad, and you need to stop living in fear like Mom."

"I'm not living in fear."

"No. It's worse than that. You're living in her shame. From her lack of self-esteem." Dan gripped the wheel, and I thought I felt him punch the gas. "If nothing else, honor her memory by not allowing yourself to be a doormat."

I gazed out the window for a while. Family vacations. Gotta love them.

Are we there yet?

NIGHT HAD BLANKETED the city while we were still en route, but it was early enough that we walked among the dog people and those who were disembarking from public transportation and heading home from work.

The first place we went after we parked the car on the street in front of my building was the liquor store on Melrose down Gardner Street. You couldn't ever, ever go to the building manager's apartment with nothing in hand. Usually I loaded up with treats from Il Ghiotto, but since I no longer worked there, I thought a quick trip to the local liquor store and behind the glass where they kept the expensive stuff was in order. I had the key guy open the cabinet and get me a bottle of Laphroaig single malt.

"I don't know why you're doing this." Dan shoved my hand out of the way when I got out my wallet to pay. "I got this. I want to see this person who has you scared to ask for the key to your own damn place."

"Madeline is nice. Laverne is the scary one. I wonder if I should have them wrap it."

"You're kidding."

"No." He'd see, and then he'd know.

It was on the way back that I began to really perceive the city.

After Nacho's it seemed deafening. Traffic rumbled along Melrose like the steady rush of floodwaters, a grinding, honking wall of noise that disoriented me. Sirens wailed in the distance. Music played from storefronts. People gathered in knots like talking, laughing, brightly colored birds, looking for fun on a Saturday night. I couldn't blame them, but after having the quiet hum of the ocean as a backdrop the previous week, it was like being thrown into a food processor. I already missed my pie ladies. I missed the firehouse and the easy camaraderie of the men there, and I missed Nacho's Bar. A helicopter flew overhead, and I used that as an excuse for why I had no idea what Dan had been saying to me.

"What?" I glanced up at him and caught his knowing look. "I'm sorry."

"You didn't hear a word I said."

"No," I admitted. "I seem to have my mind on other things."

"Would those other things happen to be back in St. Nacho's?"

"I'm afraid so," I told him honestly. "It seems noisy here."

"It is noisy."

"And the smog is really something if you haven't been in it for a while. Although it made for a cool sunset while we were driving down."

"There's that," Dan agreed. He was definitely not used to the city anymore either.

I felt a million miles from my heart. "For some reason I don't remember why I live here."

Dan frowned, then threw a reassuring arm around me. "Then it's time to leave. Let's go beard the lion, shall we? It should come in handy having a Daniel around."

THE BEST PART of the visit with my landladies was Dan's face. Madeline let us in, and I was immediately—once again—reminded of *What Ever Happened to Baby Jane?*

Lucky us. It was prom-dress day, and Madeline, having apparently won the coin toss, looked elegant and attractive in a fetching confection of lavender satin and tulle. Laverne, on the other hand, sat in a white wicker chair that was upholstered in vivid green-checked fabric, flanked by twin tables made of glass supported by white marble elephants. She was stuffed uncomfortably into a red silk and lamé number, looking part dragon lady and part...*Island of Dr. Moreau.*

Madeline rattled on about how awful it was that Sander, whom she called "that beautiful golden stud" had been such a "horrible, physically violent man." She said it like *physically vah-ha-hilent man* while biting her lip. I swear I saw a droplet of drool trickle onto her breast.

This was followed by an uncomfortable silence during which Madeline presented Laverne with our gift. Laverne waved it away, toward one of the elephant tables, and motioned for us to sit.

There was nothing for it but to get down on the ground because she didn't have any other chairs in the room. Dan and I complied, sitting cross-legged before her like worshippers, which was exactly how she liked it.

Laverne clapped her hands, and Madeline brought her a pack of Dunhills, red box. Elegant as always. Then she pulled a big crystal ashtray from the space between her ample hips and the chair cushion. After she had placed a cigarette between her lips, she offered us one. Whether we both shook our heads, I couldn't say for sure because I didn't take my eyes away from Laverne long enough to find out. Later I would explain to Dan about landing an apartment in the Norma Desmond Bates Hotel as I called it, and the fact that it was fully two hundred dollars a month cheaper than comparable apartments as long as you were willing to go along with the charade. These weren't merely the building's managers; they owned the place and had since it was built if the story was to be believed.

I wished I could have seen Dan's face when Laverne opened her mouth for the first time and a Harvey Fierstein voice came out like the growl of earth-moving equipment, but I still didn't dare look away. Sixty-odd years of smoking and—probably—shouting at her sister had taken their toll.

"You boys look like twins," came the pronouncement.

"I'm quite a bit older," Dan said carefully.

Laverne fixed him with her piercing gray eyes. "Do we look like twins to you?"

Ohcrapohcrapohcrap, the twin thing...

"Twins? Come on. You can tell me." Dan handled Laverne like the pro he was. He leaned in and said quietly, "She's your mother, right?"

Madeline gave a shocked gasp at this, but I could see Laverne was pleased. "No, no. Gotcha, you dear boy. We *are* twins."

"*She's* older by twenty-four minutes," Madeline insisted.

Laverne let loose a string of smoke and profanity that would have singed our eyebrows if we had been sitting closer.

"Well, you are." Madeline's lip jutted out. "Older." I wished for their sakes they had a normal sister. Who would be Olivia de Havilland? When all was said and done, like the Munsters, they needed a *plain one.*

"I take it from your visit that you have something to tell us?" Laverne asked.

"I need to move. I'll give you my thirty days' notice in writing before I leave."

"I'm sorry to hear that." Laverne gazed at me thoughtfully. "It will be sad to see you go. Madeline will be very unhappy. She enjoys the cannoli, Jacob, very much."

"I'm sorry." I looked down to where my hands squeezed my knees. "I no longer work at Il Ghiotto."

"I see." Another thin stream of smoke filled the air. "Yes, I see."

Then there was a silence, which seemed interminable until Dan spoke. "I'm going to hire a company to pack Jacob's things and move them. Afterward someone will clean. We'll be leaving now." He got to his knees stiffly and pulled me up.

"Wait just a moment." Laverne's voice could strip stucco off the sides of buildings. I wouldn't have been surprised if she'd asked me to kill the Wicked Witch of the West and bring her her broom. Instead she held out her hand politely, and when I took it, she said, "You're a mensch. I'm going to miss you."

Laverne told Madeline to show us out, which she did, foaming toward the door in a lavender cloud and bubbling about how it would be a major disappointment to have one less so very attractive man around the place.

Dan was mostly silent on the way up the outside stairs and down the gallery to my apartment. *Former apartment*. It wasn't home after everything that had happened there. Just before we got to the door, though, he burst out in wildly uncharacteristic, boyish laughter. He actually held his sides as he slumped against the wall of the building, and I thought, if nothing else, his reaction to the weird sisters was an unusual one.

"Jakey! When we're old, I want to be exactly like that. I want to be a pasha in some tiny corner of the world we've carved out for ourselves. I want to smoke with impunity and wear silly clothes. I'm leaning toward a *Wild Wild West* theme. Fancy vests and long coats with aviator goggles." Dan looked about fifteen years younger and laughed like he was directing the audience of a sitcom.

"Who *are* you?" This was *not* my brother Daniel.

"I want to build computers out of vacuum tubes and old typewriters and talk through funnels attached to long rubber hoses. Life can be so *fun* if you have nothing better to do with your time."

I considered him carefully. It was entirely possible that he'd finally snapped, but if I had to guess, he was just enjoying a freedom from responsibility that he'd never experienced before, even as a kid. Maybe St. Nacho's had gotten to him a little too.

I liked it on him. "Don't expect me to be your Madeline."

CHAPTER TWENTY

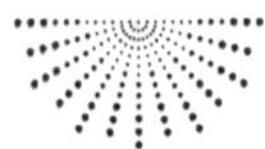

My apartment depressed me. Sander had mown through all our things, dumping the contents of bedroom drawers, riffling through papers and mail, and scavenging in our media center. I noticed a lot of my least-favorite DVDs remained, but the James Bond movies were nowhere to be found.

The kitchen—which was untouched because he didn't set foot there except to eat—was arguably worse. He'd left everything alone, but the bright white room was still exactly as I'd left it after our horrible fight—chairs turned over, one of the cabinet doors hanging drunkenly off its hinges where I'd grabbed hold to keep myself from going down, and blood spattered on the backsplash and countertop tiles. Where I'd fallen, there was a dark, damning stain. Suddenly I could hardly bear to have my brother see it.

He stepped past me and looked around for himself. "Dear G—"

"It looks worse than what it actually was." I sagged against the door frame. "I had a head wound. Mostly bluster."

He turned to me, white with shock. "You know how crazy

that sounds? Minimizing...this." His gesture encompassed the whole grisly tableau. I could see right where Madeline's little foot had slipped.

"Yes." I stared at his mouth, which was easier somehow than meeting his eyes. It tightened to a thin, light line.

"You definitely need to seek professional help."

I nodded. "I understand."

"If you can't do it with the group, then do it privately."

"I will."

The silence grew while he appeared to be making plans. Then he sighed. "Get everything you have that has any value. If you need boxes, I'll get some. We'll take what you can't bear to lose and trust movers to pack and relocate the rest. I don't want to stay here one second longer than I have to."

"All right."

"Do you have a phone book?"

"In the drawer by the phone," I told him.

I didn't want to step into the kitchen. I had good knives. Great pans. I stood in the doorway trying to think whether I had anything I had to take right away. Not from the kitchen. I went into the bedroom and grabbed a large duffel bag and threw in the rest of my clothes and some toiletries I hadn't packed when I'd left the first time. I took a first-aid kit, which seemed funny somehow.

I retrieved my zeyde's old Swiss watch from the nightstand drawer and put it on. It didn't work, but it didn't matter. Once I had it with me, there was nothing left in the apartment I had any attachment to one way or the other. I found Dan in the kitchen where he was just hanging up the wall phone. He had his wallet and iPhone out, and he seemed engrossed in making notes. I hated to interrupt him, so I hung in the doorway again.

"Now." He put his things away. "What can I help you with?"

"Nothing. I'm ready. We can go."

"Really?" He eyed my duffel. "You have everything?"

"Yeah…Or rather I don't *have* much of anything. Nothing I care about anyway."

"You always did travel light."

"Yeah."

The silence built up between us, and for once, I had nothing to fill it with.

"He could have killed you here, you know. Nothing would have stopped him from taking one of your expensive damned knives and ending your life."

"You don't have to tell me that."

"Don't make me ever, *ever* tell you again, Jakey." I heard a catch in his voice and saw that his eyes glittered with tears. "You're all the family I've got."

"I know." I couldn't bring myself to go into that kitchen, even though I wanted to. I wanted to wrap my arms around my brother and reassure him that I'd never be that stupid again, but I couldn't cross the threshold. "Can we go?"

He stood so quickly the chair slid backward, scraping across the tile. "Yeah." He pulled his keys from his pocket. "We need to drop this and the key off with Madeline. I don't think that will require an audience with Her Imperial Highness."

I heard teasing in his voice. "You liked them, didn't you?"

"Yeah." He grinned. "I've adopted them as role models."

"I hate to say it, but me too," I admitted. "I'll miss them."

"It's not like I believed for a minute you'd buy single malt whisky for someone you don't like."

"Found out." I closed and locked my apartment door for the last time and felt little more than I had felt about my job really. I was sorry to leave it behind but ready to go.

"I'll drop the key off with Madeline," he said, handing me the keys to his car. "I suppose this is as good a time as any to ask. Do you have a driver's license?"

"Yeah. I just don't have a car. Insurance is too expensive, and parking is fucked-up at Il Ghiotto. I'd have had to pay monthly fees at the bank next door. And the bus stops right outside the place practically."

"Good. In that case you drive back. We'll take the I-5 this time, yeah?"

"Yeah," I agreed. "Nothing to see at night."

THE DRIVE UP the 101 was uneventful, but the fog got thicker and thicker. As we neared Goleta, we could hardly see at all; even fifty feet was difficult. We took it slow, but I think Dan knew I was nervous, so we pulled off for a cup of coffee at a gas station, and I gave in to the urge to buy some junk food. Once back on the road it was a slow, nearly blind drive toward what I'd begun to think of as home.

"I checked around a little before we left St. Nacho's. It looks like there are some places available for lease. I wanted to ask what you had planned—if anything—before I got ahead of myself, but if you want, I'll take a place there that's big enough, and we can share it while we figure out what comes next."

"That's—" I broke off when I thought about what it might mean to share a place with Dan. "Won't you be uncomfortable if I have an overnight guest?"

Dan snorted. "Seems like your overnight guest—who sneaks in on foot so no one will see his truck and then slinks out again before dawn—will be more embarrassed than I will. What the hell are you doing with a guy like that anyway?"

"I don't know." I replied honestly. "I find him attractive in—"

"Yeah, yeah," Dan teased. "I can see why you'd think he was hot, but there are other guys—that firefighter Cam for example. He's hot too, and he's out, it seems."

"Yeah, he is. Charming too. He did ask me if I wanted a ride on the Camshaft."

Dan laughed. "You've got to be kidding me."

I risked a quick glance his way to see if he thought it was as amusing as I did. "I couldn't begin to make that up."

"So?"

"Who can say? JT is fine, like…fine wine, fine food. He's a generous, good person. He's gentle and caring, professional. Heroic. But his fear is tearing him apart, and I feel for him. He thinks he's sinning against God, and it's not like I'm his rabbi. I can't tell him he's not."

"Yeah, well. It's hard for all of us."

Again I glanced over. "I assume you mean to express a sense of solidarity. Hard for everyone to be honest in relationships, but—"

"No, Jakey. I don't mean that. I mean it's hard to man up and admit you're gay. It's especially hard to admit it when you've finally gotten the balls and the freedom to do something about it and your asshole *freshman-in-high-school brother* practically comes out on the six-o'clock news, and you realize that ends any hope you ever had of being able to live your life the way you'd planned."

"What?" I snapped. That I didn't accompany it by sailing the car over the rocky cliffs and into the Pacific remains one of the great mysteries of my life. "What?"

"Did you know Mom called me at school just frantic? 'Jacob is gay. What can we do? It's so dangerous. It's so unnatural. I pictured grandkids. What will Zeyde say?'"

"I didn't have a clue. She didn't seem…" I realized what must have happened. "She did all her angsting on the phone with you, didn't she? And then she came to me all cool and glued together."

Daniel tapped his nose. "You got it in one."

"Fuck." I felt sick. "I never…Why didn't you tell me?"

"What could you have done? It's not as bad as it sounds. I did actually—at one point—think I loved Bree. That I could love her enough."

"How long did that last?"

"Really? Until she laid down the law about kids. What a joke. If I'd wanted to adopt, I'd have stayed gay in the first place."

"That's not funny," I snapped. "It's not a fucking choice. You make it sound like—"

"No," he agreed, subdued. "It's not. I know better than anyone it's not."

"I can't believe you didn't tell me."

"What would you have done?"

What would I have done? I didn't have a clue.

"I'm getting those red cigarettes your friend Laverne smokes next time. They smelled like money." He pulled out his pack of cigarettes and lipped one from the carton. He lit it with a cheap lighter from the gas station and blew a thin stream of smoke through the barely open window. How come I never knew he could be so different from what I'd always believed? How could he hide himself so completely from me?

"I can't believe I didn't know—"

"Now you know why I love the movie *It's a Wonderful Life*. You're Harry Bailey."

The fog was too thick, and I had to keep my mind on the road, but his revelation made me more than a little sick inside. We moved through patches so dense we couldn't see beyond the hood of the car, inching along carefully. The car had headlights that dimmed when other cars approached and did other smart-car things that were entirely useless in this situation. I don't know exactly how fast we were going. There were not very many people on the road besides us, and I was grateful for small favors.

"I'm sorry." It felt like we were on a ride in an amusement park or something, like we'd entered a silent wormhole in space. We pressed on through the thick void together, and it might have seemed for a minute that we really were the only two people in existence, or that we'd slipped beneath existence, between the cracks of time and space entirely.

I turned on the radio and tried to find something good to listen to but got bad reception. I didn't trust my brother's taste in music at all, but maybe in this, as well, I would be surprised.

"Eerie," I remarked. "Do you have any music CDs?"

"I just have audiobooks."

"Figures." Audiobooks. Probably all about getting ahead in the real-estate game or something. "I don't think it's a good idea if I fall asleep."

"Asshole." He grinned and looked away. "I don't usually drive with music. I always feel like I should be learning something."

"You're right. We are a pair of fucked-up losers." The radio offered nothing but the insistent buzz of static.

"HID retrofit lights," Dan said. "They fuck up reception."

A mere second later, a microsecond, the Lexus slammed into the back of a vehicle I hadn't seen at all until I was right on it. The air bags deployed, a blast of fabric and gas, hot and disorienting. The collision jerked us around in our seat belts like dolls as the car spun, our momentum still trying to carry the back around whatever we'd hit.

I don't know how long we sat there, silent, sideways, watching dirt particles float in the glow from the dashboard lights. We were both still restrained in our seats, and the windshield was cracked but intact. It was impossible to see what we'd hit.

I groaned and felt around to release myself from my seat belt. Dan caught my hand and stopped me. I looked up at him to see why, but his head was turned the other way, looking out the window.

And then I knew.

I saw it.

Another car, the headlights barely like the glow of candles in all that mist, coming straight for us on my brother's side.

"Jakey," he called, "keep your seat belt on."

"No, man. We have to get out."

"We can't. We don't have time.

I had just found him.

I had just unearthed the brother I'd always wanted—had always dreamed about—from the one I thought I knew, and I wasn't about to lose him. I tried to start the car, but it was hopeless.

At the time of impact, I was screaming, "*Fuck this shit.*"

It all happened in an instant, and it took forever. The thing that frightened me most was the calm way Dan looked at me when he gripped my hand. I clung to him, to the calm in his eyes, as the other car slammed into the passenger side and the lateral air bags deployed.

CHAPTER TWENTY-ONE

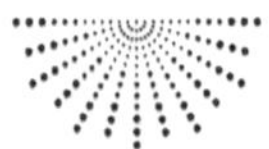

I don't really know what happened to the time we spent in that car. It couldn't have been long, but things passed that I wasn't aware of until I heard someone tap on the window with a flashlight. I couldn't remember how to open the windows or the doors to let myself out.

At first, I thought the people trying to get my attention must be the police, but it was other men and women, emerging like shipwreck survivors, gathering the things they had on hand, and trying to help, to do what they could while they waited for emergency services to arrive. Outside my window an older woman held one of those small plastic pouches of tissues out to me like she was offering it, and I made myself think how I should answer. The entire situation was confusing and absurd.

"I don't know what to do." I gestured to her in a daze. "Can you help me?"

She bit her lip and tapped the window again. She called, "Undo your safety belt." I wasn't sure what she was talking about. Then I looked down and saw that my hand was still clutching Dan's, painfully white-knuckled. It took a minute to let go, then more to get the feeling back in my fingers. When I finally had it, I pushed the button that unlatched my seat belt.

My hand felt strange, buzzy, and not at all like I was in charge of it, but my seat belt came free.

I smelled gasoline and antifreeze and brake fluid. The situation became clear fairly quickly after that. I knew I had to get Dan out, but that would be easier said than done. He wasn't conscious and had taken the impact of the second car on his side. There was no way to tell if he was too injured to be moved, but I could smell *heat*. Dan had dropped his cigarette, and it was burning the carpet or the upholstery or something. Smoldering somewhere. I prayed it wasn't in his lap, on his skin, burning his flesh, but I didn't smell that…exactly. And I would have known. I'd smelled it before.

I unlocked the door and opened the latch on my side, and several people's hands reached in to help me out. I wasn't injured, at least not specifically, but I wasn't feeling my body at all. I might have been a corpse walking around for all the sensation I had in my skin.

"I need to get my brother out," I said, turning back to see what I could do to get that started.

"I agree," a man said behind me. "It's not safe here. We need to get him to the side of the road."

No one had to tell me how difficult and dangerous that would be. I knew it. At any moment another car could slam into the wreckage. Someone like me who hadn't seen anything until it was too late. I climbed back in and knelt on the driver's seat, unlocking the seat belt that held Dan in place. The rudimentary training I'd had in first aid kicked in, and without thinking, I felt for a pulse. His eyes fluttered open.

"Oh, *Danilo*." I spoke his childhood nickname and nearly sobbed with relief. "We have to get you out of here."

"Give me a minute." He licked his lips.

I looked out the window, but I saw nothing. "I hope we have a minute."

"You get clear. I can't move."

"What?" I searched with my hand, feeling in the barely lit car for something—anything—that would tell me what he meant.

"I'm…My arm is wedged. Trapped." He swallowed hard.

I sat back on my heels. "What can I do?"

"You need to get to the side of the road. The car behind me will absorb the impact of another and so on. It will accordion around me but protect me from the force, and as soon as help arrives, they'll get me out."

"I'm not going *anywhere*." How could he think it? How could he think I would leave him alone like that?

"This isn't the time to be stubborn. It'll be all right."

I shook my head. "I'm not leaving you here."

"No. Get to the side of the road, as far away from the wreckage as possible. You have to be smart. Do the right thing."

"I can tell you're thinking *for a change*."

Dan gave a pained laugh. "Yeah."

I looked behind me and saw two faces peering into the car. "He can't leave," I told the woman with the tissues. "He's pinned by his arm."

She looked anxiously behind us at the road where any traffic would be coming. Someone was lighting flares and placing them behind the wreckage, moving far enough away that I couldn't see them in the mist. Maybe if they burned brightly enough, it would stop people from just speeding headlong into the crash.

"It's all right," I told her. "I'll stay here with him for a while."

The man behind her said, "That isn't a good idea."

"My ideas rarely are," I agreed. My head was swimmy; the sensation of being underwater instead of wrapped in an intense fog was worsening.

"You really should—"

"I'm staying," I said, tight-lipped. "It will be all right. Get to safety and flag down the EMTs for us the minute they arrive, all right? I think my brother's going to need to be cut out of the car."

"Go," my brother tried to shout, but it didn't sound too fierce. "*Go*."

"And miss your face when they use that big saw on your Lexus? Never."

I could tell Dan was in pain, yet I wanted to keep him talking to me. I couldn't bear to see the light in his eyes go out, even to escape his pain. I was too scared he wouldn't come back to me.

"Tell me about everything else. Legs?"

"Peachy." He shot me a killing glance. "When we get out of this, I am going to use them to kick your ass."

More faces peered curiously at us as they passed the car, and I began to wonder how many people were involved. How many cars? How many were injured or killed?

"You can try," I told Dan. "Weren't you just telling me this morning that I need professional help and I shouldn't be a doormat?"

He laughed weakly. "You picked a fine time to stand your ground."

"I agree completely. What about those legs? What do you feel?"

"Not much."

"Dan—"

"No, it's not that. I'm not really…I don't feel much of anything. That's probably good."

"Or not," I said grimly.

He reached for me with his free hand again, and I focused on that for a while. We sat there clinging to one another, listening to the *drip, drip, drip* from the Lexus's cracked radiator and the noise from a couple of radios. Farther from where we sat, we heard the sounds of pain. A man moaned over and over.

Someone was crying. I became aware of the sound of a car horn going off at intervals like an alarm, probably triggered when the car was disabled in the crash.

My heart stuttered in my chest when I caught sight of more luminous balls of light in the fog—headlights—heading our way. Deliberately, I let out the breath I was holding. We had no more air bags to deploy. We were crushed between two cars. It was a foregone conclusion that when this car came our way, if it saw us and was unable to stop, it would crush us further. It was inevitable. And my brother was on the side that would take the worst of it.

"Fuck, Danilo. More cars."

He sighed. "I see them."

"It's…torture, isn't it?" I said. "The waiting."

"Yes."

"I love you," I told him. "I wish—"

"Me too, man. I love you too. You'll be fine, Jakey. No matter what, you know?"

"No, *Dan*—"

"I took care of some things with my lawyer a while ago when Bree and I first hit the skids…"

No. "Don't talk like this is it."

"I don't have time to be delicate. Buy your bakery," he told me. "Get a house and find your man. Live happily ever after. Promise."

"Dani—"

"Promise me."

I didn't answer. Those fucking lights were coming, but they were crawling so slowly. Hanging in the mist like fucking ghosts were walking toward us holding lanterns. It was enough to drive me out of my mind. My heart rocketed inside my chest, and I wanted to scream, *Just do it already, just fucking do it*, so it could all just be over.

But then I heard it. The grumbling purr of a fire engine. Hope ignited within me like someone had lit a match.

"Danilo, I think it's emergency services," I said, but when I looked, his mouth was slack and his skin clammy. "*Dani*!"

I put my hand on his neck and found his pulse weak. "Jeez." I turned to the window when I heard someone approaching. I could hear police radios, and there was the sound of men's voices. Orders and replies. "Hey," I called out to them. "Hey, can I get some help? Can you help me?"

If being the world's most egregious *nudje* would get me some action, then that is precisely what I planned to do. I banged on the window so there was no doubt where I could be found. "Help me, please! My brother is pinned, and we can't leave the vehicle. He's going into shock!"

I heard the heavy clomping approach of metal-reinforced bunker boots, and when I turned toward the sound, Cam's face dropped into view just outside my door where my tissue lady had been standing what seemed like hours before.

"Yasha." He frowned and pulled the door open. He knelt in front of me, using his gloved hands to smooth down my shoulders to my arms, very much like you would soothe an anxious horse. Then he grinned. "You should have called first to see if I already had a date." He turned and shouted instructions to someone, then pulled me forcefully from the car.

"I can't leave. Dani's hurt. His arm's caught somehow. He said he's stuck."

"You'll do as I say, or I'll have Officer Andy shoot you."

"I can't—"

Cam gripped my shoulders gently—for him anyway—and I winced. "I promise you I'll take care of your brother." I was shaking my head, but he caught my chin. "I will. You'll see, but later. Let me and the guys do our job, all right? Like you said about that other time when you needed to just step aside."

I clenched my teeth because I thought they were beginning to chatter. "In Tel Aviv."

"Sure." Cam smiled at me. "Whatever. Right now, I gotta do my job, Yasha, okay?"

"Yes, I'm sorry." I shot a glance back into the car at my brother, so still and pale but breathing. I could see that, and I allowed myself to be led to the side of the road where the EMTs were setting up a triage area. "Please take care of him, Cam."

A look of tenderness came over Cam's face as he glanced past me. "You bet, Yasha. Like he was mine. All right?"

I took one last look back at the Lexus. It was horribly crushed between a passenger sedan and a heavy-duty pickup truck. I could just make out the flashers on the fire engines. The EMTs had parked their truck on the side of the road and set up tarpaulins, which they seemed to be using to sort casualties.

"Jeez," I whispered to no one in particular.

"Sir." Gloved hands reached for me.

I turned to find JT's warm green gaze on me. The look in his eyes went from indifferent concern to surprise to panic in a nanosecond. "*Yasha*?"

"I—"

"I thought you were in LA." We both looked back toward the massive wreck on the highway. His fingers tightened on my wrists reflexively, I thought, jerking when he comprehended what exactly I'd been through.

"My brother," I whispered. I couldn't tell if he heard me over the noise.

"Is he…?"

"Cam's taking care of him. His arm is pinned."

He took my arm and began to pull me toward one of the tarps. "I have to do triage, Yasha. I have to take care of people here according to their needs. There are ambulances on the way."

"My brother is still out there."

"Cam will get him out safely and bring him to me here."

"He's hurt." I sat down where he told me to sit, next to a man with cuts on his face and my tissue lady. "His arm—it's caught, and he can't—"

"Trust me, Yasha. Let me do my job. Cam will bring him to me, and I'll take good care of him, all right? Just like I'm taking care of you here, okay?"

My throat closed over with emotion and shock. Between the first crash and the fear of the second, I'd given little thought to my own injuries, but the pain was becoming insistent in muscles tightened by terror before the point of impact and wrenched hard in the ensuing collision, especially across my chest where I'd been restrained by my seat belt.

"How are you doing? Anything barking at you?" JT knelt next to me. He wrapped a cuff around my arm to check my blood pressure. I know I just stared at it as though I'd never seen one before. After that was finished, he held my head with one gloved hand while he irritated me by shining that little light of his into my eyes. I wanted him to understand.

His busy hands kept moving, kept fluttering over my skin. I flinched when he pressed on my chest where the seat belt had been, and his hand faltered. I looked up to find him peering closely at me. I wondered if he realized just how much his very brusque—albeit necessary and properly impersonal—inventory of my person was hurting me.

"Dan is all I have."

JT froze. Very deliberately—even solemnly—he leaned over and kissed me, in full view of everyone there. Even in the fog he attracted a lot of attention. I caught sight of a few surprised faces before I closed my eyes and gave in to the urgency of that kiss. He pulled me into his arms then, running a gentle hand up and down my back.

He broke off the kiss to speak softly, but his actions were unmistakable. "No, he's not all you have. You have me, Yasha.

I'm so sorry I haven't had the balls to make that really clear to you. I swear, if you only have a little faith in me, I'll never let you forget it."

JT brushed the hair off my forehead and pressed a gentle kiss on my skin. Then apologetically, he left me to help the next person.

I watched him. I took in every move he made, every gesture of comfort, every disarming smile, every frown as he went from one casualty to the next, efficiently caring for the people on the tarpaulin with me. Every so often he glanced my way or shot me a cautious smile. I caught them like a lifeline, using them to anchor myself between one moment and the next, until finally, I saw Cam and two other firefighters bringing my brother toward us on a backboard.

After my brother was free, everything was a blur, and it wasn't easy to keep up. Eventually I ended up in an EMS rig—not JT's—with Dan, who needed to get to the hospital quickly. Once there, once I established myself as Dan's brother, all that was left was the wait while they stabilized him and sent him to radiology for his arm, which was going to take most of the night. It seemed that no one in the pileup had died, but several patients trickled in with injuries, from simple lacerations to compound fractures and one possible heart attack brought on by stress.

Dan's arm appeared to have been broken extensively. From what I could see, he was awake and already badgering the nurses for his cell phone so he'd have a way to research the best doctors for the job of fixing it. I realized he was running on adrenaline and fear, free of the worst of the pain because of very effective drugs but not at all out of the woods. It was almost dawn when I called and left a message for BreeAnna on their house phone, but I didn't know whether she would come. I didn't have her cell number; I had never thought I'd need it. I wished to hell I'd gotten it.

I must have dozed off for a long while because when I woke up, according to the clock, it was nearly noon.

"Hey, is this seat taken?"

I looked up and found Cam looming over me. He peered down into my face with concern in his fine blue eyes. "No, sit. Take a load off."

He still wore his turnout pants, but he had shucked his coat and helmet somewhere. "That was a mess, Yasha. Thirteen cars and two big rigs."

"I must have been toward the end."

"The California Highway Patrol will figure that out. I just had to clean it up and get it off the road." He rolled those big shoulders, and yep, he was wearing red suspenders, but they were draped around his hips. Some lucky boy was going to give him a rubdown later, I hoped. He looked exhausted.

"What a mess."

"How's your brother?"

"The arm is broken. They took him to radiology right away. They'll bring in a specialist if they need one. He phoned his family physician, a friend, who is making calls on his behalf."

Cam nodded. "I honestly don't know how he was still conscious when we got there."

"He can be a pretty determined guy. I've never seen him so calm. The wrong Livingston definitely went into the Tzahal. He'd have made a great fighter pilot or something. Nerves of steel."

Cam's brows came together in the middle. "He'll need them. That arm's going to hurt like fuck for a long time."

"That's—"

"They'll take care of him. I'm here to take care of you."

CHAPTER TWENTY-TWO

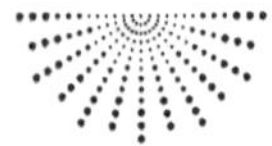

"How long since you ate?" Cam asked.

I shook my head. "I had coffee when we turned off the I-5, I think."

"JT asked me to come here and get you. Said you'd need to shower and rest and eat, but he wanted to talk to his dad for a bit…"

I remembered his kiss. "I guess."

"Look, I could take you to the SeaView, but my place has a hot tub. It would probably help you relax."

Since I had checked out with no real injuries besides a tremendously sore body, it didn't seem to be a bad idea.

Cam looked me over when I got slowly to my feet, still carrying the laptop case he had taken from Daniel's car before it had been towed off the freeway. He took it and put an arm around me. "Gotta hand it to the Lexus. It's pretty safe. Your brother wouldn't have even been hurt, but his arm got twisted between the seat and the door. That was kind of a freak thing."

"I didn't see it before you guys wrapped it. How bad was it?"

"It was a crush injury. He'll need a good orthopedist and probably a lot of physical therapy. Is he right-handed?"

"Yeah," I told him.

"Shit. He's got his work cut out for him. What does he do?"

"He's a concert pianist," I said, deadpan. I could never have expected the response I got, not in a million years.

Cam's face drained of blood, and his eyes flooded with tears. "Oh *fuck no*!"

"Whoa, Cam. Calm down, buddy. I'm sorry. *My bad*. I was kidding."

Cam scrubbed the heels of his hands over his eyes and took a deep breath. "*Jeez*...fucking mess with me."

"I'm so, so sorry, man. I didn't mean...I just wanted to lighten the mood."

Cam was silent as he led me to the parking lot.

"I'm really sorry."

"It's been a long day. I guess I'm tired."

"You can go home without me and sleep. The nurses said that they have Daniel sedated and he's likely to be out for a while. I could go back to my motel room," I offered.

"You shouldn't be alone right now. You need some food, Yasha, and someone to look out for you."

"Because you're normally such a mother hen."

"Because I care," Cam said, and I noticed his gaze strayed back toward the hospital. "Because I want to help."

"Thanks, man." I put an arm out when we got to the truck and let him help me up. He could probably bench-press my weight anyway, and I wasn't feeling very strong. I didn't have pain meds on board, but I felt weak and shaky anyway.

We drove the short way to his place in silence. It was one of the apartment buildings I'd noticed by the beach—small buildings, three up and three down on either side. They would normally be built around a courtyard, but this one had a gazebo that sheltered a hot tub. I imagined the number of hookups Cam brought here and hoped they chlorinated early and often.

"I'll get you something to eat, and then we can come down here."

"I don't have swim trunks."

"Wear your boxers. No one cares. I'm sure I have something that will fit you after."

I laughed. "Because between now and then I'll grow a foot and gain eighty pounds?"

"Because people leave shit here all the time," Cam countered. He unlocked his door, and I followed him inside. Nothing could have prepared me for the shock of Cam's small and tidy apartment.

I don't really know what I expected. Maybe…early Gold's Gym with a dash of *Rocky* and possibly, maybe, a reptile habitat. A turtle he could talk to. Something that would hibernate half the year and give him no trouble. Something for which he could leave lettuce and apple peels out during the rest of the year.

But *no*. Cam's living room was a soothing, neutral gray-green with white crown molding. He had art on the walls, and it wasn't there simply because it matched his tan leather couch or his subtly plaid green and tan recliners. It was black-and-white photographs by Ansel Adams and interesting portraits of legendary jazz musicians. He had throw pillows and a muted, faded-looking area rug that covered his light oak hardwood floors. And it felt like heaven when I took off my shoes—as he did in the vestibule—and stepped on it in my sock feet. There were shiny living plants and pictures of him and his friends from the department. A few of the local PD. Nobody who looked like family. A beautiful spotted cat rubbed up against his legs, and he picked it up as gently as if it were a baby and rubbed his face in its fur.

"What the hell kind of cat is that?" I peered at the thing. It looked like a tiny wild leopard or something. It seemed as happy to see him as a puppy would have been.

"It's an ocicat. It's a domestic breed that's spotted like a wildcat. I pulled her out of a fire when she was a kitten. She has a scar, see?"

I noticed a place on her hind leg where her fur was disrupted and reached out to stroke her soft head. "Oh, poor baby."

"The house belonged to a breeder, and we got them all out safely, but Spot here got singed. They get thousands of dollars for these cats, but because she was scarred, she can't be shown or anything. They let me keep her. She's like a dog really. So I called her Spot."

"I see," I said. Yeah, right. That, my friend, is a cat.

"You don't believe me."

"Not really. She looks a lot like a cat to me."

Cam smiled and set her down on the floor. He peered around one of the recliners and found a crinkly little ball.

"Go get it, Spot." He threw the ball so it sailed down the hall toward what I presumed were bedrooms, and the cat fairly flew after it. She brought it back and dropped the ball at his feet. "You were saying?"

"Nothing, man. I have never seen a cat do that."

"Spot's special," Cam said. "Aren't you, baby girl?" He cooed some more, uncharacteristically unselfconscious as he herded me toward a spacious and colorful kitchen with the same beige-colored walls and a beige-and-white-checkered tile floor. He had more photographs on the walls back there, mostly of children, a lot of whom were climbing play equipment, and I recognized some of the local law enforcement and fire department personnel with them. He brought me a beer and jerked a chin at a particularly fun-looking picture of some kids in a pie-eating contest.

"That's the local park. Every Fourth of July there's a big picnic, and last year—thanks to Mary Catherine—we had a pie-eating contest. You should have seen those kids. They were so happy."

"I'll bet it was something."

"Are you going to move here?" Cam asked as he moved back to the refrigerator and took out cold cuts and condiments, lettuce and tomato. "Sandwiches okay?"

"Fabulous. You have no idea." I was salivating just looking at the food. Until that moment I hadn't realized how hungry I was. "I plan to move here. I like St. Nacho's."

"It gets to you, doesn't it?" Cam agreed and took a brief swig of his beer before he grabbed some bread and started assembling a meal. "You start to think you'll find answers here."

I simply stared at Cam as he expertly cut our sandwiches in fourths and served them with the points up like in a restaurant. He put some chips in the center and a pickle on each plate.

"What?" His hands slowed when he realized I was gaping.

"You are two different people," I said.

He grinned. "I get that a lot. Do you mind if I talk freely?"

"No, of course not."

"JT is telling his dad he has feelings for you today."

I felt my beer kick in. Or maybe it was just nerves, but I sat in one of the tall kitchen chairs at the counter because my knees felt a little unsteady. "Yeah?"

"Yeah." Cam took a swig of his beer. "I know Carl, and I don't think it's going to be a problem. But I know JT too. I saw him kiss you in front of everybody. That was cool, but he's been hiding who he is a long time."

"I know." I colored. I felt it creep from my chest to my neck, and it wasn't from the beer.

"He's never been happy about how he feels about men. It's a feeling I have. But I want you to be careful with your heart. I'm not sure he's someone you can trust it with. Your dick? Sure. But hold on to your heart for a while."

I watched Cam take a huge, satisfied bite of his sandwich. Turkey, ham, swiss. I don't know what all he put on there. It was about four inches thick, and his eyes rolled back into his head when he chewed. He swallowed and then broke a piece off what was left for Spot, who climbed up onto the chair next to mine, gazing at him like he was the last bird in North America. Spot apparently had no trouble with the idea of being hand-fed by Cam, any more than I would have had, I guess, if I had never met JT.

Cam peered at me. "Okay?"

I shook my head. I was so tired. "Do you think I could just sleep on the couch for a bit?

"How about you take a quick shower while I change the sheets? Then you can sleep on the bed. It's big enough for both of us." He rolled his eyes when I lifted my gaze to his. "I'll leave you alone."

I wondered how many people he'd said that to. "I'm too tired to stop you if you don't."

"And that's precisely why you can count on me to keep my distance. I never go after the wounded gazelle except to bring it to safety."

"You like a little fight, huh?"

"I like a lot of fight, actually." He blinked a little. "Usually."

"Let's go." I put the sandwich down after only eating half of it. "I would like to go back to the hospital tonight before visiting hours are over."

"That's fine. If we get some shut-eye, I'll run you back there."

"Thanks, Cam." I helped him wrap my sandwich for later. "You're a really, really good guy."

"That's what I tell everyone," Cam said. "Towels are in the cupboard in the hall. There's new razors and toothbrushes in the top drawer next to the sink."

"You're well prepared."

Cam shrugged those big shoulders. "Boy Scout."

"I'll bet." I headed for the cupboard he'd pointed out and found a stack of fresh, fluffy white towels. "Do you realize that you're the most domestic damned person I've ever met?"

"That has been said before." He blushed. "Firefighters are often highly organized and motivated to keep things neat.

I stuck my head back around. "The only person I've ever met who is this domestic is my sister-in-law. She's driven. She makes Martha Stewart look laid-back."

"Sister-in-law?"

"Yeah. Daniel's wife, BreeAnna."

Cam stood like a statue in the hallway. "Did you notify her? Was she at the hospital?"

I turned before I closed the bathroom door behind me. "I left a message at their house. They're going through a divorce. Things got messy recently, and Dan said she might not care enough to come."

"I see."

I shrugged. "What can I say? They've been married for a long time, and it hit the skids. She was never really warm and fuzzy." I turned and entered the bathroom, and as I closed the door behind me, I thought I heard Cam talking to the cat.

"People suck, don't they?"

CHAPTER TWENTY-THREE

If I'd expected JT to come and claim me wearing a gay-pride T-shirt and rainbow suspenders, I would have been disappointed. As it was, Cam and I had a two-hour nap and hot-tubbed for a soothing hour or so before he took me back to my motel room. I felt like an idiot, a teen being driven back from a youthful indiscretion with my zipper chafing my privates and wet boxers in a plastic Ziploc bag and nothing to show for it but a boyfriend I hadn't seen since he'd asked me to trust him.

I think Cam sensed my discomfort, because after he turned off the engine, he sat with me for a silent minute just watching my face.

"Thanks for everything, Cam," I said finally. "Especially for the way you took care of Dan. I'll never forget it."

"It's just my job."

I half expected him to say, *Aw, shucks.* "You ought to hear how much it means to the people you do it for at least."

"Thanks."

I looked around and pulled on the handle of his SUV to let myself out. "My duffel was in Dan's Lexus."

"Someone will let you know where it's been towed, and you can get your things from it."

I'd heard horror stories from others about theft from those impound yards. "If it's still there."

"Did you have high-ticket items in the trunk? Audio equipment? Electronics?"

"No. You gave me my laptop case." I patted the item in question. "Just clothes."

"You're probably fine, then. Don't worry."

"I'm not worried. There's nothing in there I can't replace at the thrift store." I stood leaning into his car. "It was just clothes."

"What are you going to do now?"

"I thought I'd change and then head back to the hospital." I glanced around. "I guess I thought—"

"I'll wait here and give you a ride. Hop to it. I'm going back on shift, and I've only had two hours' sleep."

"Okay, thanks again, Cam."

"You're welcome." He waited in the car while I hurried into my motel room and changed. The phone was the kind that had a button indicating voice-mail messages, but nothing was lit. I picked up a jacket and shoved my feet back into my Vans and headed back out the door to find Cam talking with Carl.

"Hi, Yasha," Carl said. "Helluva thing that was last night. I'm so glad you and your brother are okay. How long do they think he'll be in the hospital?"

"I don't know yet. They hadn't finished consulting about his arm. He's going to need a specialist."

"I was sorry to hear he'd been hurt. Cam was just telling me about that. Every so often we get a major pileup in the fog. I wish someone would invent something to prevent that."

"I think some cars have a sensor. Maybe they'll start coming with radar."

"I'm still waiting for the flying car they promised me." Carl's eyes didn't seem to be sparkling like they normally did, but other than that his behavior was completely normal. I wondered whether JT had talked to him. It didn't seem to matter, because we said all the polite things, and then I got into Cam's SUV and we headed off.

"That might have been awkward," I said. "But it didn't seem to be."

Cam shrugged.

"You don't think much of JT."

"I didn't say that." Cam didn't look at me.

"You don't have to. It's pretty obvious by what you're not saying."

Cam rolled those big shoulders. "Look. It's never been any of my business, but I don't have a lot of respect for a guy who uses girls like he does, then goes all 'undercover lover' with guys."

I sighed. I didn't either for that matter. "You're right of course. I need to focus on Dan right now anyway. He was talking about getting a place for the two of us here."

"Sounds good. You want me to look around?"

"I thought I'd put Ken Ashton on that, since he seems to be real-estate savvy. Ordinarily I'd let my brother do that, but he's—"

"You should just let your brother get better."

Surprised, I looked over to where he clutched the steering wheel with both hands. "I will. Of course I will."

"He's going to be in pain. And he's going to need to learn to do things with his left hand that he's used to doing with his right."

"I know."

"His wife will probably want to look after him if he's really injured, huh? Don't you think? She'll probably want to be there for him, won't she?"

No way. Was Cam sweet on my brother? "Cam—"

"At any rate there's probably going to be a line of chicks a mile long at your door bringing you soup and shit."

"Probably." I wasn't going to tell Cam my brother had come out to me. No way. Let him find out for himself. "We'll be sure to put it in a mug. It's easier to drink that way wrong-handed."

Cam shot me a look like he wondered if I was making fun of him. Since I sort of was, I thought I'd try to look innocent.

"What?" I asked when he stared at me through a green light and people behind us started to honk.

"Nothing. Never mind." He took off when the light was perfectly orange, and after that neither of us spoke until we pulled into the hospital parking lot.

I got out of the car and leaned in to say thank you. "Thanks for all the things you've done, Cam. You're a good friend."

Cam smiled briefly and turned to look behind the car, clearly indicating he was done with talking for now.

"I'll tell Dan you said hi and that you wish him well," I said before closing the door. His eyes found mine, and we both knew how important that was to him. He jerked a nod, and I waved.

I watched him back out of the parking space, and then I headed for the front door of the hospital.

I'D HAD those dreams as a kid, where you're naked and have to stand in front of the class and recite the Gettysburg Address or something. I'd dreamed I was trying to get somewhere, and no matter what happened, something prevented me. But I'd never been the kind of guy to dream that wherever I went, everyone hated me.

Yet that's exactly the reception I got at the hospital, from the volunteers at the registration desk to the nurses' station to the girl in scrubs taking my brother's blood pressure when I entered his room. It was the same story. Chilly silence followed by either a murderous glare or the quickest exits I'd ever experienced outside of a bomb threat.

When the nurse left the room without responding to my cheery hello, I blinked in surprise. "What the hell?"

Laughter rumbled in Dan's chest like a groan. "I know something you don't know," he sang. He looked tired but in good spirits. His arm rested immobilized in what looked like a huge baffle. His pupils were huge and his speech slurred.

"What?"

"Closet Lad is breaking hearts all over town." He said it like *heartsh.*

"What?"

"The news is spreading like wildfire, and you're persona non grata right about now."

I slumped into the chair next to his bed. "Just great."

I had to give JT points for trying if that's actually what was happening. "It's probably all your imagination."

"I understand he's just finishing up with the *As.*" Dan swallowed hard and tried to smile, but I could see he was in pain.

"Should I call someone?" I asked. "Do you need something?"

"No."

I sat still for a minute, but the urge to fidget was keen.

He shot me a speculative look and grunted. "What's up? Out with it."

"I guess I expected to see JT at some point. But he sent Cam to come get me."

"He of the Camshaft."

"Yep." Little do you know, Dan, that you have a ticket to ride if you want it. "I guess I just wanted my moment, you know? When he chose me."

"The *Officer and a Gentleman* moment? That was one of Bree's favorite movies."

"Figures," I said unfairly. "The only thing I remember is the guy who died in the closet."

"What are you going to do if he doesn't pick you? What if he never wants to be demonstrative in public? What if you never get that evening out, or he can't bring himself to hold your hand when you walk down the street?"

My heart tightened. "I don't know." But I did know. I didn't want a guy who wasn't out. Period. JT held my heart, but that wasn't enough for me anymore. I wanted something real, not something convenient. Being with Sander had taught me that. I felt like I'd wasted a year. I would have been just as happy with no one as I'd been with Sander.

"I think about that a lot, you know."

I held a cup of water out so the straw dangled in front of Dan's dry-looking lips. "Do you?"

He took a healthy sip and swallowed. "Sometimes I wonder if I have the guts. It's all theory really, until you have to dance with a man in public or kiss him goodbye at the airport."

I hadn't thought about that. I'd never felt I had a choice, so I'd never hidden my sexuality. Even in high school. But it hadn't been exactly easy. "It's not a picnic."

"I know," Dan said grimly.

"But it gets easier."

"Does it?"

"You get tougher," I admitted.

"Good to know." He looked not only tired but disheartened. I wished I could paint a better picture of what he had to look forward to. The truth was I'd always envied the ease of his existence. Well-to-do, trophy wife, temperate, intelligent, personable. He was socially bulletproof. While I knew he didn't have a happy marriage, I had at least thought it suited him to be married to a beautiful woman. Now that I knew he'd been acting all along, it hurt my heart to think of him trapped in that existence, eyeing men he was attracted to. Men he could never have.

"You don't have to answer this. When you were married to Bree, did you ever…Were you ever with a man?"

"Yes," Dan whispered.

"So..."

"I have a dirty little secret or ten to atone for, yes." He looked away. "It's different when you connect the dots."

The dots? From Dan to some nameless, faceless guy who could have been—probably was—exactly like me? A man who was falling in love, maybe. Attracted at least. Deserving of a lot more than a quiet hookup in a hotel room while Dan was away from home on business. Definitely. A man who had a right to be more than someone's midnight booty call.

Maybe Dan's apple hadn't fallen too far from our father's tree after all.

"Don't look at me like that."

"But the infidelity clause—if you violated it first—"

"The difference is mine were tricks. Some of them I paid for. I never had a relationship outside my marriage. She did and with someone I knew. Someone I thought was my friend. I did one-night stands, and their affair has lasted for eight months, that I know of. It's not the same. And even if it were, I never got caught, and she did. I'm still trying to be generous and end it on a win-win."

"I'm sorry. You cheated on her. You didn't get caught, but in my book that doesn't absolve you. I don't understand how you can make the distinction."

"I don't either," he said petulantly. "Maybe I was wrong. What about all those women of JT's? They can't have been aware he was seeing you after their dates."

"That's wrong too, and I know it."

"Maybe we were all due for a karmic correction." He turned his face away. "Maybe I'm just tired. Can we talk about this later?"

"Sure...I'm sorry."

I was tired too. I knew I was over being the kind of guy whose lover visited him after dark and took off before dawn. After only a week I was done with that. Both Dan and I deserved better than what we'd had, and we had some atoning to do for what we'd taken. And now we had the chance for a fresh start without reservations.

"You and me? We're going to be fine, Danilo," I said, even though my brother was drifting off to sleep. "No more waiting for happiness to come from outside, yeah?"

"Yeah, whatever," he growled. "As long as there's painkillers, I'm your guy."

I pulled the sheet up a little, just fussing. There wasn't really anything wrong with how it was. I just wanted to tuck my brother in.

My big brother, Danilo.

"Night. I'll be right here."

"Night." Hospital noises were the only sounds for a long time. "Don't judge me too harshly."

"How can I without taking a good long look at myself?" Maybe that wasn't something I wanted to face either, right then.

CHAPTER TWENTY-FOUR

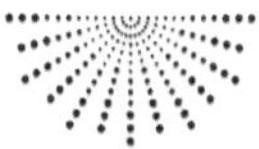

I slept in the chair next to my brother, and no one disturbed me until I woke up at the hour I generally slogged to work. I left the building and stood in the cold so I could use my cell phone to call Mary Catherine, who agreed to pick me up. When she drove up, she pushed the button to unlock the passenger-side door, and I got in gratefully, rubbing my hands together against the cold of the chilly night mist.

"The first thing I'm going to need to do is get car insurance and rent a car. I don't think Dan's going to be driving for a while. His car is totaled."

"I'm so sorry."

"We're alive." I felt more gloomy than usual. Normally I liked the fact that my job started before the rest of the world was up and pouring its first cup of coffee. But that day, even with Mary Catherine chatting amiably in the driver's seat next to me, instead of feeling like I was paddling ahead of a great wave, trying to catch a ride into the day, I felt like I bobbed alone in a vast becalmed lake. "Dan and I are thinking about finding a place here."

"Yeah?" Mary Catherine looked at me at the stoplight. I

could feel her studying me and wondered what she was thinking. Not enough to ask.

"Dan likes it here."

"What about you? Do you like it here, Yasha?"

I thought about it. "I *love* it. Muse says that means St. Nacho's wants me."

Mary Catherine chuckled. "I see you've heard about Minerva at Rune Nation and her seat-of-awesome-spiritual-power theory."

"Yeah." I laughed too. I wanted to meet Minerva. That was definitely going on my to-do list. "What's your take on that?"

"I think the sound of the waves mellows people out," she said. "And whatever nature doesn't cure, Nacho's Bar and their famous blue Adios Motherfuckers will."

By the time we got to Miss Independence Pies, the girls were already on the doorstep waiting on us. As always Candace and Bianca were bickering and Muse was looking on, waiting to jump in if it came to blows and bloodshed. Analise stood under the security lights, wearing a really attractive sparkly sweater with a matching scarf in a vivid purple color that I'd never have imagined her wearing the week before."

"Well, well, well." Mary Catherine sighed.

I sensed that Mary Catherine was observing the same thing I was. At one point, fear had sucked all the color and life from Analise. Now it was like watching someone who'd drowned take a first choking breath of air, like watching the color fill her cheeks and the life return to her eyes as oxygen returned to her system.

Muse ran to the car when I got out and wrapped both tattooed arms around me, burying her face into my solar plexus. "You are not allowed to be squished."

I tilted my head and leaned back so I could see her face. "I wasn't."

"See that you aren't." Muse growled at me, "I hate that shit. Hospitals."

"My brother got hurt," I said. I felt a little hollow, like if I didn't have her to hold me up, I might not be able to stand. Maybe that's why she did it. At that point I gave in and hugged her back hard as if I'd known that little girl for a hundred years. "Thank you."

Mary Catherine unlocked the door, and we all went forth to make pies. The rhythm of a bakery, the mixing of the dough, creating the fillings, the sheeting and cutting, the placement in pans, and the crimping of edges took me to the place I often go, where my hands work and my mind finds peace.

I looked around. Bianca and Candace were enjoying a brief respite from bitter conflict by the sink. They were drinking coffee and waiting for the caffeine to kick in. Muse was processing apples, and Analise was making the custard filling for the pecan pies. Mary Catherine had gone into her office to work on her business plan.

A gust of chilly wind came from the door, and I looked up to see JT standing there in his uniform. I felt every eye on me as he advanced.

"Yasha." He stood before me with his hands behind his back as if he were at parade rest.

"JT." I turned off the mixer. I pulled the bandanna from my hair because there are some moments you don't want to experience with a food-safety head covering, even if it's way cooler than a hairnet. I hoped this was going to be one of those. JT looked so solemn. When he pulled his hands from behind his back, he held out a single red rose. It was perfect—its velvety petals were still crisp and dewy, its long stem free of thorns. It was a big, fat, tightly closed bud, just beginning to open at the top. It looked like lips when I bowed my head to breathe in the scent.

"I came to ask you if you'd care to go out with me tonight,"

JT said. I suspected he projected his voice a little so the girls could hear. "I thought we'd go for a nice dinner, maybe do some dancing?"

"Yeah?" I thought about my meager wardrobe and the fact that Dan was in the hospital, and my heart sank a little. "Maybe now's not such a good time."

Candace hip-checked me right out of the way and stood in front of JT, grinning like a clown. "He accepts."

"Wait, I—"

Candace fired a look at me that shut me up. "What time?"

"Uh…" JT looked from me to Candace and back to me. I shrugged. "Seven?"

"Perfect," she told him, taking his arm. "That will give him plenty of time to do a little shopping and then go see his brother to make certain he's all right. You can pick him up at the hospital, okay?"

"Candace—" I implored.

"Okay, then." JT allowed her to hustle him to the door but caught the frame before she could shove him out. "Hey, wait. *Yasha*."

I saw him when he realized he had my undivided attention. "Yeah?"

His lips curved upward into a smile, and his eyes held such sincere warmth they caught my heart on fire. He gestured to me and then to himself. "*Mizpah*."

I nodded. *Emotional bond*. It was a covenant between us. It looked like I had my *Officer and a Gentleman* moment after all.

After the door closed behind JT, everyone started talking at once. Mostly it was a chorus of surprised giggling. Muse smacked my arm with a tiny fist.

Bianca put a halt to the whole deal when she told everyone, "We have pies to make, and we'd better be quick if we want to get done in time to take Yasha shopping."

I put the bandanna back over my hair.

"Wait, *what?*"

IN THE END I went along with Mary Catherine and Muse on a delivery run that took us about a half hour down the coast to a town with a fairly big discount-designer-clothing store. I was able to purchase a pair of black gabardine trousers and a guayabera—that lightweight-linen camp-style shirt with the tone-on-tone embroidery but without pockets. The kind intended for nice occasions in tropical environments that I always think of as Mexican wedding shirts. I managed to find a nice belt and a pair of black loafers that were casual yet still elegant. I even had to buy dress socks.

I hadn't dated since long before Sander. What I mostly did was feed men and let them stay over. I wondered if I even had the skill set for a regular evening out, and I pictured Muse texting me like some small but equally fierce Cyrano de Bergerac to tell me what she thought I should say.

Muse interrupted by holding a bottle of cologne that smelled like lemon peel in front of my face. "Here, try this."

"That's nice." I checked the price tag. "I can do that." Really, I was having a hard time processing. I'd never liked to shop, and I didn't think I could take much more.

Muse eyed me shrewdly. "That's enough," she stated and allowed me to take my purchases to the counter to pay.

"You've been through a lot lately," she said as we walked out the door to wait for Mary Catherine to swing back by and pick us up in the van. "Maybe you need some kind of talisman. A healing crystal."

"I don't think I believe in stuff like that, Muse."

"Well, I'm not sure that matters as long as someone does, and I do." She took a chain from around her neck with a little glob of amethyst on it. "This is supposed to protect you against intoxication and seduction."

I pushed it back. "Why the hell would I want that?"

Muse giggled. "It was also said by Moses to be the spirit of God when it was placed in the official robe of the high priest of the Jews."

I gaped.

"Seriously, you can look that up." She hooked the thing around my neck and clasped it. "You've been having a pretty legendary run of bad luck. It might help."

This time I laughed. "Yeah. I guess. At any rate it couldn't hurt."

Mary Catherine pulled up in front of the store just before a gentle rain began to fall. Maybe my luck was looking up after all.

SINCE I WANTED to visit Dan in the hospital, I got ready for my date and got a ride there from Bianca. She dropped me off with a saucy wink of approval and a scary kind of feral growl I took as a kind of go-get-'em-tiger noise. I knew that in a little bit JT would be picking me up. In the meantime, I wanted to find out what else Dan had learned about his arm from his doctors.

Dan did a double take when he saw me in my date finery. "All dressed up for me? I'm flattered and frankly alarmed. What do you know that I don't?"

I acknowledged his joke with a roll of my eyes. "I have a date."

"JT came through?"

"He brought me a rose at work this morning."

"Classy." He held his hand out for water, and I gave it to him, holding the straw so it wouldn't fall out of the mauve plastic cup.

"I thought so." I avoided his eyes. "He seems to be on the level."

Dan smiled. "You really like this guy."

"Yeah." *Shit.* Family can make you feel like you're in sixth grade again. "He's nice."

"But something is different about him. You're into him in a big way."

"I know." I swallowed. "He makes me feel safe.

"You're a big guy, Jakey. What do you need with—"

"Not like…safe from danger or anything, because no one is *safe*. He makes me feel like if I put my trust in him, if I told him my secrets and my dreams and my darkest fears, he'd never let me down."

"That's a lot to ask from a guy who shows up in the middle of the night after he leaves his girlfriend at her door."

"I'm a Jewish homosexual. There's nothing I like better than a paradox."

Dan winced but said nothing for a long time. He finally lifted his shoulder in a shrug that meant he'd given up trying to talk sense. "You're an idiot."

"I know. But you got my back, Danilo."

"Just like you got mine." He held out his left hand, and I grasped it, giving it a gentle squeeze. I stared at it for a while.

"This your jerk-off hand?"

"Like I'd tell you." He grunted. "*No.*"

"Sucks to be you, big man."

I laughed all the way to the lobby, where I received a text from JT.

On my way. C U.

CHAPTER TWENTY-FIVE

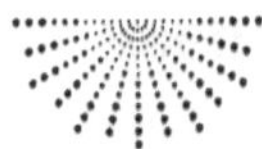

I saw that truck coming, and my heart did a perfect dive from my chest straight toward my dick, making a flawless entry into the waters of my libido, no splash. That's probably a bad thing when you want the truck as much as you want the man. For me, JT was the total package. I knew it was hopeless, and if he was kidding himself, or planning to play in my sandbox until the rest of the playground beckoned again, my heart would be shattered into a million pieces.

It was the height of irony that I'd been trained to survive chemical warfare only to be completely blown away by an ordinary man in an old red farm truck.

He pulled up to the curb and got out, looking awe-inspiring in a dark suit with a subtly striped burgundy tie, and I worried he'd think I was underdressed. Where was he planning to go? I had figured we'd go out for a drink and maybe have dinner at Nacho's, but no one wore suits there. Before I could even touch the handle, he was around the truck and opening the door for me. It was a testament to the fact that he normally dated the kind of girl who waited on the curb to be helped in. I let him. I planned to ease him into the understanding that I didn't need the same kind of cosseting his Barbies required—until he took my hand with such gentle caring and helped me up into the passenger seat. Maybe I'd try out being one of his girls for a while if it got me that kind of shy appreciation and the gentle kisses he placed on my lips before closing the door between us.

When he came around the front of the truck and got in, only the way his hands shook when he put the key into the ignition and the quick glance he made around the parking lot gave any clue how hard being with me was going to be for him.

I cleared my throat. "You know, you don't have to start by yelling, *Ta-da I'm here, I'm queer, get used to it.* It's perfectly acceptable to take it slow."

He left the engine running but took his hands off the wheel to rub his face. "If I take you out and don't treat you like a date, it feels disrespectful." He turned and looked at me. "As if I think less of you in some way. So the way I see it, I ought to treat you better than I've ever treated anyone I've dated, since…" He trailed off but his eyes seemed to implore me to understand.

I took a deep breath. "I see. Thank you."

"Yeah. Well." He grimaced and put the truck in gear. "You look nice."

"Am I dressed okay? I didn't have a lot of choices and—"

"You look great."

"Are we heading somewhere I'm likely to need a jacket?"

"No, I thought we might head down to Santa Barbara for dinner, maybe. Bouchon is a nice place. I made reservations."

"I've heard of it. Sounds excellent. It's a long drive though."

"I thought maybe on the way we could talk."

"Really?" I asked. "What did you want to talk about?"

"I"—he glanced over at me quickly—"I don't know."

I thought of a smart-ass comment or two, and a couple of dumb ones. "Me neither."

"You can tell I'm trying though, right?"

"Trying what?"

"Whatever it is I'm supposed to be doing?"

"What *are* you doing?"

He drove for a few minutes in silence—until we reached a turnout that overlooked the ocean. Then he pulled the truck to a stop and turned off the engine. Without the dash lights and with nothing but the moonlight outside, it was hard to see his face.

"Are you trying to make this difficult?" he asked.

"Me? No, I was trying to make it easier. I just wanted to know what you want to talk about. When you said you wanted to talk..."

All at once JT shook his head and started laughing. "I didn't *want* to talk. I said I thought maybe we could talk. That's always my opening gambit. Usually once I say that, I can just drive while I'm led through a conversation where all I have to do is acknowledge the speaker every so often."

"No shit?"

"Seriously. I've always picked outgoing girls because they take care of the talking. That comes from knowing I make a better impression with my mouth shut."

"I like it when you talk to me. What other misconceptions do you have about yourself?"

"I'm actually pretty self-aware."

"Says the uncrowned King of Narnia."

He sagged a little.

"I'm sorry. That was a shitty thing to say."

"But true."

I tried to see his expression in the darkness. "My own brother came out to me a couple of days ago. He hid his sexuality for years. Maybe everyone has to do things in their own time and their own way. Who am I to judge?"

"You're the guy who never lied."

"Is that what you think?" I asked. "That I never lied? For me coming out was easy because I gave fuck-all about what anyone else thought. But I lie about things all the time. I make excuses for a guy like Sander, who screwed around with everyone in the neighborhood and shut down each argument we had with his fists. I let you in the door of my motel room and tell myself it's okay if you don't want to stay. I pretend that I trust people. I lie all the time, except...maybe only to myself."

Word vomit happens. I rarely let anything out that I don't want others to see, although sometimes it's like food poisoning and I regurgitate the most toxic things as a defense mechanism. I shut up, embarrassed.

JT spoke then. "I thought if I was a better Jew, God would keep the temptation away. I used religion as an excuse to deny my nature. I thought maybe I'd get the strength to say no if I studied the Torah and believed."

"Imagine being cockblocked by God," I muttered. "That's a scary thought."

"I prayed hard for an answer, Yasha. I have to at least consider the possibility that he sent me a gay Jew named Jacob who was wrestling with his own questions and ready to ask me for help."

I smiled, but I doubted he saw it. "I don't remember much of that night."

"I do. You called me 'grandfather,' and then you kissed my hand."

"Besides Daniel, you're the only person I haven't had to lie to myself about."

"Probably because I was lying enough for both of us."

"No. That's not it. Maybe it wasn't about me anymore. Maybe I just...love you. And whatever you do, wherever you end up, nothing will change that."

"Jeez, Yasha," he whispered. "Surely I don't deserve that."

"Maybe you don't. But I can't help it. I love you, JT." My mouth went dry. "Do you think you can just take me home?"

"Home?" JT asked.

I bit my lip. “Somewhere we can make love.”

JT pressed his lips against mine, and I felt him smile. I opened to him, letting him tease and taste, exploring him back as though we had all the time in the world parked there on the side of the road. Finally he broke the kiss and gazed down at me. His knuckles brushed the side of my face.

“Home.” He keyed the ignition to start the truck. “Instead of dinner?”

“We’ll figure something out,” I told him as he waited until it was safe to pull away from the turnout and head back the way we came. Pretty soon the SeaView Motel was in sight on the highway, the *V* and the *I* still out on the sign. “How long has that sign been like that?”

“Always, off and on. I can’t remember that far back.”

“Your dad’s a subtle prankster.”

JT flashed a grin. “That he is.”

I had a sudden inspiration. “Has he met Mary Catherine?”

“I’m certain he has. Her son stayed at the SeaView, and Dad helped pack his things when he was still in the hospital.”

“Has he…? Did he ever get the chance to be social with her?”

“Are you *matchmaking*?” JT asked.

“I believe I am,” I answered. “I think they’d be perfect together.”

“My dad is older than she is by what…ten years?”

“Who cares? Your dad is a Charlie Brown Christmas tree, and he needs a little love.”

JT grinned. “You may be right.”

We pulled up in front of a classic brick-and-siding, ranch-style house painted white with green shutters. It was such a homey, painfully American kind of place that it tugged at my imagination instantly, from the welcoming door at the top of the porch stairs to the basketball hoop that hung from the wide eaves over the garage.

Once we parked in the driveway, JT and I sat for a minute

just looking at it. He reached for my hand, and I got the feeling hardly any of his dates ever ended up there. JT opened his door and got out. I shouldn't have been surprised, but for a minute I was still looking at the house, so when I went to open the door on my side, JT was there, opening it for me, placing his hand on my upper arm as I stepped down. He laced our fingers together again and led me to the front door.

I waited for him to take out his key. For the longest time he stood there.

"A hundred boys must have kissed my sisters under this porch light."

"You have sisters?" I knew both Lents men, and this came as a surprise to me, although I don't know why. We'd never really talked about the family much.

"Yeah. Two. They're older. One is in Seattle, and the other lives in San Diego."

"I didn't know."

He gathered my hands in his. "I used to come down and watch from that window over there and imagine their boyfriends were kissing me."

I looked where he was pointing, toward what was probably the living room, obscured by sheer drapes of an old-fashioned variety, lacy and regal looking. "Yeah?"

"Yeah." JT flushed slightly.

I knew what he was saying. Whatever was between us, there were no rules yet established. He might pick me up in a suit and zip around to help me out of the car, but he might also want me to pull him into my arms under his parents' porch light and kiss him like it was prom night. He was too new to have a modus operandi, and I was too experienced at this to want one.

I took him in my arms then and kissed him like I meant it. The minute my lips touched his, he relaxed, opening for me, sending his tongue out to play with mine. He locked his arms around my neck while I slid mine up to cradle the back of his head. I let one of my hands slip down, all along the indented column of his spine, to rest at its base and press his hips to mine. He arched into me with a whimper.

JT would be a dream to dance with if he ever allowed it. So responsive to the slightest touch, so willing to be led. So acquiescent.

"JT," I murmured into his lips. He had no trace of a beard since he'd probably just shaved before he picked me up.

He opened his eyes, dazed with passion, and focused on me. "Hm?"

I suppressed a small smile of satisfaction. "Maybe we should go in?"

"Oh." He lifted the keys he'd been holding and turned with a yes.

When he opened the door, I asked, "What would your sisters do next with their boys?" I admit that wasn't really the question for which I wanted the answer. I wanted to know what he'd want me to do next. Should I stand back and wait? Should I move in? Should I use every excuse to touch him and seduce him, or did he want to do the same to me?

"Well, that depends. If my parents were home—"

"Wait. Are your parents home now?" I asked, absurdly. I knew his mother was dead and his father was at the motel. It just seemed like he was somewhere else—somewhere in the past—and he wanted a do-over.

He hadn't turned on the light, but I saw him swallow hard before he spoke. "No."

"Then what would your sisters do?"

JT took my hand then and led me to his room. It was juvenile and tidy, featuring a lot of books and some swim trophies. Lots of ribbons with medals and certificates on the wall, which I took to mean he excelled at his sport. He sat on the side of his bed and just looked at me. His eyes held mischief, maybe a little fear, and some indefinable faith in me that I wanted to honor by getting everything exactly right.

I sat next to him, lifting a knee to the mattress top so I could face him better when I took hold of his tie. "This is very nice."

"Thanks," he said breathlessly as I slid the knot down and pulled it off.

I unbuttoned his suit coat and helped him slide it off, then placed it carefully onto the foot of the bed. While I pulled the hem of his shirt from his trousers, I nibbled at his jaw, his chin, and his neck as far as I could reach, until I had that top button open and his chest was mine to explore—at least that part of it that was exposed by his undershirt. I felt down his sleeves and was delighted to find French cuffs with cuff links, which I pulled out and placed on the nightstand.

"Such a classy, classy man," I whispered, liking the heft of the fabric as I peeled his shirt off him and put it with his jacket.

"Hey, how come I'm the only one getting undressed?"

"You want to undress me too?"

"You know I do," he said, raking me with his gaze. "May I?"

I stood at this, wanting to stand tall while he looked at me with hot eyes. "Of course."

He began with my belt, using fumbling fingers to unbuckle it and lower my zipper. By then my cock had leaked a slick circle of moisture over my briefs, and he leaned in to mouth it as though he couldn't help it. As though he was unable to stop himself. I cradled his head in my fingers, brushing his brows lightly with my thumbs.

"*Baby*." I breathed a sigh, bowled over by the sweet way he nuzzled me. I leaned over to capture his mouth with mine, and together we slipped and slid our way to the pillows, until we were lying together on his double bed, stretched out and straining to get rid of what was left of our clothes. His breath came in puffs of air he tried to control. He gave little gasps and shudders as my fingers played along the hard planes of his chest until I dug my fingers into his undershirt to remove it. He unbuttoned the tiny pearlescent buttons on my shirt with shaking fingers and pushed it off my shoulders. When his nails scraped over my nipples, I sucked air deep into my lungs and arched so he would do it again. He laid the flat of his tongue where his hands had been, and I pulled his head close until I felt the thrilling rasp of his teeth there.

"Yasha," he whispered uncertainly.

"Shh," I whispered. "I know what you need."

"I don't have"—he waved his hand around—"anything."

"I do. Find my wallet." What happened next was classic. Two men, cocks bobbing, taking time out to fumble through discarded clothing for a wallet until I found it and dropped a couple of condoms and two pillow packs of lube on the bed. When we were finally skin to skin, he let out a deeply contented sigh.

I readied him quickly, watching his face for cues. "How are you doing?"

He bit his lip on a cry and nodded tightly. "Fine."

"I haven't even done anything yet," I teased. He looked away. I waited for it.

"*Ah,*" he cried out. "*Jeez.* Do that again."

I felt around for the rough bundle of nerves and stroked it again.

"Yasha!" JT was frankly begging now.

I pulled his legs over my forearms and nudged him. "Put a condom on me."

He tore the packet open and did it by feel more than anything, giving me a couple of solid pumps that made me groan. "Easy," he warned.

"No worries." I went carefully, bumping him, pressing in gently, and sliding past the ring of rigid muscles only when they let go enough to admit me. "Ah, fuck, you feel good."

"C'mere." He pulled my head down to kiss me, and I went

willingly. He stroked and soothed me as he combed his fingers through my hair, moving down to my shoulders, kneading the muscles there deeply as they swirled over my skin. It felt heavenly. I clung to him, put my head on his shoulder, and simply let him embrace me. We kissed, and we fucked. We lit a slow fuse that burned all over my body until my skin was flushed and slick, and he had beard burn on his neck and dazed eyes.

I gripped his ass in my hands then, grinding hard. My rhythm was off; it was jerky and frantic. JT clawed at my back and cursed in my ear. His cock was trapped between our bodies, and he dragged in a shuddering breath just seconds before I felt the first spurt of wet heat between us. His muscles tightened until I spasmed inside him, filling the condom, driving into his sweet heat as far as I could go.

He said my name over and over, whispering it like a prayer while I let myself fall limp in his arms. "Yasha." He spoke with each rock of my hips against his, his lips open while he tasted the sweaty skin on my neck. "*Yasha.*"

I don't know how long we lay there entwined like that. Finally, as my skin cooled, drying in the whisper of a breeze from the open window, I rose to my elbow and pulled out gently, then tossed the condom into the trash next to the bed. He curled into me, and I cradled him in my arms. "Okay?"

"Yeah"—he gave a nervous little laugh—"maybe a little scared."

"Hm?"

"It's a new life. A new thing. Guys at the station, folks who know me, people I've known all my life are going to think I'm a liar or an idiot or something now that I'm out."

"You told your dad?"

"Yeah."

"What about the girls you were dating?"

"I talked to the ones I've been out with lately," JT hedged. "I didn't want to take out a fucking ad."

"Are you sure this is what you want, JT?" I cared about the answer a lot, so I didn't try to hide it.

"It's not so much what I want as who I am, isn't it?" he asked.

I remained silent.

"What?"

I thought about it. "Can it be both? I feel like I've launched a new ship."

He kissed me gently, opening me up for the briefest contact between our tongues. "I'm not sailing off to new adventures, Yasha. I feel like I've come into home port after a long trip at sea."

"Yeah?"

"Yes." He put his head right under my chin then, where I could clearly imagine it landing every night for the rest of my life, locked in like the piece of a puzzle I didn't realize I'd been looking for. "Sleepy," he whispered.

"Gotta clean up," I told him. "We're going to be stuck together."

"Yeah," he answered, but he didn't let me go. We were both going to sacrifice some body hair in the morning if I didn't get up, but I was lulled to sleep by his deep breathing, by the contentment I felt with him in my arms, and I drifted off, swept away on the tide of happiness that was only just beginning to rise in my heart.

"I love you," I told him as he tightened his arms around me and began to snore gently. "Love…love you."

WHAT TO READ NEXT?

If you enjoyed Yasha and JT's story, please leave a review. The more reviews a book has, the more likely it will pop up on other readers' sales pages, meaning they'll get the opportunity to enjoy it too!

Reviews are the #1 way for you to help me keep writing the stories you love. Review Jacob's Ladder today!

If you want to linger in the sleepy town of St. Nacho's try **The Book of Daniel**, book four in the St. Nacho's series.

He has a choice between doing the right thing or making a fortune. Will a hot firefighter and his growing love of the small town way of life help him decide?

Daniel Livingston is finally free. He's come clean about his passionless marriage and moved to St. Nacho's where he can spend time with his brother. Now he's ready to explore the endless sexual buffet being hot and rich and single has to offer.

The problem is a firefighter named Cameron Rooney who haunts his every waking thought and half his dreams. No doubt about it. Cam is going to require a level of honesty Dan has never before considered, and in order to achieve that, he will have to turn his life inside out.

Will forging a new path could cost him everything or net him the most important score of his life?

If you love hot firefighters, cool businessmen, family drama, and watching men find love that will last a lifetime, buy The Book of Daniel today!

After you read the entire **St. Nacho's Series,** try the first book in the brand new spinoff series, **"Men of St. Nacho's—A Much Younger Man.**

One man is older and not quite wiser. The other is young and living rough. Can they ignore the critics and let their hearts decide?

Veterinarian Linden Davies gets on better with animals than men. After a lifetime of always putting work first, he's resigned himself to one-night stands and shallow blind dates. But years of heartache evaporate when he offers a handsome young busker a free health check for his companion Labrador.

Christopher "Beck" Beckett vowed to care for his late friend's loyal dog. After falling out with his parents and ending up on the streets playing music for tips, he longs for a warm embrace and a compassionate kiss. Linden is perfect, and he takes Beck under his wing, but his hangups over a relationship with someone half his age have Beck's head spinning.

As Linden lets the sweet wayward guitarist into his world and gives him renewed purpose, he battles disapproval from his friends and family. And when Beck realizes the kindhearted vet could well be his true soulmate, he fears that their love is probably doomed.

Will this perfect match transcend the judgment of others?

A Much Younger Man is the first book in the tender The Men of St. Nacho's gay romance series. If you like heartfelt chemistry, unequal partners, and emotional rollercoasters, then you'll adore Z.A. Maxfield's poignant tale.

Buy **A Much Younger Man** to throw societal expectations out the door today!

If you like stories about tough men and hard choices, I suggest you try **The Brothers Grime Series!**

Life is full of dirty jobs. That doesn't mean you can't fall in love while doing them.

After disability ends his career as a firefighter Jack Masterson still helps people in crisis. Jack's company cleans crime scenes and biohazardous waste so victims don't have to. The job is all Jack wants or needs, until he gets the call about old flame Nick Foasberg's suicide.

Ryan only understands part of what happened between his cousin Nick and Jack Masterson in high school, but after Nick's suicide, Ryan agrees both he and Jack need closure. They decide to clean the scene together and despite the tragic circumstances, passion flares between them.

Jack is keeping a painful secret and fighting his attraction to Nick's lookalike cousin, Ryan. Ryan calls himself a magnet for lost causes and worries Jack might be the next in a long line of losers.

Jack gives Ryan something to look forward to, and Ryan gives Jack a reason to stop looking back.

Will love be enough to keep Ryan and Jack together?

ACKNOWLEDGMENTS

I could never have begun to rerelease the St. Nacho's series—and create a series spinoff—without the help of Susie Selva, who dove into the first four books to create a story bible, and then reproofed the original manuscripts.

To say this was a Herculean task is an understatement. I wrote those books, and even I couldn't keep anything straight in my head.

I have long been aware that the little town of Santo Ignacio drifts up and down the coast from book to book. I know the highways I used to get there don't actually go there, or they're the longest, most circuitous routes. If I hadn't learned the roads first hand driving my daughter up and down the coast to the University of California at Santa Cruz, I might still be utterly ignorant.

So, for the sake of continuity, I've put a pin in the map for my little fictional town. It coincides with a place that strategically and visually resembles the town I imagined. (Sorry Cayucos, but you're just irresistible!)

Also, a great big thank you to LE Franks, Morticia Knight,

Belinda McBride, and Sue Brown for being my partners in Writerly Shenanigans. For all you do to help foster an environment of commerce, cooperation, enthusiasm, and community, I love you all!

ALSO BY Z.A. MAXFIELD

Novels

Crossing Borders

Drawn Together

Family Unit

ePistols At Dawn

Gasp!

The Pharaoh's Concubine

Rhapsody For Piano And Ghost

The Long Way Home

Home the Hard Way

The St. Nacho's Series

St. Nacho's

Physical Therapy

Jacob's Ladder

The Book Of Daniel

Men of St. Nacho's Series

A Much Younger Man

A Flighty Fake Boyfriend

The Brothers Grime

Grime and Punishment

Grime Doesn't Pay

Partners in Grime

The Deep Series

Deep Desire

Deep Deception

Deep Deliverance

The Bluewater Bay Novels

Hell on Wheels

All Wheel Drive

The My Cowboy Series

My Cowboy Heart

My Heartache Cowboy

My Cowboy Homecoming

My Cowboy Promises

My Cowboy Freedom

Honky Tonk Hellion

The Stirring Series

Stirring Up Trouble

All Stirred Up

Novellas

Lights! Camera! Cupid!

Blue Fire

Fugitive Color

Through the Years

Holiday Stories

I Heard Him Exclaim

Lost And Found

Secret Light

What Child Is This?

ABOUT THE AUTHOR

Z. A. Maxfield is a fifth generation native of Los Angeles, although she now lives in the Inland Empire.

She started writing in 2006 on a dare from her children and never looked back. Pathologically disorganized, and perennially optimistic, she writes as much as she can, reads as much as she dares, and enjoys her time with family and friends.

If anyone asks her how a wife and mother of four manages to find time for a writing career, she'll answer, "It's amazing what you can do if you give up housework."

Look for ZAM on Social Media!

COPYRIGHT

Jacob's Ladder

Published in the United States of America.